SHOT

Also by Camryn King

Stiletto Justice

Triple Threat

Published by Kensington Publishing Corp.

SNAPSHOT

CAMRYN KING

KENSINGTON PUBLISHING CORP.
www.kensingtonbooks.com

DAFINA BOOKS are published by

Kensington Publishing Corp.
119 West 40th Street
New York, NY 10018

All Kensington titles, imprints, and distributed lines are available at special quantity discounts for bulk purchases for sales promotion, premiums, fund-raising, and educational or institutional use.

Special book excerpts or customized printings can also be created to fit specific needs. For details, write or phone the office of the Kensington Sales Manager: Kensington Publishing Corp., 119 West 40th Street, New York, NY 10018. Attn. Sales Department. Phone: 1-800-221-2647.

Dafina and the Dafina logo Reg. U.S. Pat. & TM Off.

ISBN-13: 978-1-4967-0224-1
ISBN-10: 1-4967-0224-7
First Kensington Trade Paperback Printing: January 2020

ISBN-13: 978-1-4967-0225-8 (ebook)
ISBN-10: 1-4967-0225-5 (ebook)
First Kensington Electronic Edition: January 2020

10 9 8 7 6 5 4 3 2 1

Printed in the United States of America

SNAPSHOT

1

The Bahamas. Sun and sea. Gentle breezes. Tasty drinks with floating umbrellas. Paradise. Kennedy Wade thought about the refreshing drink brought by the kind boat captain as she placed her foot on the boat's gunwale and braced herself against the boat's gentle rocking to snap a round of pics. She was relieved that the showers from that morning had passed over the island, leaving behind fluffy cumulus clouds floating in a bright blue sky. She looked forward to enjoying her last day on the water, as she'd intended. For the past two days she'd crisscrossed the island, documenting its beauty, and writing up the accompanying article for a spread set to appear in the *Chicago Star* newspaper's upcoming Memorial Holiday Sunday edition. But today was for her. As she took in the beauty of the Caribbean, with its pristine white beaches, turquoise waters, and verdant countryside, a rare, philosophical thought assailed her. Kennedy wasn't necessarily religious, and had no real concept of heaven or hell, but if for whatever reason she landed in the latter, at least she would have caught a glimpse of paradise.

"What are you doing, girl? You're supposed to be relaxing."

Kennedy smiled. Clinton's lyrical phrases drifted toward her on the wings of the wind. The boat captain had helped make the time pleasurable during her ten to twelve-hour work days. He regaled her with colorful stories about famous people who'd visited the island and engaged in shenanigans they hoped would stay there—just like Vegas.

She lowered the camera. "Taking pictures like this is relaxing." Not like the other days, while waiting for the right light or searching for the perfect shot, then returning to her room to spend another few hours crafting the words that would bring the reader fully into this idyllic world. "Today I can just take in the beauty and capture the magic when it happens." She looked beyond Clinton and motioned with a nod of her head. "Like that."

Raising her camera, Kennedy placed the colorful lines of a perfect rainbow squarely in the middle of her lens. She adjusted her aperture to enhance the color, then engaged her long-range lens for a clearer shot. She took several frames, pulled out a bit to include a small island, and shot a few more. Her finger hovered over the shutter when a flash caught her eye. *What was that?* Instinctively, she pushed the shutter in rapid succession before lowering the camera, squinting as she shielded her eyes from the sun. They were a good distance away from the island, which was dense with brush and tropical trees. She looked for Clinton, who'd returned to the helm, then back at the rainbow. It had shifted and begun to fade. She joined the captain up front.

"These smaller islands all around. Are they inhabited?"

"Some of them, but not these out here."

"Are you sure?" She nodded toward the rainbow, now behind them. "What about that one, directly in front of the rainbow?"

"Someone owns it, but as of right now it's uninhabited."

"I could have sworn I saw a flash while taking pictures."

"It could be anything," Clinton said. "Most likely something reflecting against the sun."

"Like what?"

The captain shrugged as he waved to a tourist boat passing by. "We've had hundreds of years for all kinds of things to have washed up on these shores."

"That makes sense." Kennedy spent the better part of an hour photographing the beauty that surrounded her. Satisfied, she sat on a bench facing the water and rested her head back to look at the sky. "This is the life right here, my friend. You are so lucky to call this home."

"Easy enough for you to do too, if you want it. Plenty of people want their picture taken. You could set up a little stand on the beach, get a printer, make it work."

"You make it sound so easy."

"Everything's easy in the Bahamas."

Probably true, Kennedy imagined. Not like back in Chicago where freelance photographers and writers outnumbered White Sox fans, making both industries dog-eat-dog. Or where she'd just unraveled herself from a complicated relationship that had continued long past its expiration date. Even in paradise, there was no escaping serial liar/cheater, Will's incessant texts begging to be given one more chance. She'd blocked his number, but he'd only used a friend's phone or bought burners to continue his pleas. It would be a hassle to change a number she'd had for more than a decade, but maybe that time had come. Because after too many chances to count, Kennedy was done with the brother named Will. Done with him, and for the moment, done with thinking about him. She reached for the decadent rum punch she'd saved for this moment, settled herself against the bench's far side, stretched her legs out and allowed the water to rock away the stress of the past few days. She thought of her friend Gwen who worked in advertising for the *Star,* and had given her the inside info that led to this plum assignment and her being rocked like a baby in the ocean's arms. She needed to find a gift of thanks before leaving the island.

"Wake up, sleeping beauty. It's time to go ashore."

I went to sleep? Kennedy blinked her eyes against the setting sun as she righted herself on the bench and accepted Clinton's outstretched hand.

"I can't believe I was that tired."

"You've been working hard, lady."

"I know but still . . . I planned to see more on the return trip than the back of my eyelids."

"Plus," he added, with a nod toward the empty glass that set on a table. "You were sipping at sea, and you know what they say?"

"No, what do they say?"

"Bahama rum packs a punch."

Said with such infectious glee and in that rhythmic accent, Kennedy joined Clinton in laughing out loud. While doing so she noted his pristine white teeth, the dimple peeking through a five o'clock shadow, and the cute little crinkles surrounding his sparkling onyx eyes. To make sure she was healed from Will, she'd sworn off casual dalliances and one-night stands. Was she sure that extracurricular was out?

His voice dropped an octave as he added, "And rum is not the only thing packing."

One thought kept Kennedy's resistance from breaking. That same type of package is what had kept Will in her life for two years—a year, ten months and two days longer than he should have stayed. Yes, she was sure.

"Your offer is tempting," she replied with a smile to not leave his ego bruised, then reached inside her pouch and pulled out a tip.

He raised his hands. "Oh no, that's not necessary, beautiful lady. Squiring you around was my pleasure."

"And mine, too, especially since you arranged for me to be your only passenger. That cost you sales."

"Not really." Clinton glanced at Kennedy and continued a

bit sheepishly. "Today was my off day. So, your lone fare is more than I would have normally made."

"Clinton! You shouldn't have used your free day for me."

"Like I said, it was my pleasure."

While appreciating the obvious flirtation from the Caribbean cutie, Kennedy knew the teasing was as far as she'd go. She reached into her purse again and pulled out another bill to add to the one in her hand. "I'm greatly appreciative. It was a wonderful ride." She held out the money. "I insist."

"Okay, beautiful lady. Thank you."

They stepped on to the landing. Kennedy hugged Clinton, allowed him a selfie and took one of her own, then strolled down the ramp to a line of awaiting taxis. Feeling the captain's manly muscles reminded her how long it had been since one had been inside her. It heightened her awareness of the island men's looks. Suddenly, they were all gorgeous, including the dark chocolate bar who smiled and opened his cab door so she could slide inside. *Must be that packing punch rum.*

The hotel was only five minutes away. On the ride there, she planned out the rest of her evening—order room service, do a final read through of her article before sending it off to the travel section editor, upload photos to her cloud accounts, enjoy an eight-plus hour date with her pillow. She entered the lobby and walked over to the concierge.

"Hello, Hank."

"Hello, Kennedy. How are you today?"

"Deliciously tired. I spent the day on a boat."

"Ah, the water. A great lover."

"The best. A perfect way to enjoy my last day here."

"Leaving so soon? You only arrived."

"I feel that way, too. I'll be back."

"And staying with us, I hope."

"Most likely. You guys are amazing."

"What can I do for you this evening?"

"Recommend something great from the room service menu, or a restaurant nearby that delivers?"

Hank looked aghast. "On your last night in paradise? Oh, no, my lovely lady. You mustn't spend this last night all alone in your room. At the very least you should enjoy a delicious meal and glass of wine while taking in a view of all that you're leaving. I know just the place to recommend, only a short, five-minute walk from our front door."

"I'm exhausted, but your suggestion is hard to resist."

"You won't be sorry, I promise you."

Kennedy watched as Hank pulled a card from several stacks on his station. She accepted it, gave a wave and headed to her room. After checking off the items on the evening's to-do list, all except the pillow date, she took a quick shower and donned a striped, cotton mini and flat leather sandals adorned with shells. Simple silver hoops and bangles completed the outfit and a quick shake out of her natural curls, a dash of mascara and a swipe of pure plum lipstick completed the look. She grabbed her pouch, checked for her ID, debit card and cell phone, and after a quick internal discussion decided to leave her digital camera in the room.

Five minutes later, and Kennedy was glad she'd taken Hank's advice. The shower had revived her and now a warm breeze caressed her clean skin. The azure blue sky had slid into indigo. Stars twinkled and disappeared as she joined tourists and natives strolling down the paved pathway. As she reached the steps leading to the restaurant on a hill she paused, pulled out her cellphone, and captured the moment. Once inside she was quickly seated on the establishment's veranda where a row of seats faced the ocean. She ordered the seafood dish Hank had recommended and took the server's suggestion for a fruity white wine. While eating, she became engrossed with the latest news on social media, DMing friends and posting pictures of the island taken with her cellphone. So much so that she didn't notice the handsome stranger who had been seated beside her until he spoke.

"I hate eating alone," he began without greeting, while looking out on the waves gently crashing against the shore. "But if I have to do it, having a gorgeous woman beside me makes it infinitely more satisfying."

Only then did he turn toward her with a smile.

Well, damn. Kennedy was prepared to be aggravated at the tired line, but the man was gorgeous in a way that was free and unscripted, a face that suggested, "I woke up like this."

"Thank you."

"I was thinking about ordering that dish. Is it good?"

"It's delicious. The concierge recommended it and he was spot on."

"Where are you staying?" Kennedy told him. "How have I missed seeing you?"

"You're staying there, too?"

"For the past week, though mostly I've been down at the beach soaking up the sun. What are you doing here if I may ask, and more importantly, why are you eating alone?"

Kennedy turned and swept her arm across the occupied tables. "I'm not alone."

The stranger smiled, revealing pearly whites that sparkled, just like his eyes, the color of the sky in her earlier photographs. The brilliant shade of blue against tanned skin, combined with a head of thick and curly brunette hair, and Kennedy once again considered ending her penis drought.

A server arrived, set down a drink, and took the man's order. Afterwards, he held out his hand. "Jack Sutton."

She picked up a linen napkin and wiped her hands. "Kennedy Wade."

"Nice meeting you, Kennedy."

"Likewise."

For the next forty minutes the two casually chatted. Kennedy learned that Jack was an engineer from Rhode Island, recently divorced, taking his first vacation in more than three years. He was intelligent and funny, easy to talk to, and seemed to genuinely listen as Kennedy talked. When he suggested they split a dessert, she agreed. When he offered to pay the tab, she said yes to that, too. When he asked her to join him for an after-dinner drink back at the hotel, Jack was three for three. They sat in the cushy chairs of the lounge in the lobby and swapped tall travel tales. A yawn reminded Kennedy of the next day's early rising. She finished her decaf caramel coffee and reached for her bag.

"Thanks for a great evening, the dinner and the conversation. I enjoyed it."

"Are you leaving?"

"Yes," she said, and stood.

"Then so am I." Jack also stood and reached for his wallet.

"Oh, no. You did dinner. I've got this one."

"Are you sure I can't talk you into extending the evening? The company is amazing and it's a beautiful night."

"I agree on both counts, but tomorrow's alarm rings early. I have a plane to catch."

They bantered back and forth a bit more, but Kennedy wouldn't change her mind. After paying the tab, the two walked to the elevator and got in. Jack's finger hovered over the floor buttons. "Which one?"

"Seven."

He pushed seven for her floor, and ten for his. Later, when asked, that would be the last thing she remembered that night.

2

Bright sun streamed into Kennedy's room. She stretched, turned her head, and blinked her eyes against its incessant beam. She sat straight up and immediately regretted the quick action. Granted she wasn't much of a drinker, but she'd only had the rum punch and last night's glass of wine. Why was there a hammer in her head? Then, another question popped up between the banging.

What time is it?!?!

Her mind screamed these questions, but her body refused to perform with the urgency belied by these words. Kennedy closed her eyes, blindly reaching for the cellphone while easing her head to the pillow. Feeling only the nightstand's bamboo top, she gave her head the slightest turn and took in the table with the one eye opened. No phone.

Dear God, do I have to move again?

Kennedy perched herself up on an elbow and eyed the clock. The digital display confirmed what the sun had announced. It was mid-morning. She'd missed her flight. As that misfortune sank in, two observations slammed into her so hard her stomach clenched. One, the ever-present cellphone she'd groped for wasn't on the nightstand. Two, she was naked. She never slept naked. Ever. Even after having sex she'd at least put her panties back on. A slow sense of dread began to ooze through her body, like poisoned sludge invading the pure waters of peace that yesterday's boat trip created. She forced herself out of bed, wincing against the relentless throbbing. She pulled the light throw from the foot of the bed and wrapped it around her, dazed as she walked around and took in her surroundings. The clothes, strewn across the sofa. Her small purse, open, its contents spilled over her cushions. The laptop from which last night she'd sent off files and uploaded pictures—gone—along with the digital camera she'd left beside it. Her cellphone, nowhere to be found. Images flashed through her mind, blurry, disjointed. A soft, easy smile. Deep blue eyes. Dark, curly tresses. Manicured hands. Steaming cup lifted to tempting lips.

Jack?

The palms of her hands lifted to her forehead. Kennedy slowly massaged it, trying to bring the snippets of what she remembered from last night into one, cohesive picture. She opened her mouth. To speak? To ask the empty room, the air, what happened? Only then did she notice how dry her mouth was, and the aftertaste of something acidic, or acrid, at the back of her tongue. Definitely not the taste of last night's coffee. Had she been drugged and then assaulted? The mere thought made her heart drop. She clutched her Kegel muscles. There was no soreness and given it had been months since she'd had sex, there would be. Still, she wouldn't take a shower. Doing so could wash away potential evidence. She'd watched enough crime TV to know that. Will was heavily endowed. Maybe Jack wasn't. Maybe it wasn't Jack. What if it was someone else? Why couldn't she remember what happened? Couldn't have been just the wine, it had to have been something stronger, like a date rape drug. The throbbing returned full force.

Her wallet lay open, on top of the purse. Kennedy snatched it up. The clear pocket that should have held her driver's license was empty. Credit cards, debit cards, even her grocery store reward cards—gone. But the twenty-five dollars from the ATM she'd taken out for tips was still in there? WTH? To take charge cards but leave the cash made no sense at all. Anger at being ripped off spurred her into action. The faster this crime got reported, the better chance police would have to catch whoever violated her room. Maybe her body. Definitely her trust.

Instinctively, she headed toward the nightstand to grab her phone. That led to a growl of frustration and quick strides to where last night's clothes had been tossed on the couch. She dressed in seconds, then headed downstairs without thought for a card key. The elevator doors had barely opened when she shot through them and strode straight to the front desk. She met bright eyes and cheery smiles with a statement that quickly shifted the mood.

"I need the police. I've been robbed."

The reaction was shock. Not only from those behind the counter, but from the couple beside her who'd just checked in. Not a great public service announcement. Kennedy hadn't even noticed them there. Her focus was direct, and singular. Police. Investigation. Rape kit. Justice. Now.

"Ms. Wade! I'm so sorry." The woman, seeming barely a girl, really, spoke from her heart with her hands to her chest. "Where were you coming from?"

"My room. That's where it happened."

A woman appeared from the office behind them. Her stride strong, her back straight, she bypassed the counter and walked directly to Kennedy.

"Excuse me, miss. I'm Darlene Gardner, the front desk manager. I overhead your statement. Can you please come with me into the office?" Her voice was no nonsense, but her eyes were kind. She turned and headed back that way without waiting for an answer.

Kennedy followed her, and for the first time noticed other guests in the lobby. And Hank's face, creased and troubled, staring at her from across the room. He'd recommended the restaurant where she'd met Jack. Was he in on what happened? Had it been smiling, friendly Hank who removed her clothes and took her belongings?

The woman who'd come for her quietly closed the door. "Please, sit down."

"I don't have time to sit! Somebody robbed me. Maybe even raped me. I went out last night for a simple dinner and drinks and woke up this morning with no electronics, wearing no clothes and having no memory of what happened!"

"I'm deeply sorry," the woman continued, unruffled, her voice low and calm. "But before I can help you, and believe me, I want to and I will, I need to hear the whole story to know who to call."

"Who else do you call when someone's been robbed, except the police? For all I know the perpetrator could still be somewhere in the hotel. I need law enforcement, now!"

A short stare, a brief nod, and then, "Very well. But I am the front desk supervisor and having no idea what took place, I don't have the authority to make that call. The hotel mana—"

Kennedy jumped up and headed for the door. "I'm not waiting for permission to report a crime. I'll use a payphone. I'll walk to the station if I have to."

"Please! Don't leave."

Kennedy turned, her hand on the doorknob, to see the supervisor standing, too. A second of silence passed between them.

"I don't know what you've been through, but I do know what it's like to be mistreated. I am only trying to be thorough, and experience has taught us that the more information we can document as quickly as possible, the greater the opportunity to capture details that might otherwise be forgotten and left out.

"I will get the hotel manager in here immediately, and we will call the authorities, alright? While they're coming, if you please, I will begin a report on what happened."

The sincerity and compassion in the supervisor's words brought a bit of calm to Kennedy's spirit and mistiness to her eyes.

"Thank you." She walked back to the chair and sat.

"Most certainly."

"What is your name again?"

A small smile slipped past the stalwart demeanor behind a navy suit and crisp white blouse. "Darlene Gardner. Give me a moment to contact the manager." She picked up the phone and punched a few keys. Almost immediately there was a tap on the office door before it opened, and an imposing man with a serious expression stepped inside.

"Mr. Ledard, I was just ringing you."

He nodded at Darlene, but his eyes were on Kennedy. "Are you the guest claiming to have been assaulted?"

"I am the one who was definitely assaulted. There is no doubt."

"Of course. Forgive my choice of words." He extended his hand. "I'm Charles Ledard, the hotel manager."

"Did someone phone you?" Darlene asked.

"I was crossing the lobby and was notified that we had an emergency. Have the police been called?"

"I was just phoning you to have that done."

"Let's get them down here." Charles pointed toward the chair beside Kennedy. "May I?"

"Sure."

He sat down. Kennedy shifted her body toward him.

"Is it possible for you to tell us what happened?" Kennedy was struck by the way he worded the question, his mild manner contrasting with his commanding presence and with Darlene's measured tone.

"Honestly, I was hoping to wait for the police and avoid having to repeat myself."

Charles nodded. "We can do that."

No pushback. No rebuttal. Nothing about lines of command and protocol, or time being relevant. Kennedy's face remained neutral, but in that moment, Darlene became one not to trust.

The police arrived within minutes, a team—male and female—strictly business. "We'd like to speak with you privately," the woman said once introductions were made.

"I don't want to repeat this story," Kennedy interjected, as the memory of waking up naked crossed her mind. "The hotel wants me to give them a report, too. Thinking back on what happened or might have happened is difficult."

"We will provide details to them from what you tell us," the woman, Stephanie, replied. She looked at Darlene. "May we use this office?"

Charles and Darlene left. Stephanie sat in the seat Darlene had vacated. Her partner, Bayron, remained standing, notepad in hand. Stephanie pulled out a small tape recorder. "We would like to tape this conversation for documentation. Do you give your consent?"

"Yes."

"Okay, Kennedy, it is our understanding that a robbery occurred?" Kennedy nodded. Stephanie sat back in the chair. "When did this happen?"

"Sometime between midnight and this morning, I guess. The memories are fuzzy. I may have been drugged. And . . . assaulted." She couldn't bring herself to say "raped" again.

The police exchanged a look. "Tell us what happened," Stephanie said, "as best you can."

Kennedy briefly recounted what led to her visit, and then

taking an extra day to enjoy the island. She told of the boat ride, going to dinner, meeting Jack and sharing an aperitif in the hotel's lounge.

"I paid the bill and we walked to the elevator. He asked for my floor. I told him. He pushed it. Then he pushed . . ." Kennedy stopped, closed her eyes. "Nine or ten, I believe. And . . . that's all I remember until waking up today, realizing that I missed my flight, and because of that will also be a no show at tonight's fabulous Friday."

Stephanie's brow creased. She exchanged another look with Bayron. "Fabulous Friday?"

"Never mind." Kennedy waved a dismissive hand. "It's a small gathering of professional friends back in Chicago. One of their birthday's is today so tonight is going to be a celebration of that, too."

Bayron straightened and took a step toward her. "What day is it, Ms. Wade?"

"What kind of question is that? It's Friday." Concerned eyes stared back at her. "Isn't it?"

"No, Ms. Wade," Stephanie said softly. "It's Saturday."

The truth punched Kennedy in the gut. She'd been out cold for two nights.

3

Kennedy had lost over thirty hours that she'd never get back. At first, she blamed the hotel. Why hadn't the front desk called her? Why didn't housekeeping try to clean her room? Was no one aware that a guest who'd planned to check out on Friday was still there a day later? A quick investigation provided the answer. Two days had been added to her stay, courtesy of a PayPal account with an IP address linked to a Baltic country. Law enforcement recorded the information, said they'd investigate. Kennedy's thought? Good luck with that. A "do not disturb" sign was all it took to keep housekeeping out and everyone unaware of a crime.

She spent the entire Saturday with hotel personnel and law enforcement trying to piece together what had happened. An hour of that was at a medical center where she'd been given a physical exam that showed no signs of vaginal trauma as one might expect had forced sex occurred. Still, they conducted a rape kit and had blood drawn in hopes of identifying what was used to drug her. She'd phoned the U. S. Embassy and met with a representative with information on continuing the case once back stateside. By the time she boarded her evening flight to return to Chicago she'd been made glad twice—delighted to arrive in the beautiful Bahamas and happy as hell to be leaving.

Returning home, she didn't have the luxury of dwelling on what had happened in the Bahamas. Freelancing was a constant hustle and she had a mortgage. It wasn't supposed to be a struggle to pay it. That came courtesy of a man named Will and her own foolish action of believing a liar who said the condo would be a home they'd share. A call from the Bahamas on Monday morning helped her get back into the freelance flow. The rape kit results came in. She hadn't been sexually assaulted. That only left her to wonder how she ended up naked. Since there had been no physical violation, was it possible that in her drugged state she'd removed her own clothes? As improbable as that seemed, it felt infinitely better than imagining that she'd been undressed, ogled, and groped by a stranger. The more she warmed up to this take on the story, the better she felt.

The week following the incident was a whirlwind of insurance claim filings, electronics store visits, freelance website scrolling, and nonstop work. Saturday was a day of catching up with the mundane—cleaning, laundry, and her standing mani/pedi appointment. She'd also shopped for a birthday gift, a peace offering she hoped would make up for missing her best friend Gwen's birthday, even though her absence couldn't be helped. That night she went to bed early and was up at seven the next morning for a morning jog to the coffee shop. She bought dark roast java, a bagel, and the *Chicago Star*. Super critical of her own work, Kennedy gave herself a pat on this one. She felt the article accurately captured what made the Bahamas such a popular destination. The pictures backed up those words. No time to rest on her laurels, though. She spent the rest of the day scouring various websites for jobs.

By that evening, Kennedy was more than ready to meet up with Logan, a former co-worker who Kennedy loved like a brother, and her bestie, Gwen. She entered Leftovers, the unofficial new hang out of the city's cool crowd. It was just after seven. The restaurant and bar had a full house, but she weaved her way through the suits and stilettos toward the booth where her friends sat. Along the way she waved at a few familiar faces and realized it was the first time since the incident in the Caribbean that she wasn't subconsciously searching for a suspect.

"Hey, guys!" Kennedy reached Logan first.

He stood and gave her a hug. "Hey, you!"

"How are you doing, girl?" Kennedy sat next to Gwen and leaned over for a squeeze, then held out the peace offering hidden within a glittery gift bag. "Happy birthday!"

"Thank you," Gwen replied, accepting the gift even as she leaned forward, her voice low and accusatory. "Why didn't you tell anybody that you were robbed?"

Kennedy cut her eyes at Logan. "I did tell *anybody,* and obviously, *anybody* told somebody else."

"I wasn't supposed to tell anyone?" He covered his mouth. "Oops."

"Never mind that. Said the woman to the person she thought was her best friend," Gwen mumbled before asking, "What happened?"

"It's a long story, one that will go down better with drinks. But first, open your present."

Gwen's frown flipped as she removed the multi-colored tissue papers from the bag and placed them beside her. Her eyes gleamed as she reached in and pulled out a CD box set and when she saw the cover she squealed. "Aretha! You know that's my girl!"

She threw her arms around Kennedy's neck and gave her an exuberant hug, then set back and flipped over the box.

"It's supposed to be a complete set of all the songs she recorded on Atlantic Records."

"Who?" Logan asked.

"Aretha," Gwen intoned, "and if you ask for a last name, I'll cut you."

The table cracked up.

"Everybody knows Aretha Franklin," Logan said. "We've sampled her a couple times when creating beats."

"And paid her I hope."

"Of course," Logan replied, with a hand over his heart as if wounded.

"Well, whatever it was, it wasn't enough. How are you going to capture all of what she delivered in a loop?"

"Come down to the studio some time and I'll show you."

Gwen rolled her eyes.

"Her grandmother worshipped Aretha's talent," Kennedy said to Logan, hoping to ward off an argument. Logan's hip-hop obsession and music producer aspirations were as strong as Gwen's love for old school R&B. "Gwen grew up to her music. Plus, I think she's an old soul."

The waiter came around. They ordered drinks.

"Thanks again," Gwen said, before placing the box back in the gift bag and setting the bag near the wall. "I can't wait to play them. With this amazing gift, plus knowing what happened in the Bahamas, you are forgiven for being MIA on my special day. I'm just glad to see that you're alright."

Whether that was true or not was up to debate, but Kennedy let the comment slide. She wanted to be alright. Maybe if she kept hearing she was, she'd believe it.

"I read the article," Gwen continued. "It was fabulous, made me want to go online and buy a ticket right then."

"Thank you."

"Those pictures were stunning. That rainbow? Wow. Was it photoshopped?"

"No, but I can understand why you'd say that. I adjusted the lighting to bring out the depth of color. But it was even more amazing than what you saw in the paper."

"The way you framed it, with the greenery from that island

in the middle of the picture, the white sand and that sparkling blue water . . . very well done, girl."

"I hope it leads to steadier work. That's my goal."

Gwen looked at Logan. "Did you see the article?"

"I'm reading it now," Logan said, cellphone in hand.

"Can we talk about your trip at all, or is the whole island experience off limits until you get drunk?"

"Give me a break, Gwendolyn McPherson. Nobody said anything about getting drunk."

"Did you get drunk in the Bahamas?" Logan asked. "Because if you did you probably got some. You told everybody about the newspaper spread but I know the real reason you went down there was to forget about Will."

"Would you get out of my bedroom?" Kennedy asked. "And worry about who's between your sheets."

"I'm trying to get between yours." Logan backed up his audacious statement with an unapologetic stare.

"Whatever, little boy."

"Yeah, you won't be saying that after I drop the boxers."

Gwen began an exaggerated bout of coughing. "Time out, time out!"

Kennedy agreed. Logan was handsome, she'd give him that, and the kind of man she liked—tall, lanky, coffee-colored with a generous splash of crème, and sporting just the right amount of facial hair. But he'd just turned twenty-three. Even though Will was five years older than her twenty-eight ball drops, Kennedy felt she'd spent two years babysitting a child. Next round she wanted a grown-ass man.

"So how was your time on the island?" Gwen asked. "Did you like it as much as we did Jamaica?"

"It's hard to compare them. Jamaica was a vacation. The Bahamas was work."

"I saw some of your social media posts," Logan said. "That boat ride didn't look like work to me."

"You posted pics on social media, too?" Gwen reached for her cellphone, tapped the screen and began to scroll.

"Not the ones that accompanied the article."

Gwen kept scrolling. The server returned with their drinks. "Who is this in the selfie pic? He's kinda cute."

"His name is Clinton. He works for the boat rental company."

"These are nice. But you definitely saved the best ones for the *Star*."

Gwen put down her phone. "Alright, enough shop talk. Let's toast to Kennedy arriving safely back home." They'd barely finished clinking glasses and getting through half a sip before she added, "Now, tell us what happened? How'd you get robbed?"

"Honestly, I don't know."

She told Gwen the same basic story that she'd shared with Logan, the one that omitted being naked when she woke up. Even with not being sexually assaulted, she was still too embarrassed to share that part of the story. "After wrapping up the police interview at the hotel, the manager and supervisor were brought back in and informed of what happened. We found out that there was no Jack Sutton registered at the hotel. No one at the front desk remembered anyone resembling the man I described. I'd become friendly with a guy named Hank, the concierge. He talked to absolutely everybody who walked either in or out of that lobby. He hadn't seen him, either. Or so he said."

"Why'd you say it like that? Do you think he had something to do with it?"

"I don't know what to think. After finding my stuff gone from the room, everyone became a suspect. But in my gut, I think it was the man who called himself Jack. I think he's an asshole who takes vacations and preys on women and steals stuff."

Logan nodded. "I think you're right. The fact that he lied about being a guest says it all."

"So, what happens now?" Gwen asked.

"I wait to hear from my attorney."

Gwen made a face. "Are you talking about Craig?"

Kennedy laughed. Gwen hadn't liked Kennedy's attorney, ever since he had turned down an alcohol-induced invitation to join Gwen for a private party in her bedroom.

"No, a Bahamian attorney. After the police left the hotel, I contacted the U. S. Embassy. Fortunately, a duty officer is available 24/7. He met with me and provided a ton of valuable information."

"Like what?" Logan asked.

"He gave me an overview of how their criminal process operates. He had shortcuts to reporting my credit cards and driver's license stolen—"

"What about your passport?"

"Safe, fortunately. It was in a zippered compartment of my luggage, which was unlocked. But it didn't look like he rifled through it much."

"Clothes don't sell as well as phones and laptops."

"Spoken like an authority, Logan."

"Girl, shut up."

Gwen ignored him. "Is that how you found your attorney?"

"Yes. He had a list of several attorneys. I chose one who dealt primarily with my type of crime."

"How much faith do you have in the police conducting a thorough investigation, or in this attorney prosecuting the case if they find out Jack's real name, or whoever did it?"

Kennedy shrugged. "The attorney was actually out of the country, so I only spoke with him by phone, briefly, a few days ago. The police seemed concerned, focused on the details of what happened and finding out who did it. They searched the room. I think they dusted for prints and stuff. Blood was drawn to find out what was used to drug me. But I don't hold out much hope for them finding evidence that could lead to him."

"They probably collected dust balls, evidence of how long it's been since you had sex."

"Ha!" Kennedy gave Gwen a shove. "You have no sense at all. I feel as though I did everything I could do. Now it's time for the authorities and the Bahamian attorney to do what they do. Thank goodness I have a habit of uploading everything to the cloud, especially my pictures, as soon as I finish a shoot, and that I sent the article in before heading out to dinner. It could lead to steadier work from the *Star* in the future, so having to rewrite it would have been a huge blow."

Gwen's brow raised. "I think the blow is that whoever was in your room has your ID, which means they have your address and date of birth. Identity theft is a nightmare. Be sure and stay on top of your credit reports. No telling what they might try and do as you."

Kennedy sighed, shaking her head slightly as she reached for her wine glass. "I know." She took a long sip. "They have my full name and DOB. But I've used an alternative address on driver's licenses, checks, utilities, and stuff like that ever since reading this book that was written by the owner of a security company. So, if they try and track me down, they'll find themselves driving into a strip mall and parking in front of Mail, Etc."

"I know that's right!" Gwen and Kennedy high-fived.

"Not that I think Jack, or whatever his name is, will do that. He's probably more of a snatch, grab and go type of guy. Plus, he'd have to spend money to come after me and since he's stealing, he obviously doesn't have much of that. As for the phone, it was shut off immediately. That was the laptop used strictly for travel and work, so there wasn't any extremely personal or confidential information on it. Like I said, I've done everything I can do."

Kennedy spotted a former colleague at the bar, a quirky

Jewish guy with an encyclopedic memory and a wry sense of humor. She waved him over to join them at the table. He was the perfect solution to ending talk about work and burglaries. The four decided to stay for dinner, and afterwards went to an IMAX theater to catch the latest action flick. It was after midnight when Kennedy slipped the key into her condo lock, humming the song she'd just heard in her car. She stopped though, when the steady beeps on her security system that signaled an open door didn't go off. Her heart seized for a second but just as quickly she threw off the notion that something was wrong. This wasn't the Bahamas. It was Chicago. She'd lived there for a decade and dating Will was the closest she'd come to having a crime committed against her.

"Can't believe I didn't set it," she murmured, sliding the leather strap of her laptop bag off her shoulder and stopping just inside the door to take off her shoes. One would think that after what happened last weekend she'd double and triple check locks and systems. She set it, then picked up her heels by the straps and walked through the foyer and down the hallway. Reaching for the dimmer knob she turned it and increased the lighting in the modern, open concept area, then continued into the room. The living space was fine but her office, visible from where she now stood, was not the way she'd left it.

Drawers were open.

Papers from her desk top littered the floor.

Her home computer, the one that did contain personal and confidential information—gone.

Trembling, Kennedy backed out of the room, then out of her home, dialing 911.

4

Kennedy felt drained, robotic, as she walked the officer to the door. It was almost four in the morning—the police had taken almost two hours to respond.

"Is there going to be an investigation of this?" she asked him.

"We'll file the report but honestly, not likely. Unfortunately, there are so many crimes more violent and egregious that we simply don't have the manpower to follow up on simple burglary claims."

"So, if I'd been murdered during the burglary, there would be resources available to try and catch the culprit."

The officer looked her dead in the eye. "Yes."

"Thanks for being honest with me."

The officer placed a compassionate hand on Kennedy's shoulder. "I'm sorry. There has been a spate of random smash and grab burglaries in the surrounding area. We have beefed up patrol, but without an eye witness or concrete evidence to work with, that's about all we can do."

Kennedy closed the door and briefly leaned against it. She closed her eyes, feeling drained—mentally, physically and emotionally. Footsteps echoed on the hardwood floor and neared her. Logan had been her second call after the police. Firm hands gently pulled her away from the wall. Strong arms wrapped themselves around her. The dam of strength that had kept Kennedy cool, calm and collected from what happened in the Bahamas until now began to crumble. She laid her head against Logan's chest and allowed the tears to flow.

"It's okay," he cooed, rubbing her back as he walked them back into the living room. "I got you, Kennedy. We'll get through this. Do you hear me?"

Kennedy nodded. She pulled away from him and sat on the couch, her knees pulled to her chest. Logan pulled a tissue from a holder on the coffee table and held it out. She took it and blew her nose.

"I just don't understand. Does lightning strike twice? Do I have 'rob me' on my forehead? What is going on?"

Logan slowly shook his head. "I don't know. It does seem pretty weird, though, that you'd get robbed in the Bahamas one week and then get robbed at home just a week later." He looked at her, his eyes conveying the churning taking place in his mind. "Do you think they're related?"

"I don't know what to think. It appears that once again only electronics were taken—this time my desktop. My laptop was in the car from earlier when I'd decided to work from the coffee shop near Leftovers. It's not like I live in an exclusive neighborhood. So why was my house targeted? Did they see me leave and know that the place was empty? I just don't get it. Nothing logical makes sense yet thinking this is mere coincidence seems illogical and unlikely."

"I agree. Hmm . . ."

The two remained quiet, lost in their individual thoughts about a possible explanation for what had happened to Kennedy, not once, but twice.

"Kennedy." Logan's voice was low as his eyes pierced her.

"What?"

"Do you think it was Will?"

She shook her head. "Will is a lot of things but a burglar . . . I can't see it. I also can't think of why he'd want my desktop. He's a gamer and has a top-of-the-line system. No, I don't think it's Will."

"What if it wasn't about the computer? What if he wanted to do something to interfere with your career? In the Bahamas, most of what was stolen had to do with your work—camera, computer, cellphone. Last night, same thing. Work-related stuff. Maybe he's getting back at what you did to him personally by trying to sabotage your professional career."

Kennedy shifted her legs and sat up, her back against the sofa. "It's what he did to me that ended our relationship. I was always the one giving, compromising, sacrificing." She shook her head. "I don't think it's him."

"What about another ex?"

Kennedy pondered the question. "I can't see anyone I've dated wanting my computers. Maybe it was random and I'm just having a streak of bad luck."

"The officer did say burglaries have increased in the neighborhood."

"Yeah, and I had no idea."

"What about a colleague? Can you think of somebody who might be angry that you got a job they thought they should have, or have it out for you for professional reasons?"

"Right now, I'm too wiped out to think at all."

"I hear you. It's late. Why don't you go lie down, try and get some sleep?"

"You've been up all night, too." Logan's lips took a slight upturn. "No, that's not an invitation."

His smile widened.

"Will you be okay driving home?"

"I'm good. Will you be okay here alone?"

"We're about to find out."

Kennedy walked Logan to the door. When he turned to embrace her, she welcomed it. Independent and self-contained, Kennedy never felt she had the luxury of a shoulder to lean on or depending on a man. But given what she'd been through yet again, it felt good to be in the grasp of a man's strong arms.

"Call me later, alright?"

"Okay. Thanks again, Low. I appreciate you."

Kennedy crawled into bed. She took tossing and turning to a new level, but managed to catch a few winks amid the chaos in her mind. When she woke up around two o'clock, she roused herself out of bed. While taking a long, hot shower she pondered the Bahamas break-in, last night's burglary, what it all meant, and what she was going to do to stop the madness. One thing she wanted to do, but knew she couldn't, was to call her mom. Karolyn Wade would be on the next thing smoking to Chicago waving a one-way ticket for Kennedy's return home. She hadn't been a fan of her moving there in the first place. "Nothing in big cities but big trouble," she'd told her. Kennedy and her brother Karl had experienced the ease and relative security of growing up in the small Kansas town of Peyton where her mother had been born and still resided, along with Kennedy's grandmother and much of the extended family. Karl had gone to UMKC and lived in Kansas City, Missouri's largest city. They were two of the few who'd flown the coop and returned home only to visit—never to stay.

Even though it wasn't yet five o'clock, she did call Gwen. Her normally flippant friend remained quiet as Kennedy relayed last night's events. Not even a joke when Kennedy said she'd called Logan and he'd come over and stayed through the night.

Instead, this sincere comment when Kennedy went silent. "I'm scared for you."

She'd voiced the words Kennedy hadn't dared. She was frightened, too.

After talking to Gwen, Kennedy tried to put the burglary

behind her by focusing on photos. The Bahamas spread in Sunday's paper had generated more interest in her work. She sent digital portfolios in response to two email inquiries on her availability and fee—one for an organic farm's marketing campaign and website, and a very promising one from the Chi-Town's Convention and Visitor's Bureau. Securing a position with the latter organization could mean steady work for years. She also sent a resume to a new regional publication seeking an art director. After finishing up emails checking social media and freelance sites, she filled out another Apple insurance claim and fully expected to receive a phone call from a representative suspecting fraud. If two burglaries hadn't happened to her in less than two weeks, she wouldn't have believed it either. Midway through filling out the online claim, the doorbell rang.

Probably Gwen.

Kennedy opened the door. Not Gwen.

"Logan, hey. What are you doing back here?"

"Taking care of business. Can I come in?"

"Sure."

Kennedy stepped back and watched Logan's long, sure strides through the foyer and down the hall, slipping off a backpack along the way. She followed behind him.

"Did you just come from work?" Logan worked at a warehouse. Maybe there was a camera inside.

"Naw, I was off today. Come check this out."

Kennedy walked over to the sofa, watching as Logan pulled out several items from the bag. "What's all this?"

"Security. It's a four-camera system." Logan looked up and around. "I think that's enough for here."

"You went out and bought a security system?"

"Well, obviously the one you have now doesn't work." Logan stood and began walking as he talked. Kennedy followed behind him, speechless.

"One for your front door, the outside of course. One for the office. One for the bedroom and one for your patio. What do you think?" Into the silence he added, "or maybe we should place one in the garage, by your parking space. Yeah, I think that might be a better choice than your bedroom since to hear Gwen tell it, there's little chance of anyone going in there."

Kennedy gave him a look. "Oh, my bad. I should have said, given my own experience . . ."

She play-punched him. "Shut up!"

Logan dodged her punch and walked back into the living room. He picked up the set of four cameras enclosed in hard plastic. "Can I get a pair of scissors?"

"Do you really think this is necessary?"

"Don't you?"

"I very much want to believe that it's definitely not necessary. I want to believe I've had the uncanny luck of being targeted here just like I was in the Bahamas."

"I spent the day thinking about that, wondering what were the chances that someone would get robbed in a whole other country, come home, and get robbed not even a week—or barely a week—after the last incident. Those odds have got to be pretty low, don't you think?"

Without answering, Kennedy turned around and went for the scissors.

Two hours later, the security camera software had been downloaded to Kennedy's laptop and her cellphone.

"So how the video operates," Logan said while holding the instruction booklet, "is that the device is both motion and heat sensitive. So, you can have it videoing all the time, or you can set it up to turn on only when there's motion or heat, which is what I recommend."

"Why not have it going 24/7?"

"You can, but to me that would be just filling up a lot of storage space with worthless footage. But if you have it turned to the sensors, you'll get an alert when the video turns on."

"Okay, let's do that."

Logan finished the setup. He handed Kennedy the instructions. "Here you go, Ken. I think you're all set."

"Thank you so much, Logan. How much do I owe you for this system?"

"Don't worry about it."

"Oh, no. I want to pay you the money so I don't end up owing you some other kind of way."

They both laughed.

"I'll send you an invoice for my services."

"Please do. The equipment and the installation."

"Girl, I've been trying to install my equipment ever since I met you!"

"Boy!"

Kennedy couldn't ignore how good Logan made her feel. The hug at the front door was a bit longer than the last time.

"Alright, then. I'm out."

"Okay, Low. See you later." Kennedy began to close the door, then jerked it open. "Logan! Wait!"

He turned and followed her back inside. "What is it?"

"I just thought of something."

Kennedy walked into her office and over to a black file cabinet. She opened the top drawer, reached behind the folders it contained and pulled out a box.

"Hold on to this for me."

Logan took it. "What is it?"

"Insurance." She closed the cabinet and leaned against it. "There's a flash drive in there containing the backup of my premium photos, a digital portfolio of sellable prints I've either already edited or plan to."

"You don't have a cloud account?"

"Yes, and they're in it. But clouds aren't foolproof."

"They're not?"

"Trust me, I've heard stories. I only want you to hold it until

I set up a safe deposit box or some other secure place to hold them. With all the bad luck following me lately, I don't want to be the only one with a hard copy."

Logan pocketed the small box as the two walked toward the front door. "No worries, Ken. I've got you."

Logan felt light, happy, as he exited the elevator and strolled through the lobby of Kennedy's ten-story condominium building. He hated to take advantage of her vulnerable position, and he really did want her to feel safe. But he also wanted her to look at him as something other than a play little brother. Hooking her up with a security system might be the cherry on top of a two-year campaign to win Kennedy's heart. As he neared the exit doors, his mood changed. He could have sworn that the man dressed in black sitting in the lobby was the same one he'd seen across the street hours ago when on his way to her unit. He continued out the door, pulling out earbuds as though going on a stroll. But he didn't go far. Later when asked he wouldn't be able to explain why, but when he saw the man walk across the lobby headed for the elevator, Logan cut back through a side door and hit the stairwell toward Kennedy's unit eight floors up.

5

Kennedy was about to return to the task that Logan had interrupted when another distraction sounded—her rumbling stomach. With everything that had happened, Kennedy had forgotten to eat. She bypassed the office and headed to the kitchen. The insurance claims for this latest break in would have to wait. Fortunately, she grocery-shopped on Saturday and had a full fridge. She pulled out a container of prepared salad from the organic mart and a container of chicken salad from the corner deli. She placed those on the counter and reached for a package of bulkie rolls and a bag of BBQ kettle chips from the cabinet. She placed those items next to the other containers, then walked toward the stereo and turned on her favorite afternoon drive show hosted by the comedian she once called her play husband. A nice groove oozed out of the speakers and filled the room. She did a little bop on the way back to the kitchen, glanced over at her office and took a detour to look inside. Even though Logan had placed it in a very unobtrusive spot, it would take her a while to get used to seeing the camera mounted near the ceiling, against the office's farthest wall. It took in the door and the desk, mainly, giving Kennedy the idea to rearrange the room so that her file cabinet could be captured as well. The music transitioned to a love song. That Logan's face swam into her head would have been problematic had she acknowledged it was because of the song playing. Instead she told herself it was because of the security system he'd installed.

Yes, that's it. Annoying little boy.

Annoying, thoughtful, caring, fine young man who promised big things, whispered the side of her brain that she couldn't control. She smiled despite her resolve, and bopped into the kitchen. She'd just pulled a plate from the cabinet and pulled apart the roll to make a sandwich when she heard muffled voices followed by what sounded like a scuffle in the hallway outside her door. *WTH?* Frowning, she set down the roll and walked over to turn down the music in time to hear the heavy pitter patter of running feet. She raced to her door and pulled it open without thought. Her hand flew to her mouth with the sight that greeted her. She didn't know what shocked her more—Logan on the hallway floor or the blood that dripped from his face.

"Logan!"

She rushed out and reached for him, but he shook off her hands.

"I'm alright." He got to his feet and put a hand to the nose gushing blood. "Punk motherfucker," he mumbled, brushing past Kennedy and entering her place.

She followed behind his long, purposeful strides toward the main bathroom, watched as he turned on the cold water tap and began washing the blood away from his face.

"What happened?"

"Do you have some ice?"

"Yes."

"Can you get me some?"

Kennedy hurried out of the bathroom, stopped at the linen closet in the hallway and after pulling out a wash cloth continued to the refrigerator. She placed several cubes into the towel, then placed the towel under the faucet to wet it. As she turned Logan passed her, a handful of tissues against his face as he walked into the living room area and plopped down on the couch.

She joined him there. "Here." She held out the towel with the ice cubes, then sat next to him. He replaced the tissues with the ice pack, then laid his head against the back of the couch and closed his eyes.

"Are you sure you're okay?" she asked, her voice low, soft and laced with concern. He nodded. She watched him for another moment, noticed as the rising and falling of his chest became slower and steadier.

"What happened?"

"A dude was casing your house."

"What do you mean?"

Logan sat up, pulled the pack away from his nose. "Is it still bleeding?"

"Doesn't look like it, but you might want to keep it there anyway so that it doesn't swell."

"I noticed this cat when I came in here. I don't know why, just something about him that made me kind of catalog him away in my mind. When I got off the elevator and saw him in the lobby, everything in my body went on alert. But I played it cool, thought maybe it was me being paranoid for you, that maybe he lived here and just happened to be downstairs both times I was there. I had pulled out my earbuds and put them in my ear, hit the door as though I was headed away. But I stopped as soon as I passed the glass and looked back to see if he was still sitting there. That fool was headed straight for the elevators. That's when I slipped through the side door and came up the stairs."

Kennedy looked at Logan incredulously. "What made you react like that?"

"The man just felt creepy to me. I thought maybe he was the one who burglarized your place and was coming back to do something to you. I couldn't get on the elevator with him because that would obviously make him change his plans. So I took the stairs and hid in the hallway. Sure enough, he walked straight to your door."

"No!"

"I came around the corner then, my phone in hand. He was at your door, head down, focused. I think he was picking your lock."

"What? Logan, no way."

"I wanted to get a pic of his face and distract him from his task, so I called out to him. 'Hey, buddy.' He looked up, but as soon as he saw the phone he turned his head away and came straight toward me, trying to get my phone. That was a huge hell no. We started tousling. I punched dude dead in his face, and for my troubles took an elbow to the nose."

"Geez, Logan. I'm so sorry." She stood up and began to pace. "What the heck is going on?"

"I got one shot off before he saw me." Logan pulled out his phone, scrolled to photos and held it out. "Do you know him?"

Kennedy reached for the phone and studied the blurred shot Logan captured of the side of the man's face. Her eyes narrowed as she peered at it closely, willing up a memory that would help her recognize him. But she shook her head as she gave back the phone. "I don't know him."

She came back to the sofa. "Let me see him again." Logan handed her the phone. She enlarged the picture, studied it from different angles. "I swear, Logan, I don't know that man from anywhere."

"Well, he obviously knows you, and he knows that you know me. Otherwise how did he know to wait until I was gone? How did he know that you were the person I'd come here to see?"

The question sat Logan straight up. He got up, a frown marring his handsome features as he began looking around her house.

"What are you—"

A stern look accompanied the finger to his mouth as he crept across the room, looking here and there for what to Kennedy remained a mystery. She tiptoed after him. "What are you doing?" she whispered.

"Getting you out of here," he replied, just as low.

Following behind him, Kennedy had the awkward feeling that she was the guest and this was Logan's house. After checking both bedrooms and bathrooms along with the office, he returned to the kitchen. "Ah, cool. I'm hungry, too," he said, in a regular voice. "Why don't you bust out a couple sandwiches. This place has me feeling claustrophobic. We can grab those chips and go soak up some sun."

Kennedy didn't question the suggestion. Although her appetite had fled, she made two generous chicken sandwiches and reached below the counter to a roll of plastic wrap and stack of recycle bags. After wrapping the sandwiches and using some of the salad to top them she placed everything in the recycle bag, along with a couple cans of sparkling water and a stack of napkins. By the time she'd finished, Logan had disposed of the tissue and ice pack. Aside from a couple scratches, his face looked as handsome as it ever did.

"Ready?"

"I am."

He nodded toward her office. "Grab your laptop."

"Okay." She handed him the bag of food and went to the office. "Where'd you park?"

"Not far. Let's go."

Kennedy's and Logan's eyes were everywhere as they exited the elevator and walked through the lobby. She didn't notice anything or anyone out of the ordinary. Most importantly, she didn't see the man in black. There was little conversation from the condo building's door to the car. But once inside, the floodgates unlocked.

"Okay, Logan. What the hell is going on?"

"I think your place might be bugged."

"What?"

"Think about it. The dude knew I came to see you. How else would he know? He wasn't on the elevator with me. I don't think he had time to get from where I saw him to the elevator and see what floor I took. And even if he did, how would he know which apartment? Either he's been following you for days and saw us together at Leftovers, or there are hidden mics, maybe even cameras, all over your house."

"You're scaring me."

"You should be scared."

Logan drove to an area near Lake Michigan. He parked the car and reached back for the bag of food. Once again quiet became the third companion as they walked across the grass to a bench shaded by a tree that had a great view of the water. Kennedy was glad that he chose it. She was calmed by the gentle sway of the waves. As she focused on the water, she heard Logan rattling around inside the bag. He handed her a sandwich, pulled out and opened the chips and set one of the cans of water on the table.

"This is good," he said, after a healthy bite. "Did you make it?"

"No. It came from the deli down the street from my house."

"Are you going to eat?"

"In a minute." She watched the water a moment longer before opening her sparkling water and reaching inside the bag for a chip.

"I just don't get what's happening. I can't figure it out."

Logan nodded, and finished his bite. "I hear you. It's crazy, man. When I saw that guy heading for the elevator, my heart stopped. I had this feeling that if I didn't get there in time, something really bad was going to happen."

Kennedy looked at him, eyes wide. "You felt that?"

"I did. Something about him, man. Like he was a spy or a hitman or something. I'm serious! He gave off that kind of vibe. And the fact that he didn't want his picture taken? He's working for somebody."

"But who?"

"Only you can answer that question, babe."

Kennedy ate half the sandwich and while it was delicious, nerves cut the size of her stomach in half. She grabbed her water and walked toward the lake's edge, trying to draw peace from its tranquil state. *Who could have something out for her? Was the guy Logan fought the one who broke into her home and stole her desktop? If so, why?* Kennedy racked her brain, ran down the list of associates from the past six years that she'd worked in the business. The results? Nothing. Her mind was a total blank. What had she done in another life to bring on this karma? A shadow announced Logan's presence beside her. He picked up a handful of small pebbles near the edge of the grass and began chucking them into the water.

"You sure pissed off somebody, girl."

Kennedy didn't answer, just watched him toss rocks. One produced a glimmer of light across the water's surface. Something about the light niggled her conscience. Then Logan spoke.

"I say we put together all the evidence—"

"What evidence? I have none."

"Then we start from that first robbery—what they took, what you remember, and try and figure it out from there."

"Okay."

Logan turned and faced her directly. "So . . . before you went to the Bahamas, had anything unusual happened?"

"No."

"No strange phone calls, no stalker types around your building, no colleague wanting a job you got?"

"Nothing. If anything, life was pretty boring."

"Sorry to hear that."

At a time like this, Kennedy admitted that Logan was probably the only one who could make her smile.

"So, if nothing happened before the Bahamas, we have to focus on what went on down there."

Kennedy thought back to landing in the Bahamas, working twelve-hour days traipsing the island, then poring through hundreds of photos for ones that would be best in the spread.

"That Friday, I worked some more on the article and then left to spend the afternoon on the boat. I'd become friendly with the driver, or captain I guess you'd call him, and when I mentioned what I wanted to do on my day off, he gave me a good price for a private tour."

"Sure he did," Logan mumbled. He picked up another handful of rocks, stood, and began tossing them in the water in a way that made some of them skip.

"It was a beautiful day, picture perfect," Kennedy continued, ignoring Logan's response. "Clinton has lived his entire life on the island and was basically an encyclopedia when it came to all things Bahamas, and most things Caribbean. We sailed all around the big island, a bunch of the smaller ones and . . ."

Her voice trailed off as the sun glinting off a rock Logan threw caught her eye.

Logan looked at Kennedy. "Aren't you going to finish the sentence? You sailed around and . . . what?"

"Never mind."

"Oh, it's like that, huh? What happened on the boat stays on the boat."

"I wasn't thinking about Clinton just now."

"But you spent a lot of time with him, hanging out, taking selfies."

"And?"

"I'm just saying . . . seems like you got pretty cozy with that dude."

"Yeah, real cozy," Kennedy sarcastically responded.

"Cozy enough to get invited back to your room?" Logan asked.

Kennedy rolled her eyes.

"That question isn't about getting in your bedroom business. It's about who robbed you in the Bahamas and if that person has any connection with the lick that happened here, or the man who tagged me at your front door for trying to take his picture."

Logan's words made Kennedy swallow a quippy comeback. He offered a perspective she hadn't considered, one that caused her to look at Clinton's supposed acts of kindness in a whole new light. Conducting her tour on his day off. Initially turning down payment for said tour. And the drink?

"I'm right, huh?" Logan pressed. "Y'all hooked up."

Kennedy's brows scrunched together as she concentrated, watching the wind cast ripples on the water while she replayed a mental video of that Friday's boat ride.

"Well, did you?"

"No, but I never thought about him being involved either and given what you just said, maybe I should."

She told him about Clinton working on his day off, his flirty behavior, and how there was food and drink onboard. She also disclosed the uncomfortable facts that until now she'd kept hidden, about waking up naked and fearing she'd been raped.

"There was no sexual assault," she finished. "The examination suggested that, and the rape kit proved it. With all the flirting that happened between us, I can't see Clinton having the opportunity for sex and not taking it. Besides, if that were his goal, he could have done it while we were out on the water, far from prying eyes or a way for me to escape. He could have robbed me then, too. Most of what was later taken I had on the boat. My wallet, credit cards, cellphone, camera . . ."

"Maybe he assumed you had a lot more electronics in your room. They got your computer, right?"

"Yes, but that's about the only thing I didn't have with me.

Why risk breaking into my room and getting caught on video or by hotel security? That doesn't make sense. I won't cross him off the list just yet, but I don't think he did it."

"Maybe it was an inside job, someone who works at the hotel."

"I thought about that all week, the people I encountered during the time I was there, especially Hank, an overly-friendly concierge; Darlene, the suspicious-acting front desk supervisor; and housekeeping, because of their access to the room. But there were better ways to pull this off with hotel staff. While I was in the shower or down in the lobby. Why would they chance coming into the room while I'm there? I'm a fairly light sleeper. How could they have drugged me and I not wake up for even a second?"

"Didn't you say you stopped at the bar that night? The bartender could have slipped something in your drink and eased in later, once he thought you were knocked out."

"It's possible." Kennedy returned to the picnic table and sat on a bench. Logan sat on the table beside her. "I keep coming back to the guy I met that night at the restaurant, the man who called himself Jack Sutton. Everyone that we've mentioned had a legitimate reason to cross my path, except him. He decides to have dinner at the same time that I do, gets seated next to me, strikes up a conversation and is conveniently staying at my hotel. Could all of that be coincidence? I don't think so. He came out of nowhere and disappeared just as quickly. Without being seen, I might add—at any time, by anyone."

"Definitely suspect," Logan admitted. "But it doesn't jive with what you told me about being naked. Why take off your clothes and not do anything? As a man, that's more suspicious than anything else that happened."

They were silent for a moment, then Logan said, "And you're sure that guy I checked at your front door wasn't in the Bahamas?"

"I'm not sure of anything. Until I'm able to figure it out, can you do me a favor? Can you not tell Gwen, or anyone else about what happened today?"

"I won't, but only if you agree to let me install one more camera. If somebody comes down your hall or by your door, you need to know about it."

Kennedy felt overwhelmed and the beginnings of a panic attack. She took deep breaths and willed it away. There were too many pieces to try and fit together. The burglaries. Her electronics stolen. Waking up naked. Her home being cased. The possibility she couldn't ignore, that the incidents were related. But if so, by whom and for what?

Panic fled as her resolve strengthened to solve the puzzle that had become her life. She wouldn't feel safe until that happened. Freaking out would be counterproductive.

6

Zeke Foster didn't like holidays. He didn't like much of anything, or anyone. Who needed an entire weekend to focus on the dead and departed, to remember what he'd most like to forget? Wars and the men and women who'd fought them. The loved ones who'd died and ripped apart his heart. The enemies he'd killed and now haunted his sleep. The day dredged up mental pictures of growing up in the Blue Ridge mountains of West Virginia. Every Memorial Day Monday, before the sun came up, he'd climb into his grandfather Buck's blue Dodge pickup, and along with his father Matthew and brother Jerry, take the five-and-a-half-hour drive to Arlington, Virginia to pay their respects. Buck's father Daniel was buried there, courtesy of World War II. Daniel's dad, Zeke's great-great-grandfather, was there as well. Clyde Foster had been a part of World War I's American Expeditionary Force and according to stories handed down from his grandpa had personally known fellow Virginian President Woodrow Wilson. Zeke's father Matthew had fought in the early years of the Vietnam War, then spent another twenty years in the Army Reserves. Buck did his time in Korea. Zeke and his brother Jerry were fifth generation military men. The day after 9/11, a then seventeen-year old Zeke had joined the National Guard, and had enlisted in the Navy the day after graduating high school. Both Matthew and Buck were present when Zeke took the oath:

I, Zeke Patton Foster, do solemnly swear (or affirm) that I will support and defend the Constitution of the United States against all enemies, foreign and domestic; that I will bear true faith and allegiance to the same; and that I will obey the orders of the President of the United States and the orders of the officers appointed over me, according to regulations and the Uniform Code of Military Justice. So help me God.

Four years later he took the officer's oath, similar to the one he'd recited prior, but with the added acknowledgment that he'd taken the obligation freely without mental reservation or purpose of evasion. Zeke pledged to faithfully discharge the duties of the new office he'd entered.

For Zeke, both oaths were sacred, a vow stronger than the ones he'd recite on his wedding day, should he ever get married. He'd always been patriotic, always believed in God and country, America first. From the moment of the salute and handshake of the commissioning officer, he no longer bled red. Zeke Patton Foster bled red, white, and blue.

Zeke increased the speed on the treadmill and ran full out for five minutes. He slowed it down, ran another five, and then hit the weight room—his favorite spot in the gym. Placing one-hundred-pound weights on the barbell, he straddled the bench and did several quick presses in succession. He added another hundred pounds to both sides, positioned his body for the lift and raised it up, his entire focus on the strength needed to bench press twice his weight. He lifted again. Veins bulged and sweat ran as he grit his teeth and hoisted the bar. He'd just repositioned his feet and was headed for a third lift when he felt another hand clamp the bar.

"Hey, buddy."

He opened his eyes and met the baby blues of Warren, a

friend—or as close to one as Zeke could claim—and the gym's owner. "What the hell you want?"

"For you to stop being an asshole. You know you shouldn't be lifting this kind of weight without a spotter."

"I know what I can handle."

"Yeah, well, so do I, and pulling a dead body out from under the bar that cut off your breath when it fell on your esophagus isn't something I want to handle today. Got it?"

Zeke didn't answer. Instead, he swung his leg over the bench and walked out of the room. Warren followed him out. Zeke continued into the locker room, grabbed a towel from the stack and wiped himself down. He opened the locker where his things were stored, pulled off the t-shirt that clung to his body and pulled on a fresh one from out of his bag.

"Damn, man, was it something I said?"

Zeke offered a crooked smile. "Don't be a pussy."

Warren delivered a fisted blow to Zeke's arm. "That better?"

Zeke feigned to look around. "Are there mosquitos in this place?"

"Get the fuck outta here."

"On my way." Zeke hoisted the gym bag strap over his shoulder and headed out of the room.

Once again, Warren mirrored his steps. "You okay?"

"I'm good."

"I know this isn't your favorite day."

"You know more than most."

Warren clapped Zeke's back. "Alright, man. Take it easy."

Zeke left the gym, his mind cluttered and racing as usual, during the ten-minute walk home. He entered the two-bed, one-bath bungalow he shared with Ammo—a super-smart German shepherd brought back from Afghanistan—dumped the bag, peeled off his clothes and stepped into the shower. Once done he wrapped a white towel around his waist and padded barefoot into the kitchen for his daily drink duo, two fingers of scotch with a beer back. Not just any beer. Coors or Budweiser, the beer for real men. Anything not brewed in America was the type of beer losers drank. He knocked back the scotch, took a long swig of beer, then set it on the counter while he went into the bedroom and put on a pair of knee-length gym shorts and leather sandals. After heading to the back yard with a bowl of dog food, using the hose to fill up Ammo's water, and tossing the Frisbee with man's best friend a time or two, he returned to the house, left the wooden door open so Ammo could come through the doggie door, and returned to the kitchen. He opened the freezer, pulled out a dinner from three rows of precisely stacked items, zapped it in the microwave, and then took it and the beer into the dining room where several pictures were scattered about. While shoveling a forkful of steaming lasagna into his mouth he picked up one of the pictures, a close-up of an attractive woman leaving a building, glued to her cellphone, her naturally curly hair caught up in the wind. He dropped it and reached for a second one of the same woman. This time she was leaving a restaurant accompanied by a tall, lanky Black guy, a shorter White man, and another female, this one dark-skinned and curvy, about the same height as his subject. He hadn't planned on the close encounter with the guy he now knew was named Logan the other day. It was a mistake. He didn't make those often.

Zeke reached for his beer and opened the original folder he'd received containing information on his latest assignment, Kennedy Wade, the woman who may have either knowingly or unknowingly taken potentially damning photographs of a secret meeting between Ed Becker, the taciturn heir to a billion-dollar fortune, and Zeke's boss, Braum Van Dijk, one of the most powerful media moguls in the world. He knew the lengths these men employed for their alliance to remain hidden. Many believed Becker's family's wealth was tied to unscrupulous ventures and nefarious deeds that went against the mores of the loyal conservative viewers to which Van Dijk's stations catered. The friendship or partnership, or whatever it was, had surprised Zeke, too, until learning that the meeting was about dismantling a group that posed a threat to the American people and national security. From that point, Zeke was ready to do his part to ensure the country's safety, including taking a life or giving up his own. The target Zeke had met and studied didn't appear that powerful, but when Zeke pressed for details he was ordered not to question his boss's authority. "Time is of the essence," is what he'd been told, before receiving a ticket to the Bahamas and reminded that his duty was to Van Dijk and the country, in that order. An hour later he was on a chartered flight to the Bahamas and after a couple hours more he was a guy named Jack having dinner with his mark.

He placed the beer on a coaster and pulled out a sheet of paper. The information had been memorized, but he reread it anyway:

Name: Kennedy Lynn Wade
Age: 28
Height: 5'5"
Weight: 120
Occupation: Freelance photographer/writer/artist
Birthplace: Peyton, Kansas
Current Residence: 3452 N. Lakeshore Drive, #8D,
    Chicago, IL 60657
Telephone: 302-555-9790 (H); 302-555-2745 (C)
Parent(s): Karolyn (Thomas, Wade) Burnett
Carl Wade, Deceased; Stepfather, Ray Burnett
Sibling(s): Karl Wade

The paper contained the addresses and phone numbers of both Karl and Karolyn as well as their employment information, political affiliations, police history, and tax files. The folder contained their pictures, too, along with the ones he'd shot of Kennedy once inside her room. He tried to view them dispassionately, devoid of emotion, as a doctor would. But he was a virile ex-soldier, a pure Alpha male. She was an attractive woman, becoming even more so once he'd stripped her down and taken pictures that if necessary could later be used as leverage. She'd moaned a couple times initially, before the drug cocktail he'd given her had totally kicked in. She'd looked so peaceful then, and innocent. Discipline, his sense of honor, and his grandfather's lessons on character had kept him from taking advantage of her impaired state that night. That and his ability to stay laser-focused on a job. Unsure of how long it would take him to find what he was looking for in her room, he'd mixed a potent cocktail into her drink. One of the drugs was to cloud her memory, the other was to induce a deep, long sleep. The cocktail had worked, almost better than he intended. He'd placed the hotel's "do not disturb" sign on her door and spent the next four hours combing through her belongings to confiscate everything that might contain digital images. He'd then taken other items and staged the room to look like a random robbery before returning to his hotel less than five minutes away.

He flipped through the other pictures he'd taken that Sunday once she'd emerged from hibernation. Pictures of her at the front desk, and later with the supervisor and Bahamian police. He'd rented a motorcycle, its full-face helmet the perfect cover for him to stay undetected. He'd followed her to the U.S. Embassy and trailed her as she was driven to the airport for her return flight. He'd stayed another day, retraced her steps and got intel on the private company that owned the boat from which the pictures were taken. He held up a photo of a smiling man wearing a Hawaiian-styled shirt and a straw hat. The driver of the boat, a local, had no additional information to offer, a man on a mission to hustle up some extra bucks.

While finishing the beer, he returned the pictures to the folder along with the newspaper article he'd clipped last week. The article with accompanying pictures that shocked him, that got him called into Van Dijk's office and reprimanded for a job not done.

His orders had been clear—confiscate all footage from Wade's trip to the Bahamas. He was to do this at any and all cost, and had thought that after entering her room and confiscating all her electronic devices, the mission had been accomplished. He hadn't counted on a cloud account, which she obviously had, though in retrospect that should have been a no-brainer. Sunday's newspaper spread was proof that at least some of what she shot in the Bahamas was still in her possession, and so far, his tech guy had not been able to find and hack her cloud. It was time to implement Plan B and try to purchase the lot as an anonymous buyer. He hoped that move would prove successful. Because if not, he'd have to go to Plan C, and leave another family with a grave to visit on Memorial Day.

7

Kennedy entered the quaint, locally-owned coffee shop that had become a second home since the burglary at her condo. She breathed in the smell of coffee and spices swirling around her, took in the artsy, entrepreneurial types, focused on their computer screens or talking on phones, and relaxed—something she could no longer do at home. Even with the security system Logan installed, she didn't feel comfortable or totally safe. So, on a particularly frustrating morning, she'd taken a drive and ended up here, in a section of Chicago thirty minutes from where a stranger's spirit still lurked in her office, destroying the peace she once found there.

After securing her preferred table for two with chairs facing the windows and entrance, Kennedy ordered a drink and breakfast sandwich, then pulled out her phone to return the call she'd missed last night.

"Finally," was Gwen's hello.

"Good morning to you, too," Kennedy said.

"You can't not answer your phone, Kennedy, or take hours to return my call. Not after what all has happened to you. Okay?"

"I'm sorry. The ringer was off and the phone was charging so I didn't see the missed call until this morning. What's up?"

"I talked to Logan."

"I guess you know about the burglary."

"Yes, again! I couldn't believe it! What are the chances?"

"I know. It's crazy."

"It's also scary as hell!"

"I'm living proof that lightning can strike twice."

"What did these lowlifes take?"

"My computer."

"That's it?"

"That wasn't enough?"

"I'm just saying . . . it's weird that thieves would break into a gadget-filled place like yours and take only one thing."

"They probably heard a noise and got spooked, ran out before they could dismantle the TVs and stuff."

"You're probably right. I can't believe you're still in that condo. I'd have already moved my things to an extended stay hotel."

"With all the upheaval that's happened lately, I don't think I could take a move right now."

"Well, know that if you ever need a place to crash, *mi casa es su casa*."

"Thanks, Gwen." Kennedy paid for her order and returned to the table.

"Have you heard anything from the Bahamas and the investigators handling your case?"

"Not yet."

"No activity on the credit cards stolen or problems with identity theft?"

"None, thank goodness. I was able to shut them down pretty quickly and set up a block against any attempts to use my personal information. Then I filed yet another insurance claim and included a copy of the police report so they'd know it was legit."

"I'm so sorry, Ken. I hope whoever did this gets caught."

"I'm not going to worry about it, or the Bahamas crime either. With insurance, all I mainly lost was time. I'm ready to forget both incidents and put everything behind me."

A beep indicating an incoming call distracted Kennedy from what Gwen was saying. "Hey, I've got another call. It looks like a Bahamian number."

"You think it's the police?"

"I hope so. We may have talked them up. Talk later!" She rushed to catch the call. "Kennedy Wade."

"Hello, Ms. Wade."

Kennedy immediately perked up. After what happened in the Caribbean, she could detect a Bahamian accent in one syllable or less.

"Yes, that's me."

"Hi. My name is Anita Ford. I'm a PR and marketing specialist working with the Bahamas Bureau of Tourism on an upcoming campaign. I'm calling regarding the wonderful story on our country that recently appeared in the *Chicago Star*. You did an amazing job of capturing our country, both visually in the pictures that were taken and descriptively in the article you wrote."

"Thank you."

"I've been hired to redesign some of the marketing materials used to promote the island and have been given a sizeable budget to get who and what I need to complete this task in as short a time as possible. When I came across your work online, I knew immediately that using some of the work you've already completed could definitely help me meet the deadline they've imposed. It's as though nature's heartbeat was made evident in the pictures you captured—the angles, the framing, it was all very well done. And I must tell you. The rains on this island produce some of the most beautiful rainbows I've ever seen, but the one you photographed is by far the most stunning. It literally took my breath away."

"I felt the same way, and felt very fortunate to have captured its beauty."

"Of course, we're prepared to pay handsomely for the trip's entire portfolio. Would one hundred thousand be a fair price for the work?"

Is she kidding? Kennedy thought surely this was the case. She'd not made six figures on a year's worth of work, let alone shots taken and a story written over a long weekend. She was ready to pounce on this offer like a hungry cat on a trapped mouse, but she held back, tamped down the pure glee, and kept her tone strictly business.

"It's definitely an offer worth discussing."

It was an unexpected comeback, made known by the pause that followed. If it threw her, however, Anita seemed to recover quickly and clearly had thought out the offer. "I am happy to hear that. Given that this matter is time-sensitive we'll make the offer as straightforward as possible and hopefully keep discussions involving negotiation to a minimum. We are willing to pay you one hundred thousand dollars in exchange for exclusive rights to the images shot during your visit, including those posted in the *Star*, retroactively. Meaning that any images retained by the paper, if any, must be delivered to us as well."

"I retained the rights to the pictures in the *Star*, but signed a non-compete clause that states the pictures used in their article cannot be republished for a period of ninety days."

"That's fine. Additionally, we'd like for any images appearing elsewhere online to be removed. Most papers today have an online edition. We hope their removal from the website is something that can be worked out."

"I'll speak with them but make no promises. It's an unusual request."

"We only ask because of the branding possibilities mentioned. Having the work appear solely on our materials will make them synonymous with our island, a unique beauty one can see nowhere else."

"I hope I can negotiate that for you."

"I'm sure something can be worked out. If necessary, I'll speak with them as well. Meanwhile, I'll have an offer drawn up immediately. To what email would you like it sent?"

Kennedy rattled off her email address, shocked and now a bit curious about how much Anita and her company were willing to pay. "I am flattered by your offer, and at the same time feel that you must know that it goes well beyond the going rate for photography."

"We do understand, but as I stated earlier, we want to get started right away, and felt a high offer would speed up the process. Our marketing director believes the picture of the rainbow would work perfectly as the cover of our tourism brochure as well as on our website and in other collateral. As part of the brand, if you will. They are photographs that can be used in a myriad of ways for a very long time. Are you interested?"

"Yes, I am, and apologize if I came off as suspicious. There was . . . let's just say . . . never mind. It doesn't matter. I'm very interested in your offer."

"When do you think we could have an answer? Within two, three days perhaps?"

"I'll do my best and will call the *Star* right away."

"Very good. I'll have our attorney send over the contractual agreement later today."

"I'll be on the lookout for it."

"Very well. Kennedy, it has been a pleasure."

"Likewise."

Kennedy ended the call, somewhat dazed. Had she just received a six-figure offer for her photography, the highest ever, out of the blue? Maybe this was the universe's reimbursement for her trauma in the Bahamas. Kennedy called Gwen and got voicemail.

"Hey girl, I know you're still at work but give me a call as soon as you get this message. I just got a phone call that . . . just call me ASAP, okay?"

Kennedy was no longer hungry and too amped to write. Perfect energy for working out, though. She packed up her stuff and once in her car, headed home to work out in the building's gym. Anita's offer had her mind whirling. She didn't know which was better—to think too much or to not think at all. On one hand Anita's offer was exactly what she needed right now, the answer to a prayer that she'd not even prayed. She could focus on finding employment that would allow her the flexibility she craved as well as a steady paycheck. She could get away from her tainted condo for a couple weeks, and from her paranoia surrounding it. Clear her head, and decide whether to remain in the condo or put it up for sale. Maybe a relocation was in order. Nothing like a change of scenery to jumpstart one's life, and with Kennedy currently unattached, now would be the perfect time to do it. On the other hand, Anita's offer sounded almost too good to be true. The suspicion was no doubt brought on by the recent crimes against her. Before, such a negative thought may not have crossed her mind. But a man who called himself Jack Sutton had taught her that just because someone looked good and sounded nice didn't mean they were to be trusted.

Kennedy felt her phone vibrate. She engaged her Bluetooth. "Hey, Gwen."

"Hey, girl. What's up?"

"Did you get my message?"

"I didn't listen; just hit you back. Was that call from the Bahamas?"

"Yes, but not the police."

"Who then?"

"Some woman named Anita who just made me a crazy offer for those pictures I took—a hundred thousand dollars!"

"Quit playing."

"That's what I thought, but she was totally serious. She works with the country's tourism bureau and saw my work in the *Star*. They're updating their marketing material and want to use my pictures. She wants every picture I shot that weekend, along with exclusive rights to their use."

"So what are you calling me for, to borrow a pen?" Kennedy laughed. "Girl, I'm serious. Six figures? What is there to talk about? Why are we even on the phone?"

"I'm calling to hopefully use your insider connections to handle a stipulation Anita outlined, a strange request. She knows the pictures can't be used for ninety days, but wants them removed from the *Star*'s website right away."

"Why?"

"She felt it was one they could create the brand around, one that could in time become an image connected with the Bahamas or identified with the brand."

"I can kind of see that, but I'm not sure I can help you. Even if the webmaster agrees to pull the pictures, what will replace them?"

"I don't know," Kennedy said with a sigh. "I don't get why she's so adamant, either. There are many pictures I took that showcase the Bahamas, but the rainbow wasn't one of them. It could have been taken anywhere, in one of a hundred islands. But an offer like this doesn't happen every day, so if she wants the rainbow, I want to try and give it to her."

"You know I'll do whatever I can."

"Yeah, I know."

"Call up your boy, run it by him."

"Logan? Girl, stop. He's a boy, but not my boy."

"Me thinks you protests too much, like a woman trying not

to be attracted to the man. I don't know why you're fighting it. He's fine."

"Then why don't you two hook up?"

"Let him give me half of the attention that he gives you and I most certainly will. Ooh, here comes my boss. I gotta go."

Once home, Kennedy quickly changed into workout clothes. Before stepping out the door she tapped her phone, ordered a deep dish from her favorite pizzeria and then called Logan.

"What's up, Ken?"

"Nothing much. I just ordered a Giordano's and was wondering if—"

"Yep, what time?"

"In about an hour," Kennedy said amid laughter.

"Make it an hour and a half and I'm there."

"Okay, see you then."

Kennedy headed to the gym, hyperaware of her surroundings. She bypassed the stairs that were normally part of her workout and instead took the elevator, all while looking for anything out of the ordinary, anyone watching, lurking, snooping. Every face in the gym was a familiar one. Kennedy relaxed. She spent thirty minutes with weights and bands and the rest of the hour on the elliptical machine. Back home, she showered, threw on a pair of sweats, and just under ninety minutes later, sat with Logan at her dining room table gorging on what some considered the best pizza in Chicago, or anywhere. Napkins piled up as they alternated between forks and fingers, making their way through loads of pepperoni, onions and mushrooms, covered with a mountain of gooey cheese. Logan told her about the production equipment he'd recently bought. She told him about Anita and the amazing offer. His reaction surprised her.

"Six figures, huh? For a single picture?"

"For everything I did that weekend."

"Even the selfie with Clinton?"

Kennedy gave him a look. "That was taken with my cellphone and remains personal property."

"Hmm."

"What's with this weird energy? For an unknown photog like me to receive this kind of money for a picture is very rare, unheard of. You should be happy for me!"

"Hey, you know when it comes to you, I only want the best. But after what happened, I'm suspicious of everyone down there. Secure the bag, but be careful."

Kennedy made light of the warning. "I'm not going to deliver the pictures in person. They'll be transferred digitally. So relax, okay?"

"All right, cool. Congratulations."

"Thanks."

"Oh, speaking of digital files, did you get that box yet?"

"What box?"

"The one to hold what you gave me."

"What?"

He looked from her to the camera and back. "You know, what you gave me for safekeeping?"

"Oh, the flash drive."

Logan reacted, threw his hands in the air and dramatically said, "Well, why don't you tell whoever might be bugging your place everything that you don't want them to know."

"Whoever's bugging my place can kiss my ass. I'm selling the pictures," she announced to the room, then looked at the camera mounted in the corner of the room. "Go on down to the Bahamas and bug the office of tourism because these pictures are getting ready to be all over the place."

Logan shook his head. "You're crazy."

"No, but I will be if I keep living in a state of constant paranoia. I'm sick of living like that, looking over my shoulder and behind my back. I'm ready to embrace the possibility that I just ran into a wall of bad luck, that the timing of the burglary here happening so close to being robbed in the Bahamas was just coincidence. How could anybody living here know what happened to me there?"

Logan nodded as he chewed, then said, "That's a good point."

"I mean, look at me. Do I look like a threat to anybody?"

While cleaning off the table after eating, Kennedy's fax went off. She walked into the office and was surprised to see that Anita had already sent the agreement. Logan received a text from a friend having car trouble and went to help him. Kennedy spent the next couple of hours wading through almost eight pages of complex legalese. It was just a bunch of pictures for God's sake. The repeated references to total and complete release of "every picture taken between the dates of thus and so and in the location of such and such in any and every form," was overkill. The stated penalties for violating any part of the agreement came off as a threat. The tone brought Logan's suspicions to mind, and stirred up the feelings of paranoia that she'd been well on her way to talking herself out of. But the unease came back and persisted, so much so, that she tossed the agreement aside and turned on the TV to relax. Back to back reruns of a favorite 90s show was just the kind of silliness to do the trick. By the time the third half-hour episode ended, the optimism Kennedy felt earlier had returned, along with common sense. What did she care about the agreement's language? She had no intention of doing anything nefarious, like selling the pictures to Anita and then turning around to sell them again.

What are you calling me for, to borrow a pen?

Kennedy laughed at the thought of what Gwen had said, getting up to retrieve a pen. She returned to the couch and was flipping to the agreement's signature page when her phone vibrated. It was a text from Logan.

I've been robbed.

Instinctively, Kennedy looked up at the camera Logan had installed for her safety, and then at the room around her. Images flashed before her eyes, memories from the Bahamas until now. Pictures. People. Snatches of conversation. Fast, relentless, disjointed at first, like jigsaw pieces floating in the air. They slowed and crystalized into an *aha* moment, a possible answer for why the lightning of robbery had struck more than once. She snatched up the agreement, her computer and purse, and fled like the devil chased her.

8

Kennedy had no patience to wait for an elevator. She entered the stairwell with enough fear-fueled energy to beat up King Kong and took the steps two at a time. After reaching her car and speeding out of the garage, she noticed Logan had sent a second text clarifying that he hadn't been home when it was burglarized. She slowed down, and while no longer feeling the need to run red lights, she was still concerned about Logan's well-being. And with what she now believed she'd figured out, she worried about hers as well. She reached the address he'd also texted in half the time the GPS had noted. There was only street parking, which was usually a hassle. But as soon as she turned the corner, she saw brake lights, threw on her blinker, and did a haphazard parallel park into the space. She took the steps to his building two at a time, and again was blessed by timing as a couple exited the secured building and held the door so she could slip inside. The elevator seemed to take forever, when in fact the door opened mere seconds after the button was punched. Logan and his roommate lived on the second floor of a four-story building. She'd never been there before, but didn't have to look for his place. The door was open. Music spilled out into the hallway, along with Logan's raised, agitated voice.

"That's bullshit, man. I know exactly who this is. So do you. But they've messed with the wrong one, I tell you that."

"I hear you, dog."

Kennedy guessed the deep bass she heard while approaching the door was C-Dog, Logan's roommate. Logan had told her his legal name was Calvin but nobody in hip-hop used their real name. Logan was called Lowkey, a nod to his producer skills on the mixer board. And whoever had broken into their apartment was being called a whole slew of motherfuckers.

Kennedy stepped into the ransacked room. "Hey, Logan."

Logan turned, the scowl on his face intense. "What are you doing here?"

She looked over at the others in the room and resisted the urge to walk over and give Logan a hug. Instead, she adopted his casual stance, minus the hardness. "I'm so sorry this happened. It's fucked up."

"What do you have to be sorry about?"

Nothing I can share with your boys here. "I just had this happen to me, remember? I know how it feels."

"Yeah, I guess you do."

"When I asked for your address, I assumed you knew it was so I could come over. I probably should have asked you straight out. So handle your business. Call me if you need me, or when you can." She turned to go.

"Ken, wait."

She did, and watched as he walked over and said something to his homeboys, under his breath so she couldn't hear. Soon after, they ambled past her offering either a head nod or mumbled greeting. Logan walked behind them and closed the door. He seemed to relax then. When he turned around, Kennedy saw the guy she was used to. He readily pulled her into his arms.

"I'm sorry," she said again. "This is all my fault."

He straightened and stepped away from her. "What are you talking about?"

"I think I finally have an idea about why all of this happened. The robbery in the Bahamas, the burglary at my condo, and now your apartment. It's got to have something to do with the job on the island and the pictures I took."

"How do you figure somebody came and stole my shit because of something you did?"

"I gave you the flash drive with all of my pictures, including the ones from the Bahamas that somebody for some reason has been trying to steal! It all started coming together when I got your text." Kennedy paced the room, counting off on her fingers. "Their first try was the Bahamas, taking my camera, cellphone, computer, all of the items where the pics might be stored. They probably thought they'd been successful, then the article ran in the *Star*—"

"With pictures from your trip," Logan interrupted.

"That very night somebody breaks into my house and takes the desktop. But it doesn't end there. I get this call from a woman with a ridiculous offer to purchase the pictures she saw in the *Star*. But not only those pictures, every picture taken. The agreement she sent was eight frickin' pages, that went on and on about exclusivity, and huge penalties that would occur should the pictures ever be reprinted.

"You had a feeling about something and tried to warn me earlier, when you asked what to do with the flash drive. You looked at the camera almost as though you knew somebody else was listening. I all but shouted out what they wanted to know, that a copy of the pictures I had taken was here, in your house! They were looking for the flash drive, Logan. That's why you were robbed."

Logan's expression was unreadable. Then he burst out laughing, so hard that he toppled on to the black leather sofa and allowed himself a good guffaw.

"You find this funny?" Kennedy didn't. She joined him on the couch. "So I take it that you don't think our burglaries are related?"

Logan shook his head. "Last week, when we were bringing in the equipment, a couple dudes were visiting this guy we know on the first floor. He came over to help us carry the shit upstairs. The dudes that were with him were real curious about the system, asking questions and admiring the mixer and shit. I made note of it, but didn't give it too much thought because everybody in this building pretty much knows everybody else. We have each other's backs, you know? Plus, the building is secure. There are cameras. The landlord is cool, and he looks out for all of us living here. My neighbor across the hall said he's never heard of a break-in, and he's lived here for ten years. So while I can appreciate your theory, consider yourself off the hook for what happened tonight. Whoever broke in here wasn't trying to get a flash drive. They were trying to get that equipment. Hadn't been for my neighbor coming home when he did, they would have gotten what they came for."

Kennedy looked around. "They didn't?"

"Come with me." Logan started down a hall. Kennedy followed him. "This is what they came after."

Kennedy looked at a board covered with knobs and slides and not two feet long. "But they didn't take it. They tried to, but what they didn't know is how we secured the mixer to a concrete block beneath the mixing desk."

He pulled aside a black curtain she hadn't noticed to reveal what looked like two feet of solid stone. "We bore iron studs in that motherfucker and then secured it with metal rods. Don't let its size fool you. This mixer right here is top of the line, set us back three stacks. That's why we wanted to make sure it didn't grow legs. Dude would have to be Hercules to walk out with that shit."

His smile disappeared. "They still made a lick, though, got

away with about five grand. Microphones, some of the best on the market." He walked around pointing to where stuff used to be. "The computer, monitors, keyboard, a couple guitars. The main thing they wanted though was that mixer. That's what they kept asking about. I've got something for them, though," he finished, walking out of the room. "Those brothers are getting ready to be dealt with."

"I know you're upset," Kennedy said, as they reached the living room. "You've got every right to be. Being violated is a horrible feeling, it's fucked up. But the last thing we need is another brother killed on the streets of Chicago. Your equipment can be replaced, Logan. You can't."

Logan didn't respond. He sat down heavily, spent.

"Did you have . . . never mind."

"Insurance?" Logan asked, with a crooked smile. "I've got some insurance back in the bedroom that'll help me collect what's due."

His phone rang. He looked at the face and stood. "Look, I appreciate you coming over, but I've got to bounce."

"Promise me you won't do something stupid."

They reached the elevator but continued to the stairs. "Nothing stupid."

Once on the first floor, Logan headed toward the hall leading to other apartments.

"See you, later."

"Hold up, Kennedy, let me walk you to your car. That lick has got me tripping, acting like my mama didn't raise me right."

They reached her car.

"You know what, Ken? You need to follow up on what you told me just now. I don't think I was robbed for your flash drive, but you may be on to something regarding those pictures and why you were hit twice. You may have captured somebody on your camera that wasn't supposed to be there. So, check that out, real talk."

"Don't worry. I'm all over it." She clicked the fob and gave Logan a hug. "Call me, later, okay?"

He threw the peace sign over his head and headed back inside.

Kennedy's thoughts were in turmoil all the way home, mentally flipping through the pictures from her trip. That she'd caught someone in a shot was highly unlikely. She'd been on assignment for a nature shoot. Logan's cavalier attitude about his robbery was bothersome, too. He believed the culprits were his neighbor's friends. Kennedy wasn't so sure. She'd noticed a sedan parked at the end of Logan's block, one of those somber black numbers that Feds drive in movies. The car had pulled out right after she passed it. At a red light two blocks down, she could have sworn she saw it again. Taking a circuitous route to get home made a fifteen to twenty-minute drive more like thirty-five, and had her arriving when most residents were already safe and sound inside their homes, the garage devoid of witnesses. Now, getting out of her car, fear crawled up her arm and slid down her back. The garage was almost too quiet, as though even the concrete held its breath. Getting out of her car, she imagined eyes on her, and hurried up the short flight of stairs to the locked back entry. She fumbled to get her key card into the slot. There was a sound, like a footstep. Her head whipped around. She heard nothing, saw no one. But . . . there it was again. The distinct sounds of sole meeting stone. She looked again. There it was. A silhouette in shadow. Walking, slowly, coming her way. Her hands began shaking. She dropped the key card. It hit the step and slid, almost falling off the side. She slapped down her hand to prevent it going over the edge and connected with a shard of glass. It pierced her palm but she barely felt it, her focus on the card slot in front of her and the stranger behind. In her mind's eye it was Jack, right behind her, his face distorted and laughing as he slid an ether-soaked cloth around and over her nose.

The card slid into the groove. The red light flashed green. She reached for the door handle. A hand clamped her shoulder.

"No!" She meant to scream but with a lump of terror stuck in her throat the word came out in a whisper. She wrapped the strap of her computer bag around her hand and raised it to deliver a blow.

"Whoa, Kennedy! Stop, it's me Glenn." He deflected the bag headed toward his forehead and grabbed Kennedy's arm to steady her.

Kennedy clutched her heart, recognizing a guy who lived on the fourth floor, who she'd sometimes see in the gym. "Dammit, Glenn. You just took five years off my life."

"I'm sorry. You turned around. I thought you saw me."

"I heard footsteps. I didn't see anybody."

"Probably because I saw this and picked it up." He held out an earring. "Is it yours?"

Kennedy shook her head, turned and walked through the door. They crossed the lobby and reached the elevators. She was still out of breath. "Don't ever do that to a woman. Don't sneak up on us like that."

"I'm really sorry to have scared you. It wasn't my intention. I thought you saw me. I should have said something."

Kennedy was quiet during the elevator ride, barely acknowledging her neighbor when he said goodbye. Her mind was on Logan, and the "insurance" against violence that he kept in his room. Kennedy wasn't a violent person. The only thing she'd ever shot was a Super Soaker. But for the first time in her life she considered buying a gun.

9

Kennedy drove to a twenty-four-hour superstore and bought a weapon that could be purchased without a background check, a thirty-two-ounce can of pepper spray strong enough to fell a bear. She purchased more mega flash drives like the one she gave Logan and arrived home a short time later—armed, dangerous, and focused. She removed her photographs from the computer and placed the Bahamas pictures and all her other work on separate flash drives.

The next day, her first stop was at a bank where she secured one set of drives in a safe deposit box. Ten minutes later, she settled into the back booth of a random coffee shop, one of half a dozen she navigated between to work from since her house was invaded. Now that she had a focus, Kennedy was determined—borderline obsessed—with finding out if the pictures she took in the Bahamas held the answer to why she had been robbed not once but twice. A memory she recalled while waiting for her coffee, and the agreement Anita sent over, gave her a place to start. It was the day Logan had taken her to Lake Michigan, when the glint she'd seen off a rock he'd tossed reminded her of what happened when she photographed the rainbow, the reflection that showed up in some of the shots.

That day she'd said nothing, had dismissed its significance, but now she wanted to take a closer look and see if she could find something hidden and worth six figures. She inserted the flash drive into her laptop and pored over the shots for over an hour, with no success. Even after enlarging the photos and inspecting them inch by inch, she saw nothing suspicious. Other than trees, branches, and dense brush, she couldn't see anything at all.

Kennedy sat back, frustrated, trying to think of more pictures to search. She scanned through the hundreds she'd taken. Nothing stood out. She thought about returning home and viewing them on her flat screen. Then, remembering a colleague, Kennedy reached for her phone and typed a text.

Hey Toby it's Ken. I need your help with some digital files. Looking for a needle in a haystack. I know if something's there you can find it.

She reread the text and was about to send it when a subtle feeling, as faint as a feather, gave her pause. Instead of pushing send, she pushed delete and wrote another text.

Hey Toby, Ken. Call me.

That done, Kennedy focused on the few pictures with people included, hoping to catch a glimpse of the man who called himself Jack. His was a face she wouldn't forget. But she didn't see him. Nor had he been found on any of the surveillance footage, according to the attorney from whom she'd finally received an email. Maybe someone was over there when they shouldn't have been, doing something that they shouldn't have been doing. Only problem was, she had no way of knowing who this was, or why her having taken a picture of them was such a problem. The person she was looking for obviously knew enough about her to know where she lived back on the mainland. She searched blindly, without a clue as to what she sought. She'd separated every face in her pictures that could be seen clearly, isolated them and enlarged them to eight by tens. A folder marked Model Headshots held almost thirty adults of every age and race, along with the enlarged pictures of the private island where she'd snapped the rainbow. If trees could talk, and if there was a story behind the flash of light she'd seen on the private island, she needed to hear it.

After organizing the pictures, updating her chart, and saving everything to her flash drive, Kennedy left the coffee shop. It was early, just after three o'clock, and even though she was ready to chill, she didn't go home. She kept a straight back and firm voice when talking to her friends about the burglary, assured them that she was fine. She wasn't. Hadn't been comfortable in her home since the night she returned to find that someone had been there. Even with the extra security equipment that Logan had installed, and the patrol car that regularly patrolled her block, Kennedy still felt vulnerable and paranoid, wondering whether or not she was being watched. It was a feeling of pure helplessness. Not knowing who in the world could be after her out there. Not knowing why. Her phone rang. Kennedy eyed the Caller ID and smiled. She had questions that the caller might be able to help answer.

"Hey, Toby!"

"Hey, stranger! I was surprised to get your call. It's been a long time."

"I know, too long. I've been busy."

"I hear you. What's going on?"

Kennedy looked at the clock on her dash. "I'd like to get your take on something you need to see in person. Are you still working in the same place? If so," she hurried on, "Don't say the name."

"Um, yes."

Kennedy could only imagine what her co-worker was thinking. The way he'd hesitated and dragged out the "yes," he probably thought she had a screw or two loose. Who could blame him?

"I know I'm sounding all clandestine and CSI, but I assure

you, I have my reasons. Are you still at work? I'm not that far away and can meet you there if it's okay. It won't take long, just five, ten minutes."

"You've got me a bit worried, Ken, I can't lie. But you're good people and I trust you so . . . come on by."

It was nearing rush hour, so Kennedy didn't get to Toby's job as quickly as she'd planned. Reaching the tan, nondescript building brought back fond memories of working part-time and later full-time while pursuing her BA. When thinking about it, she realized she didn't know Toby all that well. He was quite a bit older than her, already married with children when they met. But he'd always been kind and a gentleman and photography was his passion. That's what they bonded over. He loved digital photography but was partial to film, and developed his own film. Had he had the courage to pursue it full time, she believed he could have been world renowned. When it came to anything regarding photography, film or digital, he was a master. Even more important for her was the monster enhancer he had in his home. It was the size of a movie screen and could blow up a ponytail enough to count the strands of hair.

She pulled into a parking space and hurried toward the building. It was a little after five o'clock, but when she walked into his office, he was there waiting.

After the pleasantries, Toby was direct. "Alright, young lady. Who did you kill and where did you bury the body?"

Kennedy frowned. "Why would you ask that?"

"Something illegal happened given how you sounded on the phone."

"As I said earlier, I have my reasons."

"Let's hear them."

What Kennedy thought would be five or ten minutes turned into almost an hour of spilling her heart. Toby was a great listener, calm and steady. He didn't dismiss her paranoia or call her flat-out wrong. Perhaps it was his comforting manner that made her trust him. She told him everything that had happened and how she felt about it from the time she woke up in the Bahamas until now. Afterwards, she pulled out the flash drive and copied several pictures to a drive that he owned.

"It's probably much ado about nothing," she said as they walked out of the building together. "But I appreciate you humoring me and agreeing to help."

"I don't need much of a reason to turn on the spotlight."

"Oh, the machine has a name now?"

Toby nodded. "And a new friend. A computer program that allows me to correct the distortion that comes from enlarging a picture a great magnitude. I just got that two weeks ago. So thanks for giving me the perfect reason to try it out."

Waiting to hear from Toby was nerve-wracking, but Kennedy managed to keep it together. There were people to see and bills to pay. She appreciated the diversions. Though temporary, they kept her from being totally consumed with who wanted her pictures, and why. Toby didn't leave her hanging for long. He sent a general text about wanting to see her. They agreed to meet the next day.

Kennedy was up and out of the house early, well before their appointment time. She drove thirty minutes to her old stomping grounds, the area near her alma mater where she'd lived and worked for four and a half years. Meeting Toby in the area made her nostalgic, took her back to a time when life threw her no curveballs. The days had a rhythm—school, study, work, study, sleep—and party on the weekends. Back then, it felt somewhat monotonous, but now she realized that it also felt safe.

She passed Pops, a family-owned diner and college student's second home, before pulling into the coffee shop parking lot. After ordering a caramel latte, she spotted a table in the corner, a perfect place to set up shop. It also provided a clear view of the entrance. Just in case the boogeyman chased her, she mused, while trying to find humor in the thought. She opened her computer and began checking emails. One of the companies she'd sent her resume to had responded, the start-up magazine. She quickly clicked on the link, read the email, and replied to someone named Monica. Would she come in for an interview? She'd love to, and looked forward to seeing her next week. There was also an inquiry from Anita. Yes, she'd received the agreement, had no questions, and would be in touch after word from the *Star*. Truth was she hadn't followed up on them removing the pics from the internet. Kennedy had been purposely vague to buy more time to check out the photos. If there turned out to be nothing to her needle in a rainbow theory, she didn't want to rouse suspicions. She wanted to get paid!

After finishing up emails and checking into social media, Kennedy went into research mode, searching out events she could photograph and sell the pics. It was an unorthodox approach to the business, almost like being paparazzi, except her targets were not celebrities and her customers weren't *TMZ*. They were magazines and newspapers, sometimes even the Chamber of Commerce. Fun for the most part, and highly rewarding. But three years into the freelance free-for-all and Kennedy was beginning to feel the effects of the grind. She returned to Monica's email and tapped the link at the bottom of the page. *Chicago Sightings* was a regional print and web publication highlighting the city—its neighborhoods, people, culture, and food. They were looking for an art director, someone to shape the overall image and presentation, a job Kennedy knew she could handle well. A complementary educational background in copy writing bolstered her qualifications. That she was also a photographer, whose *Star* spread had been seen by the owner, had worked in her favor, too. She continued researching potential shoots, but her heart wasn't truly in it. She was already at *Chicago Sightings*, working a steady job with a steady paycheck. She picked up her phone to call Gwen. It buzzed in her hand.

Can you meet me over at Dad's house?

It was Toby with a question that made Kennedy frown. She didn't know his father. Plus, she now sat at the place they'd agreed to meet. Her thumbs hovered over the screen as she thought of an answer. Her indicator pinged again.

He promises to make your favorite. Thighs and fries.

The lightbulb clicked on. He was talking about Pops, the college kid's go-to diner. But why was he acting like a Kamikaze spy? She would ask him in person, and replied with a yes. She placed her computer in its bag and headed out to meet him. Halfway to her car came another lightbulb moment. The pictures. He'd found something. Whatever it was had him sending crazy texts, the normally mild-mannered co-worker talking in code. Kennedy reached her car and started the engine, the latte curdling in her stomach as her mind raced with possibilities of what he could have found.

Kennedy valiantly tried to stay calm during what should have been a five-minute ride. But already beyond paranoid since her burglary, Logan's burglary, and a garage stalker named Glenn, she couldn't be normal. Her eyes were everywhere, and every sound outside of her car made her jump. She tried to get green lights and probably spent as much time looking in her rearview and side mirrors as she did on the road in front of her. She even made a couple unnecessary turns, taking a loopy route to the college hangout passed a short while ago, the spot that he referred to as "Dad's house" in his covert operation text message. What he'd called thighs and fries was billed on the menu as the Two-Sided Chick, a two-dollar meal boasting two thighs and two sides for cash-strapped students. To this day, it was Kennedy's favorite part of the bird, even though right now she might not be able to eat it.

Kennedy circled the block twice and then parked across the

street from Pops with a clear view of the entrance. Her eyes moved, continually looking for anyone or anything out of place. She watched Toby enter the establishment and still didn't move for another five minutes. When her phone vibrated with a text, three question marks from Toby, she decided the coast was clear and she could go inside.

It had been years since she'd eaten at Pops. It felt weird to enter and not see people she recognized working behind the counter, but her mouth watered as she stepped through the door. She saw Toby and headed to a table in the very back of the establishment, on the side facing the door. How he'd positioned himself wasn't lost on Kennedy. It cut through nerves and made her smile. He was still wearing his hat and shades and stood as she approached him.

"Hey, Sherlock," she whispered, trying to lighten the moment.

"Hey."

Toby didn't sound like himself. He sounded rattled. Kennedy had never heard him like that.

"Do you want to order something?" she asked.

"No, I'm not hungry. After you see what you photographed, you won't want to eat either."

"What is it, Toby?"

Toby looked around before removing his sunglasses, placing his elbows on the table and leaning forward. "Who else has seen the pics?" he asked, his voice quieter than a mosquito peeing on cotton.

"Which one? I copied several."

"The one of the island with the rainbow framed behind it."

"Anybody who read the Sunday Star where those pictures were featured."

Toby ran a hand over his face. He pulled a cellphone from his pocket. "Are they online, on the *Star*'s website?" Kennedy nodded, then waited as he found the site and scrolled through the pictures. "Wow, that's crazy. Ninety-nine percent of people looking at these wouldn't see anything at all. No, make that one hundred percent, unless they had the stuff I've got."

"So, you saw something?"

Toby's shoulders dropped as he relaxed a little. "My grandfather passed about four, five years ago. He was my hero, like a second father. He was strong, proud, quiet and humble. And from the time she was thirteen years old, my grandmother loved him to death."

Kennedy sat on her side of the booth about to explode. This man had sent her cryptic texts as though he were Mafia, and now he was waxing sentimental over Gramps?

"I'm sorry for the loss of your grandfather, Toby," she said softly, hoping there was empathy in her tone. "But what does this have to do with—"

"While preparing for his homegoing," he continued as though she hadn't spoken. "We hunted down pictures of him dating all the way back to when he was a boy. Many of them I'd never seen before. They hadn't been preserved properly, or at all. Many were faded, splotched, torn, fuzzy. I went online looking for a way to enhance the photographs, bring them back, as close to or better than the original. There are a bunch of them out there and I downloaded my share but none of them worked the way they claimed, the way I needed."

It was the Toby she knew now talking, his words calm and measured, warm like a blanket over her anxiety-induced chill. The story was completely incongruent with the rest of their interaction. Irrelevant yet important. She didn't know why. But that same small nudge of intuition that led her to delete the initial text to him, now led her to sit back and listen.

"I sent in several pictures of my grandfather, downloaded programs that were supposed to allow me to repair them myself. But the essences of the images weren't captured. They were often heavily pixilated, the subjects often hard to make out. You'd get an idea of their face but not a clear image. It was frustrating. That's what started my search to find equipment to solve that problem. Turns out the solution was time, giving the world of electronics enough time to evolve into developing what I needed. When that screen came out, I took money from my savings. Wife didn't speak to me for a month! But I kept looking, finding programs that worked better and better until one day I brought her a picture of her mother at the age of ten. It was the first time seeing her at that age. It brought me so much joy to do that for her. It stirred the passion to the point that it became a bit of a side business. Because of the death of my grandfather, I found my true passion and a business was born."

Toby paused and looked beyond her to the dining room. His look turned introspective before becoming resolved.

"It took conversations with God and my Grandpa's strength to even show you what was photographed. But given everything you told me the other day, I knew it was the right thing to do." He picked up his phone, slid his finger over the face and held it toward her. "Don't say anything. Don't react. Just take a look at what you've accidentally uncovered. Then you'll know why Grandpa's story matters."

Kennedy's eyes stayed trained on Toby as the phone hovered between them. Minutes ago, she couldn't wait to see what she'd captured. Now she wasn't sure she wanted to know. She took the phone, placed it on the table in front of her.

Her head came up slowly. "No way."

Toby's eyes bore into hers. She looked again, used her fingers to enlarge the cropped view. Two men could be seen, their heads close together. She squinted, her hand rising to her mouth. She stared at the image for more than a minute, one that explained everything that had happened since it was taken.

"Am I really seeing this?" Her voice was almost like that of a child's asking the question while knowing the answer. There was no Santa Claus.

Toby nodded. "I'm afraid so. Given who's in these pictures, I'm very afraid."

Kennedy continued to stare at the picture. "Is this the only one you . . ."

"There are more. That's the only one I felt . . . I could put on my phone. It'll be deleted before I leave."

"I had no idea," Kennedy said, her voice barely above a whisper. "I was taking pictures of beautiful scenery, and a rainbow so bright that it almost looked fake." She looked up, her eyes pleading. "How could I have known that a whole other world existed beyond those trees?"

"You didn't. Just like I didn't know what my program would enhance." He reached into his pocket and slid a flash drive across the table. "I will be praying for you, Kennedy, but I have a family to think about and this is way above my pay grade. When it comes to anything to do with these pictures, I don't know you. We've never met. I'm having my phone wiped to erase our messages."

He picked up said phone and deleted the picture. Then he reached out his hand. Kennedy shook it. "Maybe we can reconnect once this blows over. But until further notice, please don't contact me again."

Toby walked out of the restaurant. Kennedy didn't move. What Toby just showed her changed everything, could absolutely jeopardize her life. She was still reeling when minutes later Toby's thoughtfulness even through this trial was apparent, as a waitress quietly set a plate before her, a favorite—two thighs and fries.

The food went untouched. Phone calls went to voicemail. Kennedy sat, as in a daze. She looked out the window and watched the events of the past month unfold on her mental video. With each moving picture, reality crystalized. Now, everything made sense. Meeting the mysterious Jack Sutton. Being drugged and robbed in the Bahamas. Being burglarized at home. The exorbitant offer from Anita. The feelings of being watched and followed. These incidents were all connected to what she'd accidentally snapped while chasing a rainbow. To what Toby's amateur digital program had exposed. To what those after her didn't want the world to see—the ultra-conservative media tycoon, lord of the evangelicals, in the unmistakable, naked embrace of another man.

10

The enormity of this new reality paralyzed Kennedy. *Who could she talk to about this? What should she do?* Toby had said it was above his pay grade. The revelation definitely pushed Kennedy out of her league and into snake-filled waters. She'd known about and disliked Van Dijk for years, ever since a friend and former college classmate of hers had faced blatant sexism and harassment at one of his radio stations. Tamara Weston was one of the smartest, most determined business majors she'd ever met—male or female. She'd graduated college with a 3.9, and in grad school maintained a 4.0 GPA. In the workplace, she was the first person in the office and the last to leave, offered innovative story ideas and cost-cutting strategies for reporting that were not only implemented, but improved the bottom line. Yet she was summarily passed over for promotion, never given the chance to go beyond weekend news. When she threatened to sue, they threatened to "make her go away." The incident was so traumatic that Tamara left broadcasting altogether, left America and moved to Grand Cayman. The experiences she endured for three years were horrific. "In the morning, he'll smile and say you're the greatest," she said to Kennedy shortly after resigning. "Then, by nightfall, he'll squash you like a bug."

During the thirty-plus years of building his empire, other salacious stories made the news. How he'd routinely discriminated against people of color. How he'd stolen, embezzled and laundered money through a series of shady, nefarious business deals. How if it meant adding to his inflated image or billionaire coffers, he'd have breakfast with Al Qaeda and dinner with the Ku Klux Klan. Amazingly, he was able to power through all of these allegations, turn the tables on his opponents and convince the masses that they were lying. He believed his own hype so convincingly that others believed it, too. Classic traits of a narcissist, honed skills of a master manipulator. Kennedy had no doubt that if anyone from his camp uncovered the true magnitude of what she possessed, Braum Van Dijk would have her hunted down and squashed . . . like a bug.

Maybe they do know.

Kennedy actually heard those words whispered. She looked around. No one was nearby. There were others in the restaurant, but she felt totally, completely alone. Her body began to tremble. She could feel her sanity slipping away, her body spiraling down a rabbit hole. She secured the flash drive in her purse and raced out of the building.

You've got to disappear.

While waiting to cross the street to her car, she heard this, as loudly as one could hear a voice in one's mind. With each step she took it grew, increased like a mantra.

Disappear. Disappear. Disappear.

Kennedy reached her car, started it and turned the air on full blast. She'd never had a panic attack but felt one coming on. She gripped the steering wheel and forced herself to breathe. Even so, she still felt suffocated beneath a boulder of truth too heavy to lift off her. She needed help, to tell someone, but who? The only other person who'd seen the pictures, at least that she was aware of, had made it clear that he couldn't help her shoulder the burden. What of her friends, Logan and

Gwen? *Could they help her bear the weight of the secret she carried? Did she have the right to even ask them to?*

Slowly, the fog of fear faded enough for Kennedy to put the car in drive and leave the parking lot. She didn't know where she was going, but it was definitely not to her house. With what she knew now, she wondered if she could ever go home again. There'd been strangers in her condo, rifling through her stuff, probably bugging the place. Because she had pictures of this man—this extremely well-connected, ultra-conservative, married with children, beyond reproach saint—cavorting with a man. A truth like this getting out could ruin Van Dijk and impact his business in a thousand ways. Given the enormity of what her pictures exposed, there was no *probably* to it. Her place was *definitely* bugged. And she definitely could not go back there.

Then where?

At the light, Kennedy glanced over and realized she was near her alma mater. The library. She could go there, ask a student to log her in, and see if the world wide web could help her catch a fat, hairy spider. She put on her blinker and eased into the turn lane. After a kind driver gave her the okay, she pulled in front of the car and turned. She continued around the campus to the entrance closest to the library. Something about the largess of the campus with students everywhere was soothing. Summer classes were in full swing. It felt good to be anonymous. Once inside, she went to where three rows of computers were there for the student's convenience. Looking around, she spotted a young man with a mountain of books in front of him texting on his phone. She walked over and cleared her throat.

"Hi, sorry to bother you but do you have your student card? I need to get on the computer and left mine at home."

"Sure."

Two minutes later, Kennedy was online. *Cool, now what?* A place to stay, that's the first thing she needed to secure. She wasn't ready to put her house up for sale, but she could sublease it. Knowing she wanted to stay as anonymous as possible she did a search for leasing companies, jotted down a few, then went to their websites. The third site she visited felt like a fit. The company was small and relatively new. They'd be hungry to get business and more likely able to handle her request—complete confidentiality. That done, she thought of where she could go and remembered a sight that Gwen used on her last vacation. On Home2Home.com, you could rent a room or an entire house on a daily, weekly, or monthly basis. No photo ID or proof of identify was required. Kennedy signed on as Kim Wright, then scrolled through the listings and found a room for rent in downtown Chicago for less than five hundred dollars a month. The room was small but clean, had a private bath and the price was right. The old Kennedy would not for a moment have considered moving in with a stranger. But in this new world, she didn't want to be alone.

Kennedy also didn't want to be easy to find, even by someone as highly trained as Big Brother. After pondering several possible word combinations, she placed "how to disappear forever" in the search engine and was shocked to see several sites containing step-by-step instructions on how to leave your life. Amazing, but disconcerting. The web was a criminal's dream and right now her salvation. After customizing a list combining tips from several websites, she spent the next three hours erasing her old life and planning a new normal. First stop after the library was the dealership where she bought her car. She walked in, sold it back to them for cash, and called an Uber for a ride to the nearest check cashing location. Once she had cash, she directed the driver to a second address, where a car owner was hoping to sell in a hurry. The home was in St. Charles, one of the city's oldest neighborhoods. She arrived, paid the driver, and met the car's owner, a middle-aged White lady, whose mother had recently died. The car was old but dependable, the woman assured, with very low mileage as her mother never drove far. One look at the spotless, white Honda Accord and Kennedy was sold. Hondas were indeed reliable and somewhere she'd read that white was the most popular car color in the country. On the highway, she'd blend right in. During the exchange, the woman proudly offered a bit of the neighborhood's and her family's history. St. Charles was home to many abolitionists and a stop on the Underground Railroad. Kennedy declined the gracious offer to see the home's fake wall, behind which slaves were hidden, but driving away she couldn't help but feel as though Harriet Tubman was riding alongside her trying to help her stay free, and alive.

Before leaving the city, Kennedy pulled over and sent Gwen a text:

Sorry I missed your call. Busy. Can you come over tonight around eight? It's important.

She tapped her fingers against the steering wheel, impatiently waiting for Gwen's response. It came a few seconds later. **Girl, what is up with you?**

The answer to that question was too long to text, and Kennedy wasn't ready for that conversation. A couple seconds later her phone rang, reminding her that she hadn't set up Bluetooth in the new car.

Can't talk now. Please, just meet me, okay?

Okay.

Kennedy turned off her phone and removed the battery so that whoever might be after her couldn't use cell towers to trace her movements. She drove to Gary, Indiana, an hour away, to make the purchases that, according to the websites, she'd need to go further underground. She'd never been to Gary before. All she knew about the town was that it was the home to the Jackson Five. But one of the instructions on disappearing was to veer from your regular way of doing things, familiar haunts and habits. Gary was far enough from her normal hangouts but close enough to visit regularly if need be. Plus, this was temporary, she kept telling herself. And probably unnecessary. She thought that and tried to believe it.

Her first stop was a facility to store her personal items once removed from the condo. Next up was a beauty supply store where she bought wigs and hair dye. Then she went to a superstore for a tablet, a tote on wheels, temporary cellphones, floppy hats, sunglasses, a few toiletries and changes of clothes for the next few days until she figured out how to remove her personal items from the condo. Near the checkout was a clearance rack. She snatched a gaudy pink jacket for five dollars and added it to her loot. Back in the car she programmed one of the phones and connected it to the car's Bluetooth. Then she fired up the tablet and transferred the pictures from Toby's flash drive. Seeing the extent of what she'd captured sent her pulse racing. The photo Toby showed her had been the tip of the iceberg. *Oh. My. God.*

It was almost seven thirty when Kennedy reentered Chicago's city limits. She parked in a grocery store parking lot, placed all her purchases in the tote and caught an Uber to her house. When Gwen entered her building and saw her sitting in the lobby, Kennedy didn't have to guess what she was thinking. Her friend's facial expression said it all, and her first three words confirmed it.

"What the hell?" Gwen plopped down on the leather seat beside Kennedy.

Kennedy smiled, then pulled out her phone and pretended to text. "What I'm about to say is insane. It will make no sense to you at all. Please just believe me, or even if you don't, just go along. I'm almost certain we're being watched. My life could very well be in danger."

"Ken!"

"Dammit, Gwen," Kennedy hissed, "stop being dramatic!"

"I'm being dramatic?" The question was asked casually, as though inquiring about the weather.

Kennedy looked up and smiled. "Please," she said, barely moving her mouth. "I will explain everything later, when we're away from here. Trust me, when you hear everything that's happened today, you will understand. Okay?"

"Okay."

"I'm going to make it look like you came for this tote. Please take it."

As Gwen reached for the tote, Kennedy continued to talk, gesturing and laughing as though sharing a story. "I'm going to give you a hug, then we'll go our separate ways. I'll head to the elevator and you'll go to your car. Only I'm not staying here. I'm really going with you."

"What?"

"Yes, I know. Crazy, but necessary. Drive to the corner across the street from the doggy park. I'll meet you there in five minutes."

"Kennedy . . ."

"Just a little while longer, sister, and this will all make sense." She stood and gave Gwen a hug and quick wave as she walked to the elevator. It opened quickly.

"Hey, Ken."

"Hey, Glenn, how are you?"

"Good. Haven't seen you at the gym lately."

"Yeah, I've got something going on with my back. The doctor told me to take it easy, so for the next few weeks you might not be seeing me that much."

Glenn's concerned expression made Kennedy feel bad for lying. "Are you okay? Is there anything I can do for you?"

"No, I'm fine. In fact, I'm thinking about going to California. An old college buddy lives there and has invited me over to recuperate."

"Alright, then. Take care of yourself."

"You too, Glenn."

Kennedy arrived on her floor, resisted the temptation to go inside her place and instead headed straight for the stairwell.

She quickly pulled her hair into a ponytail and stuffed it beneath a floppy hat she retrieved from the cheap jacket she wore. At the bottom of the stairs she pulled a pair of sunglasses from the other jacket pocket, then shimmied out of the jacket and threw it in the trash. Feeling properly incognito, she headed out the side door toward the park. Anyone observing closely would have noticed the changes but if questioned, those who saw a curly-haired woman with a pink jacket go into the building would probably not equate her with the short-haired woman wearing a black tank top who left it.

Kennedy kept her head down, frowning a bit as she saw Gwen's car. Instead of parked in a space like someone shopping or walking their dog, she was right on the corner, car idling like a robbery had been committed and she was driving the getaway car. Shaking her head, she reached for the handle, tapping the window after discovering it was locked. As soon as she heard the lock disengage, she opened the door and slid in.

"Do you think you could have been any more conspicuous?"

"What? You said meet you on the corner by the doggy park?"

Kennedy sighed. "You're right. That's what I said."

"Where are we going?"

"Just drive for now. I want to make sure we aren't being followed."

Gwen glanced at her. "Where's your jacket?"

"I threw it away."

They drove a few blocks without talking. "Kennedy, you need to tell me what's happening. My constitution can't take this suspense."

"I'm sorry to put you through all of this but I had no choice. I have to be very careful. When I was in the Bahamas taking pictures of that beautiful rainbow, I also took pictures of a very clandestine meeting happening on that island. I didn't see the images then, didn't know what I'd captured until the photos were digitally enhanced."

"Who was it?"

Kennedy eyed her friend. "I'm not sure you want to know, or that I have the right to tell you. It involves some very influential people, some of the most powerful men in the United States."

"The president?"

"A political figure would be easier to deal with. These guys tell the White House what to do."

"I can't imagine who that would be."

"Few can, unless you're a truth seeker. Many believe there is a secret society that not only runs America but the entire world, and that one of their members is Braum Van Dijk, who feeds their agenda to the masses through his network."

"Are you talking some Illuminati nonsense? I don't believe that group really exists."

"You and ninety percent of the rest of the population. But it's not just who he was with, but what he was doing."

"What?"

"Let's just say his evangelical viewers wouldn't be happy. And neither would his wife."

11

Kennedy and Gwen drove around for an hour before going to the store where Kennedy's car was parked. During the ride, Kennedy told Gwen about her plans to lay low for a while, which in addition to moving and changing cars, would eventually include closing her bank account, even though she had no idea how that would work, and to stay off social media. She was going to correspond from a new email address, too. Gwen tried to sound supportive, but Kennedy knew that her actions seemed extreme. Gwen couldn't understand why Kennedy didn't just sign the contract with Anita, return the pictures and put the whole mess behind her. With the chance of a six-figure payday, who cared that a coddled media mogul and member of a secret society was somewhere naked, getting their freak on? Kennedy understood Gwen's position. Her friend hadn't seen the pictures. If she had, she'd know why Kennedy felt this was something that should not be kept hidden, and that what some might pay to take the pictures public was even higher than the pot of gold Anita offered for the rainbow. Kennedy promised that she'd be careful, and Gwen vowed to keep her secret safe. Kennedy headed to her temporary home hoping she could stay safe as well.

After meeting the delightful sixty-something owner of the condo and explaining that a large project with a tight deadline would likely keep her holed up in the room, Kennedy set about trying to finish all the items she'd compiled on her list. Disappearing was hard work! Even though temporary, she hoped to throw off whoever was after her—the government she now presumed—long enough to figure out exactly what she wanted to do. Did she really want to expose Van Dijk and topple the empire generations had built? Could she handle the pressure, the scrutiny, the controversy that would surely follow? Even if done anonymously, it was hard to keep secrets in today's electronic world. And if she decided to go through with it, how much was what she possessed worth, and who should she approach about buying it? Getting ahead of the process was giving her a headache so she focused on what she could control—setting up a company to remove her items, creating a new email address, and going on her social media to tell a few friends who'd notice that she was taking a break to get caught up. Don't shut down everything at once, one of the websites had admonished. It would look too obvious and have those you'd normally interact with wondering what was going on. She sent out a group message to her friends and another one to her colleagues and acquaintances. She was just about to leave the site when a new message arrived. It was from her college friend Tamara, one of the names on the latter list. Other than social media they'd not spoken in years. She clicked on the message.

Hey Ken! I was just thinking about you. Saw your article the other week in the Star. Yeah, I'm all GC on the outside but still Chi where it counts. Your piece was great and the pics . . . wow! I understand you pulling back from social media to get work done. I need to do the same. Would love to catch up. Call me! 555-375-9290. T . . .

Kennedy sent back a quick reply that she'd love to catch up, then ended the night with a reply to Anita's earlier query regarding the agreement.

Dear Ms. Ford, Thank you so much for your interest in the pictures taken recently in the Bahamas. As a photographer, it means a lot that a company such as yours, and the island of the Bahamas felt them of the quality that would work well in the next tourism campaign. Unfortunately, due to the constraints of the agreement as written, I will not be able to accept your offer. I would be open to returning to the island and doing another shoot specifically for your marketing efforts. Please let me know if this is something you'd like to discuss further. Sincerely, Kennedy Wade.

The next morning, Kennedy's phone rang at eight a.m. That rarely happened. Her heart jumped as she raced to the phone from the bathroom, hoping it wasn't family with bad news. It wasn't. She recognized the Bahamian prefix and knew it was Anita. Kennedy let the call go to voicemail. She'd just gotten out of the shower and hadn't brushed her teeth or had her coffee so now was not the time for her to conduct a negotiation. An hour later, however, sitting in a coffee shop parking lot with latte in hand, she returned the call.

"Hello, Ms. Ford. It's Kennedy Wade."

"Oh, hi Kennedy! Please, call me Anita."

"Sorry I missed your call earlier, Anita. Did you get my email?"

"Yes, and I must say I was disappointed with your reply and am hoping we can come to terms that would work well for both of us. As I told you earlier my clients were very impressed with your work, especially the photograph of the rainbow, and are willing to do what we can to obtain the rights and move forward with our campaign."

Kennedy wasn't surprised that Anita had zeroed in on the very set of photographs that had captured the money shots. But she wanted to be sure it was that specific picture of a rainbow, taken that day, that the "client" wanted.

"Interestingly enough, Anita, it's that very set of pictures that preclude me from being able to sign the agreement. As you know some of them were featured in the *Chicago Star*, and since their website mirrors the print editions, they are not able or willing to remove them."

Kennedy hadn't actually spoken to the *Star* about it, but this was her story and she was sticking to it.

"There is also a personal project I'm working on where that setting—the rainbow and the island—and those pictures would be perfect. The island is beautiful and I'd love to work with you. Is it possible that I could come back and do another shoot as I suggested in the email? I can research the weather patterns and plan my trip accordingly."

"Thank you for that suggestion but, no. My client wants those pictures specifically. How about two hundred thousand for those photos? I have connections in the world of publishing who may have a bit more sway than you or I."

"I'm sorry, Anita, but I will not be able to release those photographs to your clients. I sincerely apologize."

On the other end of the line, silence. Kennedy held her breath. When next Anita spoke, gone was the bright, cheery tone that she'd had at the greeting.

"Ms. Wade, I can understand how as an artist you might become more attached to some work than others. But my clients are not only involved in tourism on the island, but they are very influential in other parts of the world. It would be in your very best interest to accept this gracious offer. I will get the release from the *Chicago Star* in writing, revise the agreement to specify which pictures are being sold and amend the amount to the newly agreed upon price of two hundred thousand."

"There's no need to call the *Star*, Ms. Ford. My pictures are not for sale. Again, I do appreciate your interest. Have a great day. Goodbye."

Kennedy thought that she'd feel triumphant following the phone call. Instead her body began shaking. It took several minutes before she stopped. Fortunately, a call from Monica, the office manager at *Chicago Sightings* redirected her thoughts. She wondered if Kennedy could come in that day instead of next week. *Absolutely!* They scheduled the interview for two hours later. Kennedy returned to the apartment, changed into a casual navy suit, and headed to the area of Chicago known as Pilsen and the condo where the up-and-coming business was housed.

Kennedy arrived in Pilsen thirty minutes before the interview was set to begin. She'd done so purposely to check out the area. One of the well-known facts about Chicago was how separate and distinct the neighborhoods were. She'd lived in the city for ten years and couldn't remember having been there before. Like many neighborhoods in and around the downtown loop it was being regentrified. What was established as a German, Polish and Czech neighborhood had become one of mostly Mexican-Americans in the 80s, and was continuing to evolve and diversify, With the skill of a photographer's eye, Kennedy took in the architecture reflective of the citizens who'd lived there. The Romanesque revival style of Thalia Hall. The vibrant Mexican art. As she found a parking space near the condo and pulled in her car, she was sure that if not done already, the makings of a rich *Chicago Sightings* article was all around her.

Monica had told her what to expect upon arrival, so Kennedy wasn't surprised to see a blended combination of office and living space as she stepped inside. Monica looked totally different from how she'd imagined. From the slight raspiness of her voice which Monica blamed on years of smoking, she'd imagined an older woman with a rough exterior, hair the color of a swatch on a bottle. Instead she was a vivacious redhead with smooth porcelain skin and a spray of freckles across the bridge of her nose. There was a desk near the doorway but the chair behind it was empty. So far it looked as if the two ladies were the only ones there.

"Hi, Kennedy. It's a pleasure to meet you. We'll go down the hall to my office later but for now let's just sit here, shall we?" She motioned to a couch behind them, sleek and modern like the rest of the room.

"Sure, thanks."

"Would you like something to drink? Coffee, lemon water . . ."

"I'm fine, thanks."

"I really appreciate you rearranging your schedule to come in today. We had someone filling in for the position and she was just not working out. So, after rereading your resume and checking out some of your work on the internet, I told Scott we needed to grab you before you went to work somewhere else."

They continued to chat pleasantly with Monica outlining the art director responsibilities and Kennedy answering Monica's questions and asking a few of her own. After a while Monica invited her to come back and see the office they'd share, one of two bedrooms that had been converted into a work space.

"How does all of this sound so far?"

"Like something I could really get excited about, especially since it's a company that's just starting out. I'm starting over myself, in a way, reinventing myself. I think this would be the perfect opportunity to do that."

"Why do you feel the need to reinvent yourself? I scrolled through quite a bit of your photography. It's very good."

Kennedy paused and composed herself. Here is where she'd have to be careful. In order to stay hidden it was very important that her name not appear on the byline. This explanation had to work.

"Reinvent may not have been the best word. What I'm wanting to do is expand my brand, and in doing so make very specific distinctions professionally. As a photographer, I'm known as Kennedy Wade. Here, if I have the pleasure of being hired, I'd like to use a little-known pseudonym connected mostly with writing—KW Wright."

"Hmm, interesting. But I can understand that, I guess. We'd have to run it by Scott and if he doesn't have a problem with it, then we're fine."

The front door opened. Footsteps were heard coming down the hall. A handsome young twenty-something stuck his head in the door.

"Good morning."

"Ah, there you are. Good morning, Scott. Scott, meet Kennedy. She'll hopefully be joining us as the art director."

He walked over, his hand outstretched. "Hi, Kennedy. A pleasure to meet you."

"Likewise. And please, I prefer KW."

"Ah, my bad," Monica said. "I forgot just that quickly." Monica explained Kennedy's desire for a slight name change.

"I don't see a problem with that."

Kennedy was more than relieved. "I think what you're building here is great. I'd love to be a part of it."

"We're just about to finish up. Should I send her down to your office afterwards?"

"Absolutely."

They watched as he reached the door, did a final wave and closed it behind him.

"So . . . I'm really impressed with your skill set and think you would be a great fit. There is one thing, though. We're like family here, and are trying to build a team that can grow this paper together. You've freelanced for the past two years. I'm a bit concerned that even with the flexibility of working both in and out of the office, you might decide this isn't for you, and I'd have to do this all over again. We're looking for someone who can commit to the magazine, help us get bigger and better year after year. Five years from now, we hope to be a national magazine."

"Monica, I have thoroughly enjoyed working in a freelance capacity these past few years. But an excellent company, great group of people, shared vision and long-term security is exactly what I'm looking for. If hired, I won't be going anywhere anytime soon."

After meeting with Scott, Kennedy returned to Monica's office to work out the details of her position and agree on a salary. Monica said she'd type it up and have Kennedy sign it when she reported for work on Monday. Just like that, Kennedy was hired. She left feeling hopeful, accomplished and satisfied. She called her mom, shared the good news, and made plans to come home for the Fourth of July. After the tumult of the past few weeks, getting the position as art director made her feel anchored, secure. When she said she'd be there for a long time, she meant it. Sometimes life didn't go as we've planned.

12

That Monday, Kennedy awoke bright and early to what she hoped was a brand-new life. The offer from *Chicago Sightings* couldn't have come at a better time. Not only would she have a steady salary, but she'd have a place other than burglars and the Bahamas to place her focus for forty to sixty hours a week. She'd appreciated Scott's honesty, that it was a regional magazine taking a long shot and doing so with a shoestring budget and paper-thin staff. He'd laughed after saying this and adding, "yes, that lame pun was intended." Kennedy had assured him that what he said was not a problem, and she'd meant it. The past month had taken the thrill out of the endless search for next month's meal ticket, and made her more than ready for something different, and steady, and local, and safe. Scott had also told her that the office atmosphere was casual, probably because said office also served as his home—a two-bed, two-bath condo in the artsy Pilsen neighborhood, just miles from the Loop on the city's Lower West Side. Still, Kennedy took care with her appearance. A black linen pantsuit with wide legs and a cropped jacket was funky enough to fit the casual bill while still giving off a professional air. She paired it with a white knit top and black sandals, pulled her hair into a high ponytail, grabbed her laptop bag, and headed out the door.

Just before nine, Kennedy was buzzed into what she hoped for the next foreseeable future would become her home away from home. Voices wafted toward her as she got off the elevator. The door was open. Kennedy felt uncomfortable about that, and the fact that the door was kept unlocked. She reminded herself that she'd just begun working here, that she'd told no one except her mom about the new job, and that there was no way she could be tracked down. The self-talk didn't remove her discomfort. So she told herself to stop being silly, to pull her shoulders back and get to work.

She opened the door and entered the sparse but nicely appointed living room, smelling of sugar and coffee. The room was part-office, part-living room, as evidenced by the reception's desk by the front door where a young woman who'd not been there last Thursday smiled up from her cellphone.

"Hi! How are you doing?"

"Good." Kennedy held out her hand. "I'm KW."

"Our art director, yay! I'm Fennel." Kennedy's brow raised. "New age parents," the slim, long-haired girl explained with a wave of her hand. "I used to hate it growing up. But it grew on me."

"Nice to meet you, Fennel."

Monica came around the hall. "KW! Good morning."

"Hi, Monica. How are you?"

"I'm good. Want some coffee?"

Kennedy held up her latte. "I'm good."

"Good. Come on back to your corner of the office." Kennedy laughed at Monica's reference that one of the bedrooms was essentially the office for her, Monica and Jeff, the rarely-there owner.

"Jeff's here," Monica threw over her shoulder. "He can't wait to meet you."

Kennedy stepped into "her office." A White guy with a bushy afro, seated at one of two desks, turned around. He was wearing wire-rimmed glasses, plaid shorts, Birkenstocks and a "Black Lives Matter" t-shirt.

"Kennedy Wade," he said standing up. "Good morning! Welcome aboard."

Kennedy shook his outstretched hand. "Thank you. I'm excited to be here. And please, call me KW."

Jeff frowned. "I heard that. KW, huh? I looked you up online and all I saw was Kennedy."

"That's strictly photography. In this capacity, I'd like to create a separate brand, if you will, one that will be recognized with the region's fastest, most successful lifestyle magazine on the market."

"Alright then, KW. I like how you talk!" He sat down and took in her outfit. "Monica didn't tell you that this is a casual office?"

"She did. First impressions, first day on the job . . ." Kennedy shrugged and smiled, a bit embarrassed at how even in this sporty linen she was grossly overdressed. "I'll come more laid back tomorrow."

"Suit yourself, but when working your ass off you should at least be comfortable, right? You are ready to put in a ten, twelve, fourteen-hour day, right?"

"Absolutely."

Jeff left halfway into her first day and was gone the rest of the week. Fine by Kennedy. He asked too many questions and seemed to live online. From what he told her about her past work, information that wasn't included on her resume, she deduced that the search engine was one of his best friends. The last thing Kennedy needed right now was a nosy Nelson. Other than that, *Chicago Sightings* was exactly what Kennedy needed to get her life back on track. Layout, photography, writing, editing were all areas of magazine publishing where she excelled, and were what she loved. While appreciating the freedom and flexibility of working from home she'd come into the office every day, enjoying the camaraderie and interaction working with the team. At twenty-eight, she was one of the elders in the room. The sales force consisted of preppy college grads—progressive, idealistic and hungry. Days were long but they went fast. Before she knew it, the holiday weekend arrived.

The Fourth was on a Friday this year, so early Thursday morning, just after five a.m., Kennedy placed her luggage, computer bag, small cooler, and CD case into the Honda she'd named Harriet. She'd never named a car before, but her uncle Ernie did. She'd thought it weird until her life went bonkers. After more than a week of trying to erase herself from the face of the world, calling her Honda Harriet seemed perfectly normal. After filling up her tank she hit the road, glad she'd gotten a jump on the Loop's rush hour traffic. She'd just placed a 2000s R&B compilation CD into the slot when her phone rang. Knowing she'd be on the road for eight hours, she'd left messages with a few people who'd been neglected the past couple weeks. She didn't expect anyone to call so early.

"Logan?"

"You remember my name?"

"Shut up," Kennedy said with a laugh. "I must have called you last night with my new number. Where were you? And why are you up so early?"

"I'm just getting out of the studio. What are you doing up?"

"Headed home for the Fourth."

"You're driving?"

"Yep."

"What, they stop booking flights to that Podunk town?"

"I wanted to drive, take some time to clear my head."

"Are you sure you're not running from somebody? You sub-leased your condo, went off social media . . ."

"How'd you know about my condo?" Kennedy already knew the answer. Gwen.

"Was that supposed to be a secret?"

"What else did Gwen tell you?"

"Just that you moved. And that you'd changed your phone number, which she wouldn't give me by the way. What's going on Ken? Does this have to do with the burglaries and what not?"

Kennedy took a deep breath and released her grip from the wheel. She couldn't be mad at Gwen. Technically she'd only asked her to keep the truth of the pictures a secret. As for Logan, he'd been there from the beginning, and had been a lifesaver when she returned from the Bahamas.

"The break-in was part of it. It was never the same in the condo after the burglary. Not just about feeling safe, but about feeling violated. Knowing someone had been in those rooms, in my drawers, maybe in my bed. A few other things have come up, personal situations that I'm dealing with. I just needed a change of scenery, something new."

"Where'd you move?"

"Just a temporary spot for now, until I decide if I want to actually sell the unit or keep on leasing."

"I hear you. Just keep in touch with your friends, okay? Gwen is worried about you."

"Sounds like you and Gwen are getting rather chummy."

"You jealous?"

"Hardly." A beep announced another call coming in. "Hey, Low. There's another call coming in. I need to run."

"As long as it's not your boyfriend."

"Bye."

Kennedy smiled as she tapped the steering wheel to switch calls. Logan was such a tease. She'd liked him and missed him. When she answered, there was a smile in her voice.

"Good morning!"

"Wow, sounds like a really good morning for you!"

"Tamara, hi! Wow, another early morning riser. I'm not usually a morning person, so that people actually function at this hour, conduct business and have conversations, I find quite amazing."

"We do. In fact, I'm often up even earlier than this. Several of my clients are international so I adjust my schedule to meet theirs. What about you? I was so excited to get your text last night, saying today would be a good time to talk. It's been a while."

The two spent the first part of the conversation catching up on shared connections—their families, different classmates and teachers, boyfriends or the lack thereof. Kennedy was thrilled to learn that Tamara was engaged.

"I didn't think there were any good ones left. Congratulations!"

"Ha! There's a few. Thank you."

"How'd you meet him?"

"Believe it or not when he took a vacation here with his girlfriend."

"Stop it!"

"I was having dinner with a client when he and his girlfriend got into it. She stormed off and about that same time my business meeting was over. We ended up in the parking lot at the same time with me offering a sympathetic ear as he went on and on about the ungrateful woman he'd dated for four years."

"Sounds like he was grateful to you for listening."

"He seemed appreciative, but I didn't think much of it. Forgot about the incident, went on with my business and then about seven months ago he walked into my office, back to enjoy Grand Cayman without Ms. Ungrateful. Three months later, we were engaged."

"That sounds so romantic, like a movie! What's he do? Where's he from?"

"He's a stock broker, Wall Street, New York born and bred."

"Does that mean you'll be returning to the States?"

"With the current climate swirling around and fringe media turning mainstream? No, thank you."

"I get it. Van Dijk's a sore spot."

"I probably shouldn't still hate him after all these years, but the experience in his company scarred me for a very long time."

Kennedy listened carefully, a plan unfolding in her mind as smooth and effortlessly as a peacock's feathers.

"I've got an incredible story to tell you. But I'll have to swear you to secrecy, to share it."

"Is it about Van Dijk?"

"It is."

"Then I swear it, Kennedy. You have my word."

13

A little after three in the afternoon, Kennedy entered the town she'd fled when just shy of her eighteenth birthday. Back home she'd lived under a cloud of paranoia but here, exiting the interstate onto Sixth Avenue, which cut through the town from east to west, she truly relaxed for the first time since meeting with Toby. All during the travel process, until well out of Chicago's city limits, she'd paid extremely close attention to everyone around her, and was sure that no one had followed her movements. For the moment, the fear squeezing her brain and heart had dissipated. She'd be able to actually think. She was also looking forward to seeing her family. This wasn't always the case. She and her brother Karl were as different as rum and whiskey and she'd outgrown her mother a long time ago. Karolyn had always encouraged her children to spread their wings but in the process forgot she could fly. But you only got one mama, and home was home. For whatever it was worth, Kennedy was glad to be there.

She reached Kiowa Street. It hadn't changed much in the ten years she'd been gone. The widow Mrs. Skinner was still perched on the corner, sitting in her swing watching everybody and catching everything. She had to be in her late seventies, early eighties, Kennedy mused, but the lady still had eagle eyes. How did she know? Because when she rolled down the window and said, "Good afternoon, Mrs. Skinner," the lady leaned forward and said, "Kennedy? It's about time you came home. Tell your mama I want some of that homemade ice cream."

The driveway was full, so Kennedy pulled behind an unfamiliar truck and popped her trunk. By the time she'd grabbed her purse and her computer bag from the back seat, her brother had reached the car.

"My word, Kennedy. Where'd you get this rental? Hooptie.com?"

"Haha, very funny. Keep your day job because your comedic skills are lacking."

He pulled her luggage out of the trunk and gave her a hug. They started toward the house. "I'm serious. What are you doing in that thing? Where's your car?"

"I got rid of it."

"Quit lying."

The innocent response was like a soft arrow into her heart. No doubt she'd be doing quite a bit of creative conversing this weekend.

"I'm not. I'm downsizing debt, big brother."

"Are you in financial trouble?" he asked sincerely, before she was saved from answering by reaching and going through the front door.

"Hey, everybody!"

The first inquisition was over. Kennedy was able to settle into the comfortable zone of fun, friends, and family. She passed on Mrs. Skinner's request to her mother, who promptly set about making the first of several batches the crew would consume before the last firecracker had popped. She thought she'd handled the evening quite well, until helping her mom clean up later that night.

"What's going on with you, Ken?"

Kennedy took the moment to finish placing the container of tomorrow's potato salad into the refrigerator to embrace her inner nonchalant.

"I'm good, Mom."

Karolyn gave her a side-eye. "You can try that with Ray, Karl or some of the neighbors, but I'm your mama."

"Are you talking about me trading cars?"

"I never was a fan of cars that cost half as much as houses so, no, I don't have a problem with what you're driving."

"What then?"

Karolyn used a dish towel to wipe off the counter. "That's what I'm asking you. There's something going on. I see it on your face when you think no one's looking." She passed her on the way out of the kitchen. "And you've lost weight."

Kennedy followed behind her and assured her that everything was fine. And when it came to her vacation in Peyton, it was. Until they arrived at the quaint Main Street parade and for a split second, she thought she saw a face she recognized. *Jack Sutton.*

Her family, along with a couple neighbor families, had found space and seating near the start of the parade's route on Main Street in the town square. Her mom and Ray sat in lawn chairs. Karl and his girlfriend stood just behind them, along with Ray's brother, some cousins and a couple of Karl's friends. She'd just accepted a small flag from her brother as the band cranked out a respectable version of "Sir Duke." She waved her red, white and blue as they passed her and had just turned to view the mayor standing and waving from a horse-drawn wagon when she saw a face etched in her memory. Even beneath a cap and behind glasses. *Jack.* She knew it was him. They didn't make them like that in Kansas, and "that" didn't come to her town for a parade. Before she could think, she reacted, headed straight through the procession and across the street, narrowly missing a pile of horse poop and a float's large, protruding papier-mâché nose. She could vaguely hear her name in the distance, as though being shouted down a tunnel. Shouts and stares bounced off her armored focus. She searched the faces and the space where he'd just been, looked up and down the street, and beyond, began a quick turn around the center. He couldn't have gone far. The town was small, the square even smaller. But the man she saw was nowhere in sight. He was gone. *Poof.* Like the wind. The adrenaline rush receded. Kennedy slowed, then stopped, leaning against a building to catch her breath. She looked across the way. Only now was she aware of the people watching her, the question on their faces. Had she really darted across the street and almost gotten crushed by the Peyton Bear? She could only imagine what her family thought. On the way back to the group she formulated a story. Time for more creative conversing in Peyton.

All eyes were on her as she returned to the family. Her mother loudly asked the question all of them wondered.

"Girl, what in the world is wrong with you?"

"Sorry! I'm sorry everyone," she said to those around her, then back to Karolyn. "I thought I saw Tinisha!"

"Girl, please. Tinisha comes home even less than you do, and that's saying something."

Kennedy gave her mother a playful bump.

"You know she married a preacher," Karl said, turning to join the conversation.

Karolyn reached into a large straw tote and pulled out a fan. "She don't need a man," she said, furiously fanning the heat or a hot flash, Kennedy didn't know which. "She needs Jesus."

Those around who heard Karolyn laughed. Tinisha was a celebrity, a major one by Peyton's standards. Once well-known for dating a record producer, Tinisha found herself on reality TV. Her storyline was juicy, messy and popular, just like the Tinisha Kennedy remembered. Her star fell as quickly as it rose, though, and she ran into the arms of the Lord.

Once the parade was over, family and friends returned to Karolyn's house, ready to grub on a feast. Someone pulled out photo albums and amid barbeque, salads and a fountain of drinks, they all went down memory lane. The noise levels rose over Scrabble and spades, and once the squirt guns and badminton net came out, the festivities moved outside. Kennedy saw several people she hadn't seen in years, and took a container of food to Mrs. Skinner. She ate too much, laughed to tears, and felt the happiness that lately had been rare. By the time she joined her brother outside on the patio, she'd convinced herself that the man she saw earlier could not have been Jack.

She took a chair across from Karl, who was smoking a cigar. "When did you start doing that?" she asked with a scrunched-up nose, while waving away the smoke.

"It's an acquired taste, for sophisticated, upwardly mobile folk." Karl blew smoke rings that floated into the night.

"In that case, put it out." They laughed for a minute, then enjoyed a companionable silence. Kennedy and Karl hadn't always gotten along. He was quite a bit older than her and polar opposite in many ways. But today they'd gotten along, a refreshing change. So much so, that for a minute, a split second really, she thought about sharing a version of what had happened to her to get his opinion.

But he spoke first. "Did Mom tell you I'm running for the city council?"

"No, but I'm not surprised. You like to argue and tell people what to do so . . ." Kennedy was rewarded with a soft bop to her head. "Seriously, I think you'll make a good representative. Didn't you minor in political science?"

"I sure did."

"What party are you representing?"

"The only one that makes sense right now."

"Oh, the party for all the people. Good to hear." She looked over to see him giving her the eye. "Please don't tell me you're still leaning conservative, and still binge-watching and listening to TBC networks. Not after all that's happened the past two years." True Broadcast Corporation was an international media powerhouse offering the most "alternative" views on current events.

"Okay, I won't tell you."

"Seriously, Karl? You still think Van Dijk is a great businessman? The guy's a jerk, the absolute worst that's ever stepped in front of a camera. And I don't mean just in the United States. I mean in the world!"

"Like so many others you've drunk the Kool-Aid. I get that the man is unconventional. He's also a genius, on the pulse of the nation, plugged into the hearts and minds of the American majority."

The image that floated up in Kennedy's mind was one of Karl's hero plugged into something else. She bit her tongue to keep quiet, so hard she almost drew blood. *The Pulse* was an autobiography written by Van Dijk that became a bible among evangelicals and a *New York Times* bestseller. In it, he detailed the discipline based on biblical principles that garnered his family's astronomical success. Kennedy knew of a certain p-word Van Dijk didn't want in print.

"There are things you don't know, Karl, that if you did . . ."

"What, another witch hunt or some kind of fake news?"

Kennedy turned toward him again, serious this time. "You do know I'm in that industry, right? Not directly as a reporter or such, but I work with some form of media every day. My best friend is at *Chicago Star,* and I can tell you they work their asses off to keep America informed of what's really happening. The truth, facts that have been researched and documented."

Kennedy felt herself getting agitated. "Look, I don't want to argue. I'm not going to change your mind."

"Atta girl."

How frickin' chauvinistic! She swallowed the thought. "Where's your friend Kimora?"

"She left a little while ago."

"She seems nice."

"She is, smart too. We think alike."

"Of course."

Someone signaled that it was time to go watch the fireworks. The conversation ended but Karl's words reverberated in her mind for a very long time. He spoke the position held by millions of Americans about a man who seemed made of Teflon, where the most heinous facts—corruption, racism, adultery, abuse—rolled off like water on a duck's back. There were documents and pictures supporting those allegations, too. A fact that, for Kennedy, begged the question. Would publicizing those pictures be the end of Van Dijk's career and life as he knew it? Or would it be the end of hers?

14

Zeke waited until he heard a cheer from the crowd, then emerged from a stairwell behind the dollar store, his demeanor calm but inside, slightly shook. For the second time in this operation he'd been caught off his game. Had this been war and were he on the frontline, he'd be a casualty right now. *No Bueno.* Zeke had vowed as he threw her off his trail that it wouldn't happen again. He'd flipped his reversible ball cap and pulled the hair attachment from inside the rim. The black Yankees sign that Kennedy may have seen was now orange with a logo for the Mets. The buzz-cut blonde now sported straggly black locs. He'd slapped a large, stick-on flag to the front of his shirt and kept his head down slightly as he slipped into the alley and headed to his car parked two blocks away. Once back to the rental, he fired it up and headed straight to Kiowa Street and the home of Karolyn Burnett. Since learning she'd subleased her condo, Zeke had been unable to uncover her new location. Pure instinct had led him to Peyton, figuring she'd might go home for the holiday.

By the time he arrived at the home where Kennedy's mother, step-father, and either a half-sister or cousin lived, he was once again in all black, except for the Mets cap. Not that it mattered. Five thousand, four hundred of the fifty-five hundred residents the town boasted were standing along a parade route that went on for a mile, ending at the town's high school on the other side of town. He guessed no one would be back in the house for at least an hour. Not that it would take him that long. He pulled out his lock kit, slid a file along the patio door and unlocked it faster than someone with a key. He slipped inside, holding his alarm detector as he let his eyes adjust to the darkness. The house was small and cluttered. It smelled like a holiday. The sweet and tangy smell of barbeque sauce vied with onions, and some kind of meat. Zeke's stomach growled. He ignored it. Assured there was no type of surveillance equipment inside, he began a search of the house. There was only a slight chance that Kennedy had left her computer bag here, but he had to take it as he'd already looked in that boat of a car he saw her exit earlier, when the family arrived to watch the parade. What had happened to her BMW? Starting at the farthest point west, he entered a master bedroom. His military fingers itched to properly complete the shoddily made bed, and gather the clothes strewn on the closet floor and place them in baskets. With the military training on top of his borderline OCD, he wouldn't last more than five minutes in this house. How did people live like this? A running dialogue continued in the back of his mind, even as his focus was squarely on the task at hand. He checked purses and luggage, coat pockets and drawers. He moved methodically from room to room, ending in one with twin beds with a piece of luggage at the end of one of them. A quick check told him it was Kennedy's belongings. But there was no flash drive inside. After taking several pictures of the framed photographs and a few of the home, Zeke headed toward the patio door. He opened it. Just before stepping out, he turned and walked back to the refrigerator. Seconds later he made his exit, the smell of a barbequed chicken breast wafting up from between two pieces of bread.

There was nothing more for him to do in Peyton. He scheduled a flight back to New York and put a call in to his boss. As far as he was concerned, continuing to trail Kennedy Wade was a waste of his specialized time and Van Dijk's money. There were traitors to his country who needed to be silenced, but Zeke didn't think Kennedy was one of them.

Then there was the matter of the pictures themselves. What exactly was supposed to be on them? What meeting could she have photographed that was a threat to national security? Van Dijk had openly met with many controversial figures. He'd shunned weak allies and bolstered connections that were in his company, and in turn, America's best interest, such as Saudi Arabia and other countries in the Middle East. He'd rattled America's biggest competitor, China, and showed the Asians who was boss, that no matter how much his channels were sanctioned, America was and always would be the leader of the free world, and that TBC would be its official voice. That's what he loved about Van Dijk, that's what his viewers got that those who watched fake, watered down media did not. He led with a firm hand and a big pair of kahunas. He got the job done.

As a former member of one of the military's highest-trained personnel, one with high clearance and access to military se-crets, Zeke knew about covert operations and questionable tac-tics used against the enemy that had been successfully shielded from America for years. So who could this mogul have met with where public knowledge of such would threaten national secu-rity? And even more perplexing, why hadn't he been briefed on this person's identity? Their determination to retrieve the pictures from Wade was proof that Van Dijk felt the pictures especially damning. Who was this person? Zeke's thoughts took a turn. Maybe it wasn't a leader of a foreign government. Maybe it was someone whose relationship with Van Dijk might be one few people could understand. A member of the mafia, perhaps, or a White Supremacist organizer. As his phone rang the answer hit Zeke squarely in the forehead. Wade had a snapshot of Van Dijk with a woman other than his wife.

He tapped the phone icon. "Zeke Foster."

"Zeke, it's Braum."

"Yes, sir."

"I received your message. You're calling with good news, I hope."

"I haven't secured the flash drives containing the photos, sir. So far, my searches at several locations have turned up nothing. Our attempts to buy back the pictures were unsuccessful as well."

"Dammit. That woman is costing us more trouble than she's worth. You've scoped out enemy combatants, captured terrorist sympathizers, performed major intel. What's the problem with you handling this rather insignificant mission?"

"Insignificant, sir?"

"Not the mission," Van Dijk replied with a cough. "The person you're tracking."

"I have no problem tracking the subject, sir. I'm just leaving Peyton, her hometown, and the home of her parents. The problem is in finding the pictures, sir. She's taken them down from the cloud and removed them from any computers I've obtained. She has them on flash drives, sir, and has given them to at least one other person that I know of. I also entered his residence to potentially retrieve a drive, but to no avail.

"May I ask a question, sir?"

"You may, doesn't mean it will get answered though."

"Is the retrieval of this information for personal reasons, sir?"

"No."

"Is it a competitor, sir? Or someone on the other side of the political or moral aisle? I'm just trying to better understand the mission."

"You know enough," Van Dijk brusquely replied. "Now get those flash drives. Now!"

"Yes, sir."

"Ah, hell, Foster," Van Dijk continued, a slight accent seeping into his relaxed demeanor. "I might as well tell you since in many ways you're risking your life to help me. You're aware of my connections with MAN, the Manner Allmachtig Knights Fraternal Order, aren't you?"

"Of course, sir. My former commander was a member as well."

"One of the reasons I hired you. The founding families are very private. They keep an extremely low profile, which keeps the sheep guessing as to who holds the staff."

"Sheep, sir?"

"The masses, the followers, the ones who, but for organizations like ours, would send the world as we know it plummeting into the darkness of depravity, immorality, and inferior global positioning behind China, Russia, and only God knows who else. I was meeting with the son of one of those fathers. Now, the average person has no idea this family is a part of the order. In fact, they believe just the opposite, that they're part of the crowd bringing America down. He has successfully infiltrated Hollywood, politics, every bastion where secrets we need flow freely. To be seen with me would mean the end of that access, and usher in the end of the America that we now know.

"There is an association of world leaders who've been meeting for years, putting a plan in place to create a new global destiny, a new way to see the world. It will be a merging of power economically, environmentally, and socially, in a way that would be hugely beneficial to the American public, white and blue collar alike. This liaison would give us greater ability to fight the problems that threaten our way of life. But it's an unconventional, ambitious strategy, being carefully laid out, in secret. Those men were the men with whom I met in the Bahamas, and who may have been captured by the lady taking pictures of the rainbow. Can you imagine what the liberal media would do if they had pictures of me chatting with someone seemingly opposed to our values? Say a faggot or atheist, or one of those sympathetic Hollywood devils?"

"They'd have a field day, sir."

"You're damned right. They'd spin a web a lies the way they always do, and the next thing you know there would be yet another probe with lawyers blowing smoke up our asses trying to find wrongdoing where there is none. Those liberal stations have hated me for years. They are jealous of the power our media yields, and how we've got the real American, the patriotic, God-fearing majority on our side. They want to turn our democracy into a socialistic, communist nation full of illegal immigrants taking the jobs, and people too lazy to work living off the hard work of the tax-paying public, and make that look normal. Now I know you don't want that to happen."

"Absolutely not sir."

"That's why this mission is so crucial, son, and why I've been a bit testy about it. I don't want something that can be so beneficial to the majority ruined because of those lying liberal media networks and the fake news they air."

"I understand, sir, and now that I have a clearer vision of what's at stake, I'm even more dedicated, more committed to making sure every copy of potentially damning evidence is retrieved and turned over. I won't let you down, sir. You have my word."

The call ended. Zeke paced the room—tense, agitated—his fingers twitching to capture and neutralize his target, in this case a flash drive or the owner of such who'd betray her commander. A couple minutes passed. He walked over to a file cabinet and pulled out the folder with pictures of Wade. He flipped through them slowly, as a plan began formulating in his mind. The conversation with Van Dijk had crystalized the mission, made clear that what was at stake was their very own democracy, America, and the constitution he'd sworn to protect. Van Dijk had faith that he could do the job. Zeke did not plan to let him down.

15

On Monday, Kennedy slid into Harriet's front seat and headed to work. She was still in a good mood from the trip home. Her heartbeat was normal, with no paranoia. While she sometimes dreaded going home, this time she'd actually enjoyed herself, even the quaint little Fourth of July parade sponsored by the Peyton, Kansas Chamber of Commerce. Even with the teasing she endured by almost becoming a part of it. Thankfully, her family had bought the story that she thought she'd seen Tinisha, a former classmate and the only member of their neighborhood gang that Kennedy hadn't seen since high school. Kennedy never stayed long when she came to town, and mostly hung around family, so being able to see a person she at one time considered a best friend, especially one who'd carved out a little chunk of Atlanta society and appeared on a reality show, would have been a big deal. She'd seen just about everybody else though, including her ex-boyfriend, the "best friend" who'd stolen him, and a slew of rugrats she assumed were their children.

Seeing them, and several other of her high school haters and their families, brought back bittersweet memories. But seeing the sports teams represented made her smile. At one time Kennedy, ran a mean one-hundred-meters, and when it came to hurdles, she wasn't half bad. The high school band performed respectable versions of Prince's "Let's Go Crazy" and a high school marching band favorite—"25 or 6 to 4." A second mascot float depicting a twenty-foot bear, this one made entirely of gummy bears, was totally impressive. Kennedy even managed not to roll her eyes as the year's Miss Peyton offered a queen's wave to the crowd. Twenty-first century and the town of five-thousand had never selected a person of color to represent them in the state pageant. The more things changed, the more they'd stayed the same. Still, as they'd caravanned to Peyton Lake to watch the fireworks—her mom, Ray, Ray's brother Fred and his mistress What's-Her-Name, Karl, his new girlfriend Kimora (and yes, Kennedy felt her name starting with K had given the cute law student an edge over other women he'd dated) and his best friend Deuce (the one she'd had a drunken one-night stand with and then took a pic of his dick as insurance against him telling her brother)—she thanked heaven for her blessings, which included her crazy clan.

There were now two sides to Kennedy's life—pre-Bahamas and post-Bahamas. It felt that working at *Chicago Sightings* would help her build a bridge between the two. Less than two weeks on the job, and her co-workers already felt like family. The zany sales force that occupied what they'd dubbed the "Situation Room," but was actually the second bedroom, kept her laughing. The editorial assistant, serious and efficient, balanced them out. Scott and Monica's assistant, also the receptionist, was the youngest in the group, just eighteen. A social media whiz whose bright smile hid a slew of insecurities, Fennel brought out Kennedy's compassionate side, in many ways reminding her of the teenager who'd left Peyton to conquer the world. She'd forgotten the sense of belonging that a workplace could stir up. Maybe that's why she was at work at eight thirty, when the day didn't officially begin until nine.

She set down her computer, refilled the Keurig case, made herself a cup of java and sat down to work on the magazine's September and October issues, the first totally under her art direction. One of the new features she'd added was a page called Hindsight, where a piece of Illinois history, specifically something that had happened in Chicago, would be featured. The articles were paired with photographs, offering modern takes on the historic events and if available, a current counterpart to the history remembered. She'd found a couple interesting pieces for October—the State Convention of Colored Citizens convening in the city and the great Chicago fire of 1871. But so far, the month of September was slim pickings. She sat against the chair back and slowly sipped the sweet, caramel liquid. Her phone rang. With the office still empty, she placed the call on speaker.

"Good morning, Mom."

"Good morning."

Something in her mother's tone suggested the morning may not be as good as Kennedy thought. She sat up and placed her cup on a coaster. "How are you?"

"Not too good."

"Why? What's going on?"

"I just ran into Mrs. Skinner at the hospital. She shared some troubling news."

"Oh my goodness, is she alright?"

"She's fine, was here for her annual checkup." Kennedy relaxed. "But I'm calling because of what she shared with me. She believes that on the Fourth, while we were all at the parade, someone was in my house."

The unease that Kennedy had worn like a second skin for weeks, the discomfort she'd just shed in Peyton, came back in a flash. So did the image of Jack Sutton, the face she thought she'd seen in the crowd before convincing herself she'd been mistaken.

"Did she know them? Mrs. Skinner knew everybody. "Did she see who it was?"

"She couldn't see their face. They were too far away. But she thought it was a man, dressed in all black."

Kennedy's heart seized up. What did a heart attack feel like?

"Said he was wearing a bright orange ball cap."

Her heart muscles loosened enough for blood to flow. The guy she'd seen across the street was wearing a black Yankees ball cap. She'd immediately recognized the logo and committed it to memory. Still, she felt lightheaded. Was it conceivable that if someone indeed had been in her mom's home that they'd been there looking for her? Or the flash drive? Rushing to check emails before the parade, Kennedy had stashed her computer bag beneath the couch instead of taking it back to the guest room. She reached beneath the desk, snatched up the bag and quickly checked the inside pocket. The drive was there same as always. But had the Chicago condo burglar been in Peyton on the Fourth?

"That's crazy, Mom. I don't remember anything out of place when we got back home, did you?"

"Come to think of it, I did notice something, but at the time it wasn't a big deal. But when we got home and I pulled out the food, I remember removing the foil from the chicken and noticing some had gone missing. You weren't in the kitchen when I asked who got into the food?"

"No, I didn't hear that."

"Nobody owned up to it and I didn't press. The food was there to be eaten, so like I said, it was no big deal. But I had a funny feeling when I saw the chicken like that, like someone had just reached in with their hands and snatched pieces off."

"I'm going to go home for lunch and have another look around. Maybe the man wasn't in the house, maybe he just crossed our patio and came from behind the house, which from

Mrs. Skinner's angle would look like he may have come from inside."

"Did she see the car he drove?"

"She said he was walking. She followed him all the way down, said he turned on Tenth Street. She made a mental note of it, but said she went inside after that."

"Then maybe you're right. Maybe it was somebody who cut across the back lawns. But call me when you go home for lunch, okay, to let me know if anything's missing or out of the ordinary."

"Okay. I'll call you back."

Kennedy was in a meeting and missed Karolyn's call back, but once she was out, she returned the call.

"Hey, Mom. Sorry I missed your call. I was in a meeting, a lot to learn."

"Sounds like the new job is agreeing with you."

"It's perfect. I'm really happy to be working there. So . . . you went home for lunch?"

"I did."

"And . . ."

"Everything was normal. I didn't see anything suspicious or out of place. I visited Mrs. Skinner and assured her that everything was fine, that it was just someone cutting across the lawn."

"Hopefully that made her feel better. I know she lives alone. It's understandable that she'd be concerned seeing something like that."

"You ask me, I think it's all those crime shows she watches, and movies on Lifetime. Still, I appreciate her keen and thorough observations of everything going on within a four-block radius. The neighborhood wouldn't be the same without her."

"I'm glad you were able to make her feel better. I feel better, too."

"Good. You need to focus on your own problems rather than worrying about what's going on down here."

"Mom . . ."

"Oh, I know you're going to deny it. But I know what I saw, the frown that would creep up in unguarded moments when you thought you weren't being watched. It's alright, baby. You know your mama wasn't born yesterday. Doesn't take too much for me to know that one way or another, it involves a man."

They chatted from when Kennedy left the office until she found a place to park on the street near the apartment. Getting home when she did, finding such a spot was a nightly challenge, one of the few things she disliked about living here. But her roommate Lydia was cordial and for the most part minded her own business. Knowing someone else was in the house was a comforting feeling, as was believing that she'd shaken whoever was following her and removed any way they could find out where she lived. The cloak of anonymity had settled around her shoulders, and felt pretty good right now.

Not far away, curious eyes followed a blinking red dot as it travelled across a map on a screen. The red dot stopped. The viewer waited, then smiled, enlarged the map and took a screenshot of Kennedy Wade's current location.

16

She told herself it was silly, that there was no way anyone followed her home last night. Yes, she'd been talking to Karolyn, but Kennedy remembered periodic checks in her rear and side mirrors. Whoever was after her and the pictures didn't know she'd traded cars. Even if they'd learned that she'd moved, there was no way they could know her current address. Since revealing the situation to Tamara and employing her help, there wasn't even a bank trail on her anymore. Checks from *Chicago Sightings* were endorsed over to a non-profit run by Tamara's aunt, the money then transferred to Kennedy's account set up in Grand Cayman. All of Kennedy's business was conducted via cash or the cash Visa card the non-profit set up. For Kennedy to add money, she didn't need ID. But last night she'd dreamt that that was exactly what happened. It was in color, and detailed, and felt so real that when she woke up her heart was racing. A reminder to her that even though she felt safer she wasn't totally out of the woods. She needed to stay vigilant and take all precautions.

As soon as she arrived at the office on Tuesday, she pulled Monica aside.

"What's going on, KW? Those magazine layouts giving you

the heebie-jeebies? You looked scared." After a beat Monica added, "I'm joking."

Kennedy didn't laugh. Instead she walked over and closed the bedroom door.

Monica's mood changed. "Uh oh. Something's really wrong."

"Nothing to do with work."

"That's a relief."

"But I do want to share something that's going on. Something personal that I'd hoped had been resolved, but now believe may not be."

"Okay. What is it?"

"I might have a stalker."

"KW, oh no! Are you sure?"

"Not sure that he was who I believe followed me last night, but definitely sure about the problems I've had in the past."

"Is this an ex-boyfriend?"

"You could say that."

"Ah, man. That sucks. I've been in those shoes and they do not feel good."

"You've had a stalker?"

Monica nodded. "Years ago, when I was in college. You know that guy your parents warn you about?" Kennedy nodded. "I dated him. He was controlling, possessive, and when I finally got up the nerve to end the relationship, he wasn't ready to let go. Late night visits. Hang up calls. Things got ugly."

"What did you do?"

"My parents finally had me get a restraining order."

"And that stopped it?"

"That and his next victim. Have you tried a restraining order yet?"

"I was hoping it wouldn't come to that. Plus, I have no real proof of his identity. But it's gotten serious. My home was bur-glarized."

"Oh, you poor thing." Monica got up from her chair and gave Kennedy a hug. "I feel so badly for you. Hey, is that why you're going to use the KW Wright pseudo as a byline signature instead of the more well-known Kennedy Wade?"

"Yes."

"Geez, kiddo. Did you call the police?"

"For what it was worth. They came and took a report, but other than that there wasn't much they could do. A few stolen items is no match for waves of violent crime."

"No doubt. And you think it was your ex?"

"I can't be sure. But I don't want you to think this will have any impact on my ability to do the job. It's just that for the next few weeks, if it's okay, I'd rather not do late nights here."

"That's no problem. If there's anything that needs discussing, we can either Facetime or talk over the phone."

"Thank you, Monica." Kennedy let out a relieved breath.

Monica's eyes narrowed. "Are you in imminent danger?"

"It's probably closer to the truth to say I'm in*sane*. Last night after leaving here, I felt as though I was being followed. I kind of freaked out, took either the real or imagined person tailing me on a wild goose chase. Again, it was probably nothing but . . ."

Monica reached out and squeezed her arm. "It was something. Even if it was nothing, it's something because it upset you. Don't be dismissive about what happened. Trust your gut. Do you carry any kind of protection, pepper spray or something like that?"

"No, but I'll look into it."

"Please do. We want you here, and we want you safe."

"Thank you, I really appreciate it. And Monica, do you think that this can stay just between us?"

"Of course."

When Kennedy left work that day she didn't go home. Earlier she'd gotten a text from Gwen to meet her and Logan for dinner. So she headed to a Mediterranean spot near the *Chicago Star* offices, ready to enjoy a good meal.

Gwen was there when she walked in, and easily seen in the

near empty dining room texting on her phone. Kennedy gave her arm a playful slap. "Hey, sis!"

They hugged. Kennedy sat down. "Where's Logan?"

"He's not going to make it, decided to work overtime."

"I wonder how his music project is coming."

"Really good," Gwen said, putting down her phone. "I've heard a couple tracks, one with a girl with a voice like Mariah Carey singing in the background. You know he moved the studio from his bedroom into a building over by the warehouse."

"Really? He'd just gotten it set up in his bedroom."

"Yeah, but after that burglary things were never the same."

Kennedy nodded, understanding all too well.

"Plus, they needed a bigger space. They're doing it up large, for real. He's so proud of the new set up. The production going on there is all he talks about. I'm surprised he didn't tell you."

"I haven't talked to him since going home on the Fourth."

"How was that? How's family?"

"Everybody's good. The trip was fun. I enjoyed it." Kennedy shared the highlights and kept the phantom Jack sighting to herself. "What about you? How's your internet dating plan working? Any fireworks besides those lighting up the sky?"

Gwen smiled, shrugged.

"Ooh, there is. Don't sit there and act all coy about sharing. That's probably why you called me down here."

Kennedy sat back as the server set two waters on the table and accepted the menu given.

"Something actually did jump off, and it was totally unexpected."

"That's usually how it happens." Kennedy leaned forward. "I'm glad at least one of us has a date life. Well, tell me all about him. What's his name?"

"There's probably not much I can tell you that you don't already know." At Kennedy's frown, Gwen continued. "Me and Low are hanging out."

Kennedy's jaw dropped. "Shut. Up."

"Are you mad?"

"Why would I be angry?"

"Because y'all used to flirt around all the time. I thought you liked him."

"When he tried to flirt, I saw a little brother." Actually, she'd begun to catch a glimpse of something different, but it was too late to act on that now. "I can see you two together, Gwen. I'm happy for you."

An hour later, Kennedy left the restaurant in a hurry to get home. She was glad for the long summer days, still light after eight, but the parking situation on her street was crazy. The other night she had to park her car almost three blocks away. While looking for a space she thought about tonight's dinner conversation. Gwen and Logan. She hadn't seen that match coming and reexamined her feelings to make sure there was no regret. There wasn't. Logan was fine, and a nice young man. But the emphasis was on young. She was almost home before she realized what the niggling feeling was about those two together. Her secret. Gwen knew things about Kennedy and the pictures that she hadn't shared with Logan and vice versa. For whatever reason in certain areas they were both in the dark. The rationale might be shaky, but somehow she felt they'd be safer not knowing at all. She thought about the flash drive that Logan said was hidden at his house. How safe was it, now that he spent so much time working and away at the studio? Maybe she should send the one he had to Tamara in Grand Cayman. Something about having a copy outside the country felt like a good move.

She entered the apartment to the smell of spaghetti and the sound of cooking coming from the kitchen.

She passed by the dining room on the way to her space. "Hi, Lydia."

"Hi, Kim. There's an envelope for you on the dining room table."

Kennedy's hand froze just over the doorknob. "For me? Are you sure?"

Lydia crossed from the kitchen to the dining room wiping her hands on a towel. "It has your name on it." She picked it up and checked it again as she walked toward Kennedy. "Well, not exactly."

Kennedy let out a breath.

"It says Kennedy and your name is Kim. Close enough is what I thought. It's definitely not Lydia."

The knot jumped back in her stomach, and tightened. "Was it in the mail?" She asked this rather casually, but her voice had risen a notch.

Kennedy accepted the envelope from Lydia, eyeing it carefully. "Oh, never mind." Her question was answered. There was no postmark. Which meant whoever delivered it came right to the door. "Thanks, Lydia."

"You're welcome. Hey, it's impossible to make a small quantity of spaghetti. You're welcome to have dinner if you'd like."

"I just came from having dinner with a friend. But it smells delicious. Thanks for the invite."

Kennedy managed to keep her voice light, despite the fact that her insides were shaking. They'd found her. Whoever they were, the faceless ghost after her because of the pictures, that followed her to Peyton like the phantom Jack. The face that was there and then gone in the span of a second. It might not have been the man who'd drugged her in the Bahamas, but there was no doubt this was connected to the pictures she took. She felt it in the now ice-cold blood that ran in her veins. She entered her room, and leaned against the door, willing herself to be calm, and slowly scanned the room, similarly to what her mom had done just last week, she imagined. Was it time to go to the authorities, let someone know that someone had invaded her life? But who? That's the first question law enforcement would ask her. Why, would be the next question. And then, where's the proof?

She sat on the bed, wearily stared at the flat, letter sized manila envelope, turned it over in her hands, studied the block printing—KENNEDY WADE—and beneath the address to the place she now sat. *Maybe it's nothing.* She knew the thought was a lie. After retrieving a letter opener from the desk, she stilled shaky hands, picked up the envelope and made a careful slit. Inside was a single sheet of typing paper and two photographs. *The ones she'd taken of the very conservative, very married media mogul's homosexual tryst?*

She removed the photos. Her heart hit the floor, along with the envelope and the paper inside. They indeed were pictures, but not of Van Dijk. They were of her, taken in the room she'd occupied in the Bahamas. Her face was clearly visible. Her eyes were closed. And she was totally nude.

17

It was just past one a.m. when Zeke used a master key card to enter what the general public thought of as secure buildings and made his way to the second floor of the four-story structure. Having continued surveillance on the target off and on since she returned from the Bahamas, made easier after breaking in to take her computer and leave cameras behind, he knew that Logan fancied himself a hip-hop producer and would be at a studio across town all night long. He also knew that his plan had worked, and that paying a couple of thugs to burglarize his place for the flash drive had been at least partly successful. They hadn't found the drive, but they had pulled the blame in a different direction. Still, Zeke needed to up the ante. So far, his special delivery to Kennedy's new residence had not garnered a response. Now Van Dijk's right hand man, Theodore, was breathing up his ass. If that flash drive was anywhere in the apartment, Zeke planned to find it.

He opened the door to the stairwell with the stealth of a cat, took the stairs two at a time and slipped into Logan's apartment unnoticed. Breaking into homes like these was almost too easy. Most Americans would be surprised to learn how truly vulnerable they were, how often their rights and privacy were violated and what was known about them by people they didn't know at any given time. That was by a regular criminal's standard. Given all the tools and information the government had at its disposal, chances of privacy were zero and none.

Zeke removed a pair of rubber gloves from his pocket as he surveyed the room. The place looked like a home inhabited by two twentysomething males. Big flat-screen TV. *Check.* Game console. *Check.* Several pairs of athletic shoes strewn around. *Check.* Blunt roaches in the ashtray. *Check.* He eased down the hall and opened the door on the left. The room was surprisingly neat, with a ton of sports memorabilia. But no recording equipment though, not Logan's room. Zeke crossed over to the other door and opened it. Clearly the room was used more for recording than sleeping. A small mixer, a computer and microphones were set up on a desk, jammed against the wall. A clothes-strewn futon anchored the other side. Walking to the bed he picked up random articles of clothes, checking pockets for anything the size of a flash drive. He continued to the closet, and over to a plastic stacking unit that served as a dresser. On top of it was a picture of Logan with a woman. He picked up the picture and studied it closely. It wasn't Kennedy in the picture. Why did the woman look familiar? Then Zeke remembered those first days of surveillance and seeing Wade, this Logan kid, and another couple exiting a restaurant. He eyed the picture again. This looked like the other girl. So was he dating her instead of Kennedy? If so, had he given the drive to her?

Two hours in and Zeke had come up empty. He wouldn't have guessed the drive was stored somewhere outside the home. In the guy's car perhaps? Zeke looked at his watch. Just after three. He knew where the production facility was but one, by the time he got over there it would be almost dawn and two, there was almost always a crowd in and around the place. In frustration, Zeke kicked a speaker located beneath the desk.

The blow jarred the mesh-like screen on the front loose. After staring at it a couple seconds, he knelt and placed his hand inside. He ran a finger along the grooves on both sides and across the entire bottom. Getting on both knees he used a chair for balance while checking the sides and top of the speaker inside. His finger ran across something taped to the top. Small. Flat. About the size of a flash drive. Zeke smiled and yanked the tape from the wood. He pulled it out and saw attached what he believed to be one of at least two drives that had eluded him for a month and a half. Satisfied at achieving his goal and too stoked to give a damn about who saw him, Zeke strode out the front door, down the stairs and out the front entrance, even throwing up a peace sign to the group of teens who observed his exit.

He could hardly wait to get back to the apartment he stayed at when in Chicago. On the way there, though, his stomach reminded him he hadn't eaten for hours. He went through a drive-through for a triple cheeseburger with fries, and then stopped at an all-night grocer for a six pack of beer. Once inside the one-bedroom set-up, he pulled his tablet from the still packed luggage, brought it out to the dining room, and set it on the table. He turned it on and while waiting for it to load went into the kitchen and zapped his burger and fries. Back at the table he pulled a can of beer from the pack, opened it up and took a long swig. Reaching into his jeans pocket, he pulled out the flash drive and inserted it into the slot. He grabbed the triple-decker sandwich and took a huge bite, followed by a thick, crunchy fry. He opened the thumb drive. The contents were in a numbered list. He switched the settings to icons. All pictures, he noted, with another burger bite. He clicked on the first icon, immediately recognizing the picture that nabbed him for this assignment—a beautiful rainbow behind a lush private island, the picture he'd studied more than he'd like to remember. Several more clicks revealed the same shot from a variety of angles and distances as he imagined Kennedy monkeying around with the lens. By the time he'd gone through the burgers and beer, he'd also gone through the entire flash drive. His stomach was full, but he was totally frustrated. Where was Van Dijk and the pharmaceutical heir with secret society ties? What was threatening about a bunch of trees? Zeke popped another beer and took it and the computer into the living room. He propped his feet on the coffee table, set the tablet in his lap. He went back to the first image, blowing it up as far as the tablet allowed. He reached into his wallet and pulled out a card that worked as a high-powered magnifying glass. In one of the pictures Zeke could make out what appeared to be a human body. But enlarging the photo so extensively had made any further identification of what he looked at totally impossible. He went through all the photos again, and sat with more questions than answers. Where were the incriminating photos? Zeke had a thought, sat up, looked at his watch and reached for his phone. One of his special op buddies was also an expert when it came to all things digital. He believed, or at least hoped, that photography was included on that list. The guy everyone called Bullet was stationed in the Middle East. It was early afternoon where he was. Even if Bullet was asleep, he thought, as he tapped the screen and his friend's number, Zeke was getting ready to be his wakeup call.

The greeting was friendly, the conversation brief. Zeke knew Bullet was a patriot. He could be trusted. Knowing this was a job for the good of the nation, Zeke knew that what he told his comrade would go no further. Without sharing details, he asked his friend to use his equipment to see if anyone could be detected on any of the files that would appear threatening to national security. Zeke didn't mention names when outlining the search. Bullet woke up and went to sleep to TBC News. If Bullet saw Van Dijk with anyone, he'd let Zeke know.

After ending the call, a tired Zeke stretched on the couch,

fully dressed, and was asleep in minutes. Hours later he woke up to a message from Bullet, short and to the point.

Nothing but rainbows. Destroy the drive.

"Nothing but rainbows," Zeke muttered. *WTF?* He read the message to himself. He read it again out loud. Bullet was keeping something. What, and why? One thing was for sure, he thought as he headed toward the shower. He'd be guarding that thumb drive with his life.

18

So far, Kennedy had done nothing regarding the envelope she'd received or the message she later found once her mind stopped reeling. The message was simple. Turn over the flash drives. Turn over the pictures. A smaller envelope had been included, containing a P.O. Box in Oklahoma that could belong to God knew who. She'd also received hang up calls and once again, felt she'd been followed. About the only area of her life that felt remotely normal was work, which was where she was headed as she got a text from Logan. She pulled into the garage, locked her car and read his message as she walked toward the building.

Where u at? Come over. It's important.

Logan knew about her new job. He said Gwen had told him. So why was he asking her to come over during working hours? Kennedy knit her brow at the request and responded.

Just got to work. I'll call on a break.

She read his answer and sighed. Would the craziness of the Bahamas ever be behind her?

Not as long as you keep their secret.

For an inexplicable reason, Kennedy paused and glanced back at the garage, and Harriet. Her text indicator pinged but she waited until she reached the office and had sat down at her desk to read it.

Never mind. Meet me tonight at the studio. Ten o'clock. She read the address. **This some real shit. We need facetime.**

With a slew of photos to analyze, articles to edit and the print deadline for *Chicago Sighting*'s August issue looming, plus Jeff making a rare office appearance, it wasn't hard for Kennedy to put Logan's texts behind her and focus on work. Even without a break for lunch, the day flew by. She left around six o'clock. Once in the car and flowing with traffic, she tapped the Bluetooth.

"Hey, Kennedy."

"Hey, Gwen."

"What's up?"

"That's what I was going to ask you. Logan sent me an urgent text wanting to meet right away. Do you know what it's about?"

"No. I haven't talked to him today."

"Are you sure?"

"What kind of question is that? Of course I'm sure. Why? What do you think it's about?"

"You know there's only one thing that comes to mind with weird stuff like this. Anything unusual happening with you? Any strange incidents or people or something out of place?"

"No." Gwen dragged out the word into more than one syllable. "You?"

Kennedy had told herself she wouldn't share what happened in Peyton and the phantom Jack Sutton sighting. But she told Gwen what happened.

"You know what, Kennedy? This has gotten way out of hand. I'm seriously concerned for you. It's time you go to the authorities and get a trained professional to help you figure out what's going on. Either that or . . . ."

"Or what?"

"I probably shouldn't say anything."

"Well, after saying that you most certainly should."

"Okay, don't get upset. I'm just throwing stuff out there. Do you think it's possible that with the burglary in the Bahamas and all the stress you've been under lately, it might help to see a therapist?"

"You think I need therapy?"

"It's not the worse that could happen, Ken. You've been through some pretty traumatic experiences. I know people who've sought help for far less disturbing experiences than you've been through."

"I've never thought about it, but . . ."

"Think about it, Ken. You may be experiencing some type of breakdown and not even know it."

"Okay, wait a minute. I'll concede to maybe needing to talk to somebody but to say I'm in breakdown mode is pretty extreme."

"So is feeling as though you're being followed, or that your home is broken into, or that a guy you met in the Bahamas has followed you to your hometown!"

"You think he was a figment of my imagination? Fuck you, Gwen. I know what I saw."

"You asked me to tell you what I was thinking, and I did. I love you, girl. You know that. I'm also concerned for your welfare, in every way—physically, mentally, and emotionally. I just think it would help you to talk to somebody, that's all. I didn't mean to upset you or make you angry. Just giving you something to think about."

"Got it. Thanks."

"I'm sorry you're angry."

"I'll get over it."

"You know I love you."

"I know it, chick. I love you, too."

Kennedy ended the call, looking around for a place to have

dinner. She'd planned to ask Gwen to join her, but her friend's well-intended advice squashed that desire. She was drugged, robbed and burglarized, all in just over a week. Not to mention the compromising pics Gwen knew nothing about. Yet Gwen thought it irrational to believe she might be followed? To consider that the person who robbed her in the Bahamas, and may have burglarized her home could do the same to her mom's house in Kansas? She knew Gwen meant well but she wasn't the one who'd woke up groggy and naked with two days gone.

"I may be crazy," Kennedy mumbled as she pulled into a strip mall parking space. "But at least that kooky paranoia is keeping my ass alive."

Kennedy dawdled over a Chinese dinner, but afterwards there were still a few hours until her meeting with Logan. She got in her car with no destination in mind. Several lights later she saw a theater marquee. A dark room, hot popcorn and total anonymity. She maneuvered her car into the left turn lane. Turns out it was a discount theater offering second runs of recent blockbuster hits. Kennedy scanned the titles and decided on a Spike Lee movie she'd heard about but never saw. She'd just eaten but still bought popcorn and candy along with a drink and settled into worn but comfy seats in the darkened room. From what she gleaned in the darkness there were less than a dozen others who'd selected to watch a movie about infiltration and covert operations. Given that she herself was in a controversial situation that could upend a nation, she couldn't miss the irony, and felt the movie more than a little apropos. The deft way the director used humor to lighten a heavy topic helped her see her own situation in a less tenuous light. It also helped her understand where Gwen was coming from, and to forgive her. Not that she could laugh at what was happening in her life. When it came to the picture she'd accidentally snapped, with its myriad implications and what it could mean to the entire world, there wasn't a damn thing funny.

Over two hours later, Kennedy was back in her car and headed to Chicago's notorious South Side. She pulled up to a nondescript, brick building, and parked close to the entrance. Bass beats from another car in the parking lot cut through the night air. A group of men stood off to the side, talking. They eyed her speculatively as she approached the door. One of them—short, stocky, wearing shades after dark and a scowl that suggested "you don't want none of this" stepped away from the group and blocked her entry. She felt him ogling her through the black lens.

"What's up?" he asked her.

"I'm here to see Logan."

"Who?"

"Um, Lowkey?"

His chin rose and fell with his blatant body scan. "You his woman or something?"

She crossed her arms. "Or something. Is he here?"

"Is he expecting you? This is a private session."

Kennedy pulled out her phone. The "guard" offered a lop-sided smile, reached back for the door and opened it. "I'm just messing with you, shorty. He's on the second floor, last room on the right."

There was a stairway just inside the doorway. As she climbed to the second floor, Kennedy was greeted by a swirl of voices, a pounding bass, and the smell of weed. She passed one open door and another closed one on the way to the room from where music blasted. Inside the room, Logan stood behind a huge mixer with what looked to be a hundred knobs. Another guy stood beside him. They both bobbed their heads to the beat. Two sound rooms housed two artists—a male rapper spitting words with a rapid-fire, staccato-like delivery, while a female R&B singer crooned a hook: *Love me. Better. Love me, love me. Better, better. Love me. Lower. Love me, love me. Lower, lower.* She began making out the rapper's words. He was describing, in detail, exactly how he'd love her better. But it was too late to back out of the room, especially with the way both Logan and the guy beside him now eyed her, waiting for a reaction. *Did Logan write this, inspired by Gwen?* She kept her jaw strong and didn't give them one. She could have. The lyrics were hot, and it had been a while since she'd played lower body ping pong. But neither of those guys needed to know that. Instead, she turned to watch the performance and joined the guys in a head bob to the beat.

The song ended. Logan pulled off his headphones and stood. "I'ma take five, y'all." He came over and put an arm around Kennedy. It was a classic baby brother move but he wasn't smiling. Instead he guided them out the door.

"You alright?" she asked.

"Not at all."

They continued down the hall. Logan tried a couple of doorknobs, finally finding an unlocked door on the right at the end. He stepped back so she could go in before him. Someone's office, Kennedy noted, before turning around.

"Okay, Logan. You're acting all kinds of weird. What is going on?"

He leaned against the wall. "That flash drive you gave me? It's gone."

"Gone. What do you mean?" The comment was unexpected and delivered so calmly, she honestly had no clue.

"Gone. Stolen. No longer in my possession. Some motherfucker got into my house, went into the room and stole it."

"Damn!" The truth finally sank in. "I can't believe they broke in again."

"Not a break in really. Whoever's after you or whatever you've got is a professional. Homeboy entered just like he had a key."

"Homeboy? You saw him?"

"No, but some dudes hanging out the night he broke in did.

Tall White dude, they said. He was wearing jeans, a baggy shirt, baseball cap. They felt he was up to something, because for one thing, we know all the White people in our building and he wasn't one of them, and two, they said he turned and threw up signs. On any block in that part of town, that's some bold shit."

His eyes turned compassionate, even as she mentally cataloged the description. With nothing more than a gut feeling for evidence, she thought it was Jack.

"This situation is out of hand, Ken. You need to go to the police, the mafia, some gangs, something. Because these boys aren't playing. They've been after you for months, all the way from the Bahamas. I don't know what you've got, but you need to give that shit back. It's not worth your life, and it feels like whoever this is could actually take it."

Logan insisted on Kennedy staying until he could follow her home. He parked, walked her to the door and in a move to lighten the darkness offered to check under her bed for the boogeyman. The coast was clear. She was okay for the moment. But if what Logan felt about whoever was after her was right, she wouldn't be safe for long.

19

Kennedy was on auto-pilot the next day when she arrived at the office. All she could think about was how someone—the same person who'd done her, Kennedy presumed—had burglarized Logan's house and stolen the thumb drive. She'd initially been angry at Logan, but he was right. It wasn't his fault that someone had no scruples and would do anything to get something even he hadn't seen. When Kennedy stopped to think about it, her friendship with Logan hadn't been the same since that week after returning from the island, Logan being over, and getting punched in the face. Her eyes narrowed as she remembered the blurry picture of the stranger at the door that he'd shown her. He hadn't looked like Jack, had he? Did Logan still have that picture? Did she want to ask him for it, and involve him more? And if she asked him, would he give it to her? A few days ago, she would have bet money that his answer would be a resounding yes. Today, she might lose her money.

A light tap cut through the voices coming from sales. She looked up. "Hey, Fennel."

Fennel held up a package. "Special delivery!"

"Hi, Fennel." Kennedy waved her in. "Thank you."

"Sure."

Monica looked up. "Is that something for the office?"

"No, it's for me. But electronic devices are always getting stolen so I thought it would be better to have it delivered here, during office hours."

"Smart move."

"Speaking of moves, can I get your eye for a minute?" Kennedy picked up the board that she preferred to a computer layout and walked it over to a table. "Since that new Chicago talk show has purchased the inside cover, what about having this photo spread adjacent to it instead of the article on the jazz festival, and move that to the middle, right behind the center-fold?"

Monica picked up the pictures of famous talk show hosts Kennedy had compiled, studying them one by one. "Did you take these?"

Kennedy nodded. "I did."

"All of them?"

"Yep."

"Even this one of Phil Donahue?"

Kennedy laughed. "Even him. I was a freshman and he spoke at our school. I even have a picture taken with him."

Monica looked up. "Now that is the picture we need here."

Kennedy didn't say anything. She'd purposely changed the subject to get away from what was in the just delivered package. Bringing up the stalker-boyfriend-not-really, and the fact that she doesn't even want her name on the publication, let alone her face, may have repercussions.

Her response was non-committal. "That's a thought."

"Otherwise, I think the switch is perfect. Definitely keeps the flow, especially as we go from there to the article you're writing about our own lovely Pilsen neighborhood and those pictures you took are sensational. The way your eye captures angles and lighting and texture . . . it was like becoming ac-

quainted with this area all over again. They made me literally
get out the other day and walk several blocks just to find what
you'd shot."

"Thank you, Monica."

"I mean it, Kennedy. I know, KW here at the mag, but those
photos you took deserve your whole name Kennedy Wade, at
least in this conversation, in this room."

Kennedy held it together until lunchtime, actually getting
work done, then took her package and headed for Harriet. She
pulled out of the garage and into the bright August sunshine.
After driving to a nearby park she maneuvered her car into a
space facing away from the street and pulled the box from the
shipping container. She looked at the counterintelligence sweeping device she'd just ordered and wondered who'd invaded her
existence and where was life? Seriously, was she getting ready
to sweep the room she rented from a sweet woman named
Lydia to find if the place was bugged?

Yes.

She read the instructions. The equipment, said to be "law
grade," whatever that meant, had one of the highest detection
ranges in the industry. It could detect wired and wireless cameras, wireless mics, audio and video transmitter bugs, computer
and fax transmitter bugs . . . *Gasp and sputter! Such things exist?*
Wiretaps and . . . GPS trackers? Kennedy stilled as she considered the possibility. Was there a way that . . . no, not possible.
Surely no one had tampered with Harriet. But if they'd gotten
to the BMW then at the very least they'd know she'd sold it.
But if the phantom Jack Sutton was actually Jack in Peyton, is
that how he tracked her? Kennedy ripped the operation instructions from the box and quickly read them. She turned off
her wifi and cellphone. Then right there in the park before
God and everybody, as mothers pushed children and joggers
ran nearby, she exited her car, pushed the button and began
sweeping the underside of her car. Within seconds she learned

two things. One, the device she'd purchased worked properly. Two, there was a GPS tracking device on her car.

It was six-thirty before Kennedy could leave the office, but when she did, it was to make a beeline to a mechanic to have the tracking device removed. The next stop was her house. The gods aligned for her. Lydia wasn't home. Kennedy went to work. She covered the entire apartment inch by inch. Twice. The sweeper detected no surveillance equipment. That fact probably should have made Kennedy feel better than it did. Whoever put the envelope in Lydia's mailbox was probably the same one who placed the GPS on her car. Which meant they knew where she worked and where she lived. This was bananas. Like a movie, except it was her life. Kennedy would make a lousy criminal and doing anything under cover would be impossible. She didn't have the constitution for that life. She was tired of hiding. Tired of lying. Tired of being on the run, wanted to live loud and in color. One of the statements on the websites she'd researched was right. Disappearing was hard. Before making the decision, be sure.

Keys jangled in the lock. Kennedy jumped up. To do what? Jump out the window? Nervous laughter spilled out of her mouth as she left the bedroom. She needed to have a talk with the woman who'd kindly opened her home up and welcomed her. Hopefully Lydia's act of kindness wouldn't put her in the crosshairs of "they."

Kennedy entered the living room as Lydia closed the door. "Hi, Lydia."

"Hi, Kim." One look at Kennedy and she stopped. "Oh, honey, what's wrong?"

The maternal care in Lydia's voice almost made Kennedy cry. She moved over to the couch, rapidly blinking her eyes to staunch the flow. "Can I talk with you for a minute?"

Lydia walked over and sat down.

"I'm sorry to have to share this. I'd hoped the whole situation was behind me."

"What situation?"

"An ex." Tired of lying. "A bad breakup." Tired of hiding. "Him stalking me."

Lydia reached out, took Kennedy's hands in hers. "Oh, honey, no!"

Kennedy gently pulled back. Lydia deserved a truth that Kennedy couldn't tell her. She felt like crap.

"It's why I moved here. I have a condo and it got so crazy I sublet it, figuring that in time he'd give up and realize it's over. Somehow, he found me. I don't know how."

"The envelope. He put it there?" Kennedy nodded.

"Is he dangerous?" Kennedy looked up at the change in Lydia's tone. "I don't want any trouble."

"I understand. I don't want to cause any. I'll make arrangements to move just as quickly as I can."

"I'm so sorry for you, Kim, but I do think that would be best. I'm a single woman with no real family here and . . ."

"It's okay, Lydia. You're a beautiful person and I've enjoyed being in your home. You don't have anything to worry about. Cowards bark but they don't bite."

There was really no more to be said after that. Kennedy waited until she was inside her room, and the door was closed, to let the tears fall.

20

Bullet's cryptic message drove Zeke crazy. He'd spent hours studying the pictures on the drive to find what his friend and Van Dijk were trying to hide. Getting the call to meet with Van Dijk was a blessing. Zeke hoped that turning over the drive would mean an end to this assignment. Given what was readily seen on the flash drive, Wade was no longer a threat. One thing still niggled him, how adamant Wade was about not selling the pictures, especially when Anita doubled the rate. He'd been sure she'd jump on that. Who knows? Maybe she fancied herself a unicorn and the rainbow had special meaning. She was a creative type after all. Artists were funny like that.

Right now, all he wanted to do was work up a sweat. He'd been summoned back to New York to meet with Van Dijk, which meant a chance to work out at his favorite gym. He needed something familiar, that was in his world before being handed this wacky assignment. Zeke entered the gym and threw his bag in a locker. He started out on the treadmill at a fast clip then after five minutes slowed down to a jog. Thirty minutes later, he reached for his towel and went to the bench. He laid down, positioned himself beneath the bell bar and closed his eyes, channeling his focus to lifting the weight.

"What's going on, buddy?"

Zeke was up and off the bar bell bench in an instant, hand around Warren's throat, thumb hovering just above the internal jugular vein where he knew the right type of squeeze would render instant unconsciousness.

"Argh," Warren cried, working to remain upright while being physically propelled across the floor. "Zeke! It's me. Zeke!"

A quick shake of his head and Zeke was no longer blinded by the swirling sands of Afghanistan. The man who'd touched his shoulder wasn't the enemy, but the only civilian, and one of only a handful of people, he considered a friend.

"I'm sorry, man." Warren's own hand was on his neck now. He worked to still his breathing.

"You know not to do that."

"I wasn't thinking. It was a reflective action from how glad I was to see you. It's been a while since you've been to the gym. I know you can handle yourself, clearly, but I worry when I don't see you around."

Zeke paused, gave a slow look around the room. The scant crowd that had been gawking quickly returned to their routines. A couple grabbed their towels and water bottles and left.

"I'm really sorry, dude. You okay?"

"I probably should be asking you that question."

Warren gave off a nervous laugh, touched his neck again. "A few more seconds and I might not have been. I didn't even see you move! I'm really sorry about that, bro. You've warned me more than once."

"And I will again. No sudden touches, brother. It's a trigger for sure."

"Come on. You need somebody to spot you?"

They walked over to the bench from which Zeke had sprang up. Zeke placed a couple hundred-pound weights on each side of the bar and got into position. He curled his fingers around the bar, eased his palms over the metal's coolness, focused, and lifted. After repeating the move several more times, he sat up and reached for a towel.

"Your turn."

"No man, not today. I went skiing over the holidays and pulled something in my back." Zeke felt Warren's intense gaze. "You want an energy drink, man? I've got some in my office."

"No, but thanks. I'm about to head out, take care of some business."

"Ooh, the way your eyes changed just now, it must be serious business."

"Everything I do is serious."

"Top gun classified."

"No doubt."

Warren held out his fist. "Alright then, brother. Take care of yourself."

Zeke bumped it. "Will do."

"Better yet," Warren continued, his eyes just beyond Zeke's shoulder. "Have somebody like that take care of you."

"Let me guess," Zeke answered without turning around. "A fine female."

"With a body that looks like it could take a workout. And wound up as you are, brother? That's probably exactly what you need."

Zeke smiled, placed the towel around his neck, and picked up his water bottle. "See you next time."

"Don't be a stranger."

Zeke saw several women when he turned around but had no doubt of the one Warren mentioned. Tall, platinum blonde, tanned skin, at least six feet, her body toned without being overly muscular, with a chest that looked natural, soft globes nestled within a bright white tank top sporting the Nike swash. She met his gaze but like him, didn't smile. Instead she turned back to the mirror and balanced long, lean legs into a perfect squat. The move wasn't lost on Zeke or more specifically, his penis. It hardened and nudged his thigh in a clear message that the times between sex had been too long. Maybe later, Zeke thought, as he left the building and headed to his car. Not with the Amazon though. The look in her eyes told him she'd catch feelings. When Zeke wanted sex these days, he paid for it. That way, both parties knew exactly what the deal was.

He didn't like monkey suits, but Zeke knew this meeting wouldn't be like the rest. His world was no longer the same. Before leaving the military and being hired by Van Dijk, he had seen the world in black and white, good guys and bad guys. While he knew that large corporations, even the government, were not without a shade of corruption, and that there were incidents done by these institutions that the average citizen would never know, he believed that sometimes a lesser evil had to be performed for the greater good. Sometimes there was collateral damage.

Back home, Zeke took a quick shower, then dressed in a suit. Instead of the network offices, this meeting was being held in one of Van Dijk's many residences, this one a forty-million-dollar penthouse on the city's Upper East Side. This was only his second trip to one of Van Dijk's private residences. Usually, they met in the midtown offices of TBC. The first residence he visited was the family estate in Southampton so large Zeke felt it deserved its own zip code. That day he'd crossed paths with the president. Not of TBC News, of the United States of America! No telling who he might meet this time. He wanted to look his best. Taking one last look in the mirror, he straightened the red, white and blue striped tie set against a white shirt. He pulled at the cuff links just below the hem on his navy jacket and ran a hand over the spiky tendrils of his freshly buzzed cut. He looked at himself a second more and wondered about the man who looked back from the mirror. Thought about the military lineage of which he was so proud—Clyde, Buck, Daniel, Matthew, and his brother Jerry. What would they think of the pictures he'd seen? What would the veterans do? Their job, he thought as he left his apartment and hailed a taxi to take him across town. To the best of their ability, as they had sworn to do.

He reached Fifty-Eighth Street, a world away from his one-bedroom apartment in Brooklyn. The doorman greeted him warmly and walked with him to Van Dijk's private elevator. When the car had reached more than seven-hundred fifty feet in the air, the doors opened into a wide foyer with jaw-dropping views on one side, and priceless art on the other. He walked down a short hall to a set of double doors. They were closed. He rang the bell and was surprised when Van Dijk opened the door. Given the sensitivity and importance Van Dijk had given this matter, he'd expected a small envoy of attorneys, or more security detail, maybe even someone from the fraternal order of Knights. Instead it was Van Dijk, dressed in what looked like a robe, but Zeke knew was called a smoking jacket. It matched the pipe his boss held in one hand. There was a drink in the other. He could have stepped straight out of the 1930s. Zeke felt overdressed.

He held out his hand. "Good afternoon, Mr. Van Dijk."

Van Dijk held up his filled hands.

"Sorry. Habit."

"Come inside, Zeke." Zeke followed him into a room with a view few New Yorkers would ever see—an uninterrupted vista spanning from the East River to the Hudson, and from the Freedom Tower to the George Washington Bridge. From here, New York indeed looked like the world's epicenter, its most powerful city. Zeke counted himself lucky to work for one of its most powerful citizens.

"Have a seat, Zeke," Van Dijk said, motioning to a sitting area near one of the windows. "Get you a drink?"

"No, sir. I'm fine."

"Let's make an exception today, shall we? I just broke the label on a fifty-year-old bottle of single malt scotch. It cost seventy-five thousand dollars; fifty for the bottle and twenty-five to have it delivered by personal air courier."

Zeke felt a wave of anxiety. Expecting the unexpected always made him uneasy. He tried to relax and stop thinking negative. Van Dijk had to know he'd accomplished the task and had what had been requested. Maybe that's why his boss was pouring him a premium Scotch. Maybe they'd toast to a raise.

Van Dijk joined him in the area that looked out toward the Hudson. He placed the tumbler on a gold coaster and slid it toward Zeke. "You've got something for me?"

Zeke nodded. "Yes, sir."

Reaching into his inside breast pocket, Zeke pulled out the small thumb drive retrieved from Logan's house. He stood and placed it on the table, directly in front of Van Dijk. "I believe that's what we've been chasing, sir. They are the pictures from Wade's trip to the Bahamas, sir. However, in full disclosure, sir, this may not be the only copy of them out there."

Van Dijk neither looked at or reached for the drive. He took another sip of Scotch. "What about the girl?"

"Wade?" Zeke asked.

"No, Foster, Cinderella."

"Sorry, sir, I know who you meant. I believe that after seeing what's on the drive, sir, you'll understand why I didn't feel the need to confront her directly, as she has nothing that proposes a threat."

"How do you know that?'

Zeke leaned forward. "Because I've seen what's on the drive, sir."

"And?"

"It's the same as what is on the equipment initially turned over, sir. Photos of the island and the surrounding area. There are no photos of you, Mr. Van Dijk, of anyone or anything that would threaten this country."

Van Dijk sat back, rubbed his chin as he seemed to mull over Zeke's words. He reached for the drive, studied it briefly, then rolled it around on his fingers. Zeke felt the tension in his shoulders begin to abate. He picked up the drink, placed it under his nose and inhaled notes of oak and brown sugar and a few different spices. Van Dijk refocused his attention on Zeke, his posture casual but his eyes intense. Zeke set down the glass.

"What if I told you that information has been received from a credible source that some damning photos are in that girl's possession, and that as we speak she could be negotiating to sell them to one of the fake news broadcasters, set the nation in chaos, and make a hefty sum for herself as part of the bargain?"

"I'd say that would be quite egregious, sir."

"I'm glad you realize that, because if you didn't, what I'm about to say next might seem overzealous. The threat of exposure is too great and will cost too much. In time, I may be able to share more, but know that thousands of lives could be lost if this information got into the wrong hands or was delivered to the public in a dishonest way. That is why this directive has come from my superior, the head of the MAN. The threat has to be eliminated, Foster."

"Sir?"

"You heard me. With your background of undercover ops in Iraq and Afghanistan, we are confident that you're the man for the job."

The proposition was so ludicrous and unexpected that a breath caught in his windpipe and made Zeke cough. He picked up the Scotch and knocked back a finger, felt the burn from his throat to his stomach. "Excuse me," he said, trying to regain his composure. "Please, excuse my presumption. As someone who has tailed her for almost eight weeks, may I offer my opinion?"

"You know they're like a-holes, right? Everybody's got one."

Van Dijk smiled. Zeke did, too.

"I'm aware of that. However, I also believe I have a pretty good handle on this subject. From the contents of her electronic equipment to her home and mode of transportation, I see absolutely nothing to back up that claim. I've run intel on her family and friends, her footprint on the web. I admit to not having full knowledge of her political affiliations, but from everything I've seen and read, she does not pose a threat."

"I see." He leaned forward, placed the flash drive inside his suit coat pocket. "Alright, then. With that said you are now relieved of this assignment."

"What?" said with a shock that forewent decorum.

"I didn't say you were fired, though that could come next. A prominent European family is moving to America, part of the society. They will need round the clock protection, a full security detail. I'm sending you to set all of this up."

"If you want me to handle the Wade issue—"

"No," Van Dijk held up a hand. "I'll talk with Becker, send an agent from the group. There are several men who can handle that action. You're the only one I trust with this job."

No matter the praise, Zeke felt he'd been demoted. He hid the disappointment behind a professional façade. "Where is the family settling, sir?"

"Springfield, Missouri. You might be somewhat familiar. It's close to a military base."

"Fort Leonard Wood, sir. Yes, I'm familiar. What about this family? Would I recognize their names?"

Van Dijk shook his head. "The Kyvas are well known in Europe. Their sons are rock stars in the world of tech. They're coming here to set up a major telecommunications installation and have purchased five-hundred acres outside of town. Everything will be housed on this land, including the estate that will be built to their orders. Until then, it will be your job, and that of your team, to secure living quarters that are safe and befitting their billionaire status."

"Team, sir?"

"Yes. I called a buddy of mine who works at Fort Hood. He said he'd loan you a few hardheads if there's a need."

"Are you sure about my ending the Wade surveillance? I wouldn't want to leave a job if there is any doubt that it has not been properly completed."

"Put together a report with all the information you uncovered, contact information, locations, information on her family. Email that over within forty-eight hours. After that, your dealings with that situation is done."

Van Dijk looked at his watch and stood. "And so is this meeting. I have a wife who's had dinner alone for almost two weeks. If I stand her up with this dinner reservation, someone else might be eliminated."

"A few more questions, Mr. Van Dijk. Do you know when the family is arriving, and how long I'll be working with them? If possible, I'd like to take a few days to handle the relocation."

"I'll have Cassie send over the details. Work out the schedule and forward the moving expenses to her."

Zeke stood, and held out his hand. "Thank you, Mr. Van Dijk."

"You're welcome, Foster."

Zeke left the building, feeling conflicted. Wade, a threat to national security? A subversive who might need to be killed? Where could that information have come from? And why did hearing it make him feel so uneasy? Zeke pulled out his shades as he walked into the sunshine. He'd been officially relieved from surveilling Wade, so it was time to put that whole thing behind him. Whoever she was, whatever she did, Kennedy Wade was no longer his problem.

21

Kennedy made it through the week but as she lay awake early on Saturday morning there was only one thought: she couldn't keep living this way. Kennedy knew that this kind of stress at this continuous level was not healthy. She was beginning to feel the toll it was taking. Trouble sleeping. No appetite. Lost weight. High anxiety. Strained friendships. Maybe Gwen was right. Seeing a therapist or counselor couldn't hurt her. But seeing someone professionally wouldn't get rid of the problem. The problem was the pictures she'd taken in the Bahamas, and accidentally captured Van Dijk, owner of the conservative TBC Network, enthusiastically engaged in gay sex.

What are you going to do with what you've been given?

The longer the saga played out the more obvious seemed to be the only answer. The pictures had to be published. Not for judgment, though they would surely be judged. Not for scandal, though this would likely be one of the most embarrassing moments in the history of media. Kennedy wasn't a fan of the network, in fact she abhorred it. But that wouldn't be the reason, either. In the past ten years, Van Dijk had doubled his company's ownership of television and radio stations, and with a series of bloggers and websites, was staking claim to a large percentage of those online. His divisive, judgmental, non-compassionate message was reaching an increasingly insensitive audience. They were being fueled by his rhetoric, convinced of the "other." Largely due to his network's narrative, rights for women and people of color had been rolled back to before the Civil Rights movement. Gay marriage was on the verge of being repealed. He constantly criticized same-sex relationships while he secretly practiced the same. In short, he was a hypocrite. That's why Kennedy had no choice but to make those shots public. America, the viewers who loved him and what his network stood for, deserved to know the truth.

The physical reaction was surprising but once the decision was made, Kennedy's whole body relaxed. She'd spent this entire time until now afraid of what would happen if she released the pictures. The moment she considered what would happen if she didn't, and decided to proceed, fear melted away. There was only one problem. Even though her career was centered in news and publishing, handling something as big as this was out of her league. She knew someone though who might have some answers.

After a quick shower and an even briefer chat with Lydia, Kennedy headed out the door with her computer and the anti-surveillance detector. She'd copied her hard drive on to a flash drive last night before coming home. With Logan's no longer in his possession, Kennedy wanted at least one more person on earth to have it—the person she was getting ready to call. To be on the safe side she'd also purchased another temporary phone. If anyone heard the conversation she was about to have, this plan, maybe even her life, would be over.

She swept her car, inside and out, then headed toward Lakeshore Drive. It was a beautiful morning. She imagined the area she had in mind to stop at would be filled with like-minded people ready to take advantage of the cooler, early-morning temperatures and soak up some sun. For Kennedy that was part of it. The other part was that with so many people, translated witnesses around, the fewer her chances of being attacked or worse at the hands of her phantom Jack Sutton. On the way to the lake she stopped for a latte and feeling the appetite that had eluded her for the past couple weeks bypassed a plain bagel for a breakfast sandwich. Back in the car, she slipped a self-compiled CD into the slot, some of her favorite ladies who gave her strength, reminded her who she was, and made her proud to spell her name W-O-M-A-N. Lauryn and Jill, Erykah and Alicia, India and Bey. By the time she parked and tapped her Bluetooth, Kennedy was ready for the revolution.

"Ken!"

"Hey, Tamara. Is it too early to call?"

"It's never too early to talk to a friend. How are you?"

"Actually, better than I've been in a while."

"That's good to hear. What happened?"

"I made a decision." Kennedy paused. Once she said the words out loud, shit would get real. "I'm going to sell the pictures."

"Okay. What's the plan?"

Kennedy released a nervous chuckle. "Actually, that's why I called you. I've got several contacts in the industry but none at the caliber I think will be needed to either navigate or negotiate what's about to take place."

"I may be able to help you. Well, not me so much. My fiancé, Ryan. He's very well-connected in New York, especially Manhattan. He knows people. If he doesn't have a name to give you, he knows someone who does."

"Thanks, Tamara. It's amazing to not feel as though I'm doing this all by myself."

"That's much too great a burden for you to try and bear alone. Speaking of, where are you now?"

"By the lake, just off Lakeshore Drive."

"Do you feel safe where you are, Kennedy? Not just right

now, but I mean where you work, where you're staying. Say the word and I'll get the guest room ready."

"Ah, thank you, Tamara. That means everything, really. Right now, I feel relatively safe." Kennedy told her about the sweeping device. "I also talked to my roommate and gave her a heads up about anyone coming by, asking for me, asking questions, anything like that."

"How well do you know this roommate?"

"I don't, really. I answered her ad looking for a roommate on Home2Home."

"Jesus, Kennedy!"

"I thought it was a smart move, to go somewhere without a history. If whoever's after me can't find me, their next stop will be my friends. I signed up under an assumed name and made sure there was nothing out there connecting me to the address. Although, that veil of secrecy is no doubt off now. Someone placed a tracking device on my car. I found it this week."

"Kennedy, you can't stay there."

"Tamara, please. I just stopped being scared."

"It's not about being scared. It's about being smart, careful, and totally aware of the shark-filled waters you're swimming in. I know that man. I worked for him. He is ruthless and has no conscience. Do not underestimate how far he'll go to not be found out."

When it came to Van Dijk and the people around him, Kennedy wouldn't put anything past them. For anyone who would do or authorize what had been done to her in the past two months, there were no rules. No boundaries. No conscience. She couldn't afford to take any chances. Once she was safely in Grand Cayman, Kennedy would find a private investigator to look into who was looking into her. But she'd do it from outside the country.

That night, after talking to Tamara, Kennedy stopped at the Overnight Carrier office and sent off the flash drive containing her copied files. She sent the package overnight, insured and requesting a signature. Though not religious, she said a little prayer that the drive would arrive safely. Back at the office for the next week and a half, there was little chance to think about it. Long hours made the days go fast. Production was in overdrive as they prepared stories for the weekly website and readied the September issue for publication. Those working on the magazine developed a rhythm, with most areas coming together like a well-oiled machine. Even the home front had quieted. After a couple days to think about it, with no further personally delivered envelopes in the mail, Lydia decided she may have overreacted and invited "Kim" to stay. During the whirlwind came a message from Tamara. A high-profile publicist, someone named Dodie Ravinsky, would be giving her a call. That Thursday, after a final push to make the deadline and send the final layout to the printer, Monica suggested the team go out for a drink.

Once they'd ordered drinks and appetizers, Monica turned to Kennedy. "How does it feel, KW? The first issue totally under your supervision, just put to bed?"

"Tired," Kennedy replied.

"Ha! I hear you. You've worked hard, but you've done good work. Scott is very impressed."

"He saw the layout?"

"He's like a vampire, often coming into the office while we're sleeping to check out the day's work. The first person we hired was qualified, but she didn't have the passion, commitment, or innovative eye that you do. You're a perfect fit, KW. Scott believes we've got the team that can take us national, maybe even public. He's so happy to have you on board. And so am I."

Kennedy was touched. "Thanks, Monica. I hope to be laying out issues for a very long time."

Monica thanked the sales staff while Fennel showed up with

her rocker boyfriend. The group behaved like one big happy family as their drinks arrived and were handed out. When everyone had a glass, Monica lifted hers up and waited while the others followed suit.

"To *Chicago Sightings*," she said proudly, "and the team that rocks."

On her way home a call came in, caller unknown. She started not to answer it but quickly changed her mind. This was a temporary phone after all, not on a telemarketer's radar. The only other people possibly tracking her worked for or at least on behalf of Van Dijk.

Her voice was light and cheerful as she answered, her mood still lifted by an evening with co-workers. "Hello?"

"Kennedy Wade."

Light followed cheerful right out of the car as a sense of trepidation flowed in. The voice was male, distorted by some type of device. Any caller who felt he had to hide his identity behind a private number and a voice-altering device could not possibly have any news for her that she wanted to hear. She disconnected the call and turned up the music.

The phone rang again, and then a third time. She ignored it, tried to bring back the feel good on the waves of Logan's demo that he'd sent to her last week. But the caller had dimmed the lightness she felt. She was lucky to find a parking space just a couple doors down from the apartment. She swept the car, and once inside the apartment, she disassembled the phone the scary call had come in on and pulled out another temporary phone. She did all of that, and still felt uneasy. She'd told Monica her plans to be at the magazine forever. But something about the distorted voice warned that her departure from the city might need to take place very soon.

22

The next day Kennedy was on pins and needles. Even though she'd changed phones, she still half-expected to answer the phone and hear a robotic voice on the other end threatening her well-being. As it was, changing her number so quickly threw her life out of whack. The publicist had tried to contact her, unsuccessfully, until Tamara reached out through Kennedy's email address. A group message finally set her family, friends and workplace straight. Everyone had her new number. For the time being, all was right with the world. Turns out that time lasted exactly an hour, until Fennel greeted her in the hallway with a manila envelope in her hand.

Later she'd wonder whether it was being overwhelmed with the continual life changes or it being that time of the month that Kennedy barely missed breaking down right there. She rushed into the bathroom, turned the water on and cried. She looked up and stared at the image before her. The red eyes, concealer hiding a sleepless night and tiny worry lines on the side of her eyes. Until now she'd held up nicely, all things considered. In this moment, however, came a wave of real fear. Not that anyone would catch her, but that she wouldn't be able to hold on to herself. For the first time she gave Gwen's comment serious consideration. Kennedy felt as though she were going crazy. She needed help.

Someone rattled the door handle.

"Just a minute!" Kennedy said, trying and failing to sound alright. She ran cold water and splashed it on her face. After a last look in the mirror and a deep, fortifying breath, she put a smile on her face and opened the door.

"Jeff!"

"Hey, KW. You're just who I was looking for. You got a minute?"

Kennedy looked at the envelope. "Um, sure."

"We can talk later. Matter of fact, why don't I take care of business," he nodded toward the envelope, "you do what you need to do, and we can go grab a bite. We've never really had a chance to talk, and I'd like to."

"Sure. I'd like that, too. Meet you in ten?"

"That'll work."

Kennedy went to her office, retrieved her phone and purse, then headed straight for Harriet. Her need to cry was slowly being replaced by her desire to hit somebody, namely herself. Why was she dragging this whole thing out, having the pictures published? Once she did that the secret would be out and there would be no need to be chased anymore. At that point, whoever it was would have bigger fish to fry. She'd thought about the reasons she'd hesitated, potential danger to her family and friends, the end of her career, and possibly her life. But what kind of life could she have always looking over her shoulder. At this rate, with the constant stress she'd been feeling, she'd give herself a heart attack and die anyway.

As had been her habit, she started her car and exited the garage. Rounding the block, she found a parking space on a busy street filled with shops and restaurants. She parked and this time, instead of the careful consideration she'd given the first one, she ripped off the top of the envelope with her bare hands. The contents were not what she expected. There was no letter. No pictures. Only a flash drive.

Damn.

Kennedy looked up and down the block. She pulled out her phone and looked up an office store that offered computer use by the minute. There was one just five minutes away. She entered the establishment and went to the last computer. It was secured to the desk, but she swiveled the face as best she could. The last package left for her contained pics of her nude. There was no telling what would be on the flash drive. After setting up payment and logging into the computer, Kennedy inserted the flash drive. Just before clicking it, she realized there was something else she needed. Earbuds. With an aggravated sigh, she pulled out the flash drive and headed toward the aisle. Twenty dollars later she had what she needed. She sat back down, replaced the drive, tapped on the single file, and braced herself.

The file opened to a black screen. Which each second that passed, Kennedy felt her nerves fray a little bit more. She stared at the screen, still ominously dark. When a voice began speaking, she jumped.

This message is for Kennedy Wade.

The voice sounded familiar, digitally altered, like the one who called her last week. She gripped the edge of the table, swallowed the desire to shut the drive down, and listened.

Listen, bitch, because this message will be delivered one time, and one time only. We are not in the habit of having to repeat ourselves, and you have already been more trouble than you are worth. You know what this is about, a certain purchase that was requested, that you denied. A shame, because you have made your life more difficult than it needed to be. The message is quite simple. You will get another call, and another offer. This time you will accept it. You will sign the agreement releasing ownership of all photos taken on your Bahamian trip earlier this year. You will sign the confidentiality and non-disclosure agreements

*as well. You will then go on with your life as if this never hap-
pened. This is not a request. It is an order.*

*In case you think you have a choice in the matter. Consider
these pictures, which if the agreement is not signed will be published in their entirety all over the internet.*

As he talked, naked pictures that she'd not seen appeared
on the screen. She gasped as her hand flew to her throat, and
her eyes darted around to ensure no one else saw what she did.
What had been delivered to her had only been the tip of the
iceberg. There were several pictures, several positions, close-
ups of everything, including her face. Her body shook with
shame and anger, as the video continued to play.

*If that isn't enough incentive for you then consider the lives
of these people.*

Pictures of Karolyn and Karl, taken in familiar places, appeared and dissolved.

*Life for them can become very difficult indeed. You don't
want that, do you? All for a group of pictures showing Bahamian
islands and the ocean surrounding it. With the proceeds of the
sale, you can take another trip to the Bahamas. You can take more
pictures. Without the sale, another trip will be planned for you. A
one-way trip to hell, with no return ticket. This transaction will be
completed within twenty-four hours. Goodbye, Kennedy.*

Kennedy sat back as though she'd been punched. Emotions
of anger, sadness, helplessness, frustration, all fought for dom-
ination inside her soul. She worked to wrap her mind around
what had just happened, so deep in thought that she didn't
hear her phone the first time it rang. A pause, and then it
started up again. In that moment, she remembered.

Jeff!!

She reached for her phone and saw the familiar number for
Chicago Sightings. "Hello?"

It was Monica. "Hey, KW. You okay?"

"Yes, and I'm so sorry to be late for my meeting with Jeff. I
ran out to do an errand and it took longer than expected." She

pulled out the flash drive, signed out of the computer and grabbed the receipt. "I'm only five minutes away and on my way back now."

"Are you sure? Jeff says he can reschedule if you don't have time now."

She had time but not the strength it would take to cover up her emotions and meet with her boss.

"Actually, Monica, I'd really appreciate that. In fact, I'd like to come back for my computer and take off for the day. There are some buildings I want to capture for next month's issue." That wasn't the plan when she'd hastily left the building, but it would get her out of having to act like she was okay.

"No problem."

"Is Jeff there? I'd like to apologize."

Monica handed over the phone. Kennedy repeated the creative conversation she'd just had. She returned to the office, then to her car, and then she called Gwen. They'd both been so busy there'd been no time to meet. But today, more than ever, she needed a friend.

Panic must have coated Kennedy's request to meet because in a rare move Gwen took time off and agreed to meet at her place. She was home when Kennedy got there, concern-filled eyes taking her in before a heartfelt hug embraced her.

Gwen stepped back and closed the door. "Ken, you've lost weight."

"Not much appetite these days. Not much sleep either."

"Come on, let's sit in the living room." Gwen took her hand and led her inside. "Are you hungry? Can I fix us something to eat?"

"No, but I could use a glass of wine."

While Gwen went to the kitchen, Kennedy pulled out her tablet and placed it on the coffee table. She fired it up, then reached for the flash drive the enemy had sent. On her way over, she considered the fact that the drive might be bugged or have a virus to infect her computer. Considering nothing seemed to have happened to the one that she'd rented, Kennedy decided that for someone else to witness the threat that had been sent, she'd have to risk having to buy another computer. It was a chance she'd have to take.

Gwen returned with two glasses of red wine. "Here you go, sis."

"Thanks." Kennedy took a generous sip, cupped the goblet in her hand, and swallowed some more.

Gwen eyed her for a long second. "Let me heat something up. The way you're drinking, we're going to need food."

Kennedy barely heard Gwen speak or leave the room. She was preoccupied with the drive she'd inserted in a port and clicked to open. Nothing happened. Frowning, she pulled out the drive and reinserted it. Her screen blinked. Kennedy held her breath, waiting for the crash. But instead the home screen reappeared.

What is going on?

By the time Gwen returned with a platter of spicy chicken fingers, chips and rolls, Kennedy was mumbling to herself, her face a mask of confusion, her hair sticking up in unflattering places where she'd run nervous fingers through it.

Gwen slowly set the platter on the coffee table, opposite of where Kennedy worked on the computer.

"Ken . . . are you okay?"

"There's nothing here. There's nothing here the drive is empty, even though that's impossible because I saw the pictures and heard his voice not even an hour two hours ago what's going on there's got to be . . . where are pictures . . . how did they . . . what . . ."

Kennedy felt a hand clamp on to her arm. She looked up into Gwen's tear-filled eyes. "Kennedy, what is the matter?"

Realizing she was mumbling aloud and how confused and crazy that must sound, Kennedy looked Gwen in the eye. "I know I sound crazy, Gwen, but what I came over here to show you is not here."

Both women turned to look at the still black screen.

"So much has happened since we talked, things I didn't share because I knew you were worried and that you thought I was crazy and needed therapy, and maybe I do, but not in the way you're thinking."

Kennedy paused, took a deep breath. "Sit down, Gwen." Gwen sat. Kennedy began again slowly, calmly, in a voice she hoped Gwen would think sounded rational. "A package was delivered today, in my name, to the *Chicago Sightings* office. It's the second package I've received. I left the office, went to my car and opened it."

Kennedy paused, wondered if she should tell Gwen why she opened the envelope away from the office, afraid of what it contained. She decided against it.

"This was inside." She pulled out the now non-working thumb drive. "Because I didn't have my computer, I went to an office supply store to use one of their computers. I inserted this drive and there was a message for me. A man's voice, pictures and threats."

Gwen looked from Kennedy's serious expression to the drive she held in her hand, and back. Kennedy could tell her friend wanted to believe her, but wasn't quite there.

"What kind of threat?"

Kennedy sighed. Coming here was a bad idea. To tell Gwen anything, she'd have to tell her everything.

"I've got to go."

Gwen moved to sit next to her. "Kennedy, don't leave. Put the drive in again. Maybe it will work this time. If you just played it, whatever was on it has to still be there . . . right?"

Maybe I am going crazy. Maybe I imagined the whole thing.

She put the drive in her purse and her tablet in its case. She finished the wine and stood. "I'm sorry for leaving abruptly but . . . I've got to go."

She gave Gwen a quick hug and headed for the door.

"Ken!"

Kennedy quickened her footsteps. Her phone rang. She began to run and didn't stop until she reached Harriet, got in, locked the door . . . and felt safe.

The phone rang again. Kennedy snatched it up, defying the angst of who might be calling. She didn't even look at the ID.

"Hello!" She said in a tone that suggested no bullshit—demanding, defiant, cold.

"Kennedy?"

She looked at the ID, recognizing the New York area code, but not the number. "Yes, this is Kennedy."

"This is Dodie Ravinsky, the publicist that Tamara recommended. Is now a good time to talk?"

The question was innocuous, a polite query so as not to infringe upon Kennedy's evening. But something about the way it was asked sent Kennedy's mind on a whirlwind rewind of what she'd been put through over a set of pictures she didn't even know she'd taken, several snaps of the shutter that completely changed her life. Drugged. Robbed. Photographed naked. Hunted. Threatened. Privacy invaded. Friends and family affected. Life disrupted. No wonder Gwen was so worried about her. It was a wonder, sheer grace, that she hadn't lost her mind.

The question provoked a moment of clarity. She'd been running scared because of the power she'd given her stalkers. The very real power that Van Dijk possessed, with a slew of high-powered resources behind him. For all the consideration given, however, there was one thing she'd forgotten—the power she possessed. They'd pushed this sister into a corner. Now was the time to fight her way out of it. Now was the time to show her hand.

Kennedy closed her eyes and went with her gut. "Yes, Dodie, this is a very good time."

23

Kennedy and Dodie talked for an hour. Afterwards, Dodie insisted on arranging for Kennedy to spend the night at the Peninsula and promised she would be there the next afternoon. Kennedy drove straight there from Gwen's house, feeling the burden of secrecy had been lifted. As she drove through the streets of Chicago, she felt strength returning to her bones like warm blood upon a tourniquet's release. Upon valeting her car another thought struck her. There was no fear. Once inside the room, Kennedy made good use of the hotel phone—a brief call informing Lydia she'd be out for the night, a short chat with Scott to apologize and say that drinks were on her, and a long talk with Karolyn. While not going into detail, she finally admitted that her mother was right, that a professional issue had become personal and that legal action may be necessary to settle the matter. Her mom immediately jumped to the worst-case scenario, as Kennedy knew that she would, only this time the very worst that Karolyn could think of didn't come close to Kennedy's dangerous truth. She assured Karolyn that she'd be careful, and that she was meeting with someone tomorrow to help her strategize her next move. After that Kennedy ordered room service and a bottle of wine. She looked over the agreement that Dodie had couriered over, discussed it with Tamara and signed it. She took a long, hot shower. The food arrived. The wine was smooth, the food delicious and that night, for the first time since she boarded the plane to the Bahamas in May, Kennedy slept like a baby.

The following afternoon, just past one, Dodie Ravinsky whirled into the suite like a Kansas tornado—a deceptively beautiful phenomenon that could form in an instant, with the ability to reach a momentum that could take out everything in her path. Kennedy was prepared, both for speaking with Dodie and for the undoubtedly tumultuous path that lay ahead. Until now, she'd focused on her weaknesses, her vulnerability to an entity much bigger and stronger than anything she possessed. A formidable opponent yes, made even more so because she'd given away her power. But no more. She felt like a phoenix coming out of the ashes. It was time to rise up!

Along with talking to Tamara, she'd researched Dodie on-line before signing the agreement. The well-known publicist had been in business for almost twenty years. Her client roster included high profile politicians, celebrities, and socialites. Dodie Ravinsky had the pedigree to work in this atmosphere of rarified air. Her father was a judge in New York State. Her mother, a socialite well-known for her philanthropic efforts for children's causes. Dodie had grown up in privilege, but embraced just causes and was as comfortable in jeans and sneakers as she was in couture and Cartier. Ivy League educated, married and divorced, Dodie Ravinsky abhorred strong-armed injustice, and manipulative narcissists like Van Dijk, which made her the perfect person for the job. When Kennedy stood to greet her as she entered the suite, Dodie's embrace was genuine, her smile, sincere.

"Your story's amazing," Dodie began, after they'd shared pleasantries and settled down in an area with a view of Lake Michigan. "And with everything you've dealt with these past few months, you are one tough cookie."

"Funny you see that in these first few minutes," Kennedy said with a chuckle. "I just figured that out."

"I'm glad you did. It's a fact that you're going to have to hang on to, a strength that in the weeks and months to come you're going to have to call upon every day. I want to make sure you fully understand what you're getting into, exactly what is at stake. Because once these photos are released, there's no do-overs, no going back."

"The pictures are to be released anonymously, you do understand that, correct?"

"There is no such thing as anonymous anymore. The public may not know about you, at least not right away. But the guys who've been chasing you will know exactly where they came from, even if we use the argument that someone stole them from you. Be prepared for them to try and make your life a living hell."

"They've done that already."

"What I'm trying to say is no matter how we spin this story, your life will never be the same. Are you ready for that? Are you ready to leave the type of life you've lived until now behind you? Understand, what you've uncovered will ruin Van Dijk's reputation, certainly impact the True Broadcast Corporation, and impact his bottom line. Even more, you're exposing the Becker family and pulling the curtain back on the most secretive parts of secret society. They position themselves as a charitable, God-fearing organization, but trust me. There are some very ruthless players in that group."

"Are you trying to talk me out of releasing the pictures?"

"No. I just want to make sure that the actions you take from here on out are with your eyes wide open."

"No one wants their life upended. I would not have chosen this path for myself. But what's happened has happened, and I believe I have a moral and ethical responsibility to expose Van Dijk for the fraud that he is, to let America know the full story behind who's representing this country to the rest of the world. I don't know much about the Beckers, but the MAK's agenda to run the world, well, it needs to be exposed. I will prepare myself and those around me as best I can but yes, Dodie, based on what's happened to me so far, I have some idea of what I'm getting into, and my eyes are open. Let's do this."

Dodie maintained her serious expression a beat or two more, then offered a smile. "That's my girl."

"Oh, that was a test to see if I really wanted to go through with it?"

"Absolutely. And I'm happy to see that you're battle ready. Now that we've gotten your commitment to this process out of the way, and the agreement has been signed, it's time for me to see what all this fuss is about. Do you have the pictures with you?"

"I don't go anywhere without them."

Kennedy went into the bedroom and came out with the flash drive attached to her tablet. She set the tablet on the table and set on the settee next to Dodie. She opened the folder with the pictures Toby had given her, and clicked.

The room went totally silent. Then after several seconds, Dodie said, "Wow."

Another picture. "Unbelievable."

A few more and then the final picture. "Holy shit." Dodie looked at Kennedy. "You have no idea what you have here. I mean you do, but . . . wow. This is going to be the biggest scandal of our lifetimes. Anyone in the media would kill for these pictures, to break this exclusive. You are going to be a very wealthy woman."

"How much do you think they will offer?" When deciding to sell the pictures, Kennedy hadn't given much thought to the price.

"For these pictures? They'll pull in eight figures easy."

Kennedy's jaw dropped. "Ten million dollars?"

"At least," Dodie casually replied. "You say those pictures were shot accidentally?" Kennedy nodded. "Well, you've accidentally shot your way into becoming a multi-millionaire."

Dodie was right. She put her experience, connections, and business savvy to work. All of media took the bait. If Dodie promised, she delivered. They knew that about her. An aggressive bidding war broke out between four major network and cable news stations and more than a dozen major newspapers and national magazines. When the dust settled, the pictures sold for a record-breaking thirty million dollars. Kennedy almost passed out when she heard the news.

24

Zeke spent the week packing up his apartment, closing out business in Brooklyn, and readying himself for life at the slower pace of the Midwest. He was glad the assignment with Wade was over. But he couldn't help feeling that he'd somehow been punked. Van Dijk had told him the photos Wade possessed threatened national security. Yet all he'd seen on the flash drive were a bunch of pictures of the beach, the island, and a rainbow. Where were the potentially damning photos of Van Dijk meeting Becker? He'd broken in to three different residences behind chasing what . . . pics of Gilligan's Island? Obviously they knew something he didn't know and at the end of the day, it was none of his business. He'd done exactly what Van Dijk had asked.

And what was the thanks he got? Settling a billionaire family into life in the country? Seriously? Zeke was a soldier. He'd seen combat. He thrived on the danger of covert operations, had trouble existing in mundane life. But it wasn't his place to question the boss, or put his personal feelings ahead of what Van Dijk wanted. If he was unhappy, he could always quit working for the mogul, change his reserve status and go back in the service full-time.

Zeke took a couple days and went home to see his family.

There were always mixed emotions around doing that. He loved his kin, would die for any one of them. But they didn't always get along, he didn't like them all of the time. The relationship with his dad was contentious, largely because of how Matthew treated his mom. Zeke knew his dad was basically a good guy, but Vietnam changed him. He'd gone into rehab when he returned home to get off an addiction to pills. He drank heavily and when he did, verbal and physical abuse often followed. But he'd had a blast with his grandpa Buck and grandma Martha. He'd seen a few friends who still lived in the area. A few days was all it took before he'd had enough and returned to New York to pack up his life there for the relocation to Springfield. The one bright spot was that on his way there he'd spend time at Fort Leonard Wood, looking for personnel to create a team. Not that Zeke thought he'd need one in the short term. He liked working alone.

By early afternoon Friday, Zeke had wrapped up his life in the big city. The boxes of his other personal belongings had already been packed and shipped in a pod to a place he'd rented from an online listing. Now, less than an hour away from leaving, Zeke pulled another duffel bag out of the closet and placed it on the bench by his bed. He reached into the closet, pulled out the segment of jeans and slacks, and after removing the hangers placed them inside the bag. He placed shirts on top of them and in a final bag, packed tees and underwear. Hands on hips, he looked around the room, making sure there wasn't anything else he wanted with him in the Jeep.

Most travelers began their road trips early in the morning. Zeke liked doing most of his travelling at night. Driving relaxed him. Travelling across the country would give him time to think and unwind. Ready to get started, he decided to go ahead and get on the road. He loaded up his Jeep, filled the gas tank and at around three o'clock was ready to hit the road. He got in the car, placed his phone in an auto holder and scrolled his music library for music to drive by. Known for his love of rock, he felt nostalgic that night for a piece of home, a little West Virginia, and settled on a country station. As if summoning up his family, shortly after merging on to the highway, his phone rang.

"Grandpa Buck! You're not going to believe it, but I was just thinking of you!"

"You're probably a lying sack of shit but it still sounds good."

Zeke laughed. "Seriously! Listen to this." He turned up the stereo so that his grandfather could hear one of their shared favorite artists, Willie Nelson, belting out a classic. "Do you hear?"

"Well I'll be damned, boy," Buck responded. "Somebody sure raised you right. What's happening over there in Yankee country? You keeping those bleeding liberals in line?"

"Doing my best."

"I sure love what that Van Dijk is doing for the country. We'd be swallowing a pile of lies if not for TBC."

"That's right. Left-wingers wanting to pack people into the country like sardines, trying to stir up trouble for our president."

"Don't I know it. But between you and me, I think that draft dodger creates a pile of trouble for himself."

"Wait a minute, Gramps. I thought you were a solid Trout supporter."

Trout, a conservative, had eked out a narrow victory and taken office last year.

"Just because I support him doesn't mean I think his doodoo doesn't smell foul. Who else were we going to vote for? He was the only choice we had. His opponent wanted to take what we've fought and died for and give it all to people who just came in the country last week. We were already going to hell in a handbasket trying to be friends with everybody and fill folks' minds with the harebrained notion that the world could become one big kumbayah. Anybody who reads the bible knows that's not possible. There's been war in the world ever since Cain killed Abel. I believe if there was only one man left on the planet, he'd go find a mirror and fight with his fool self."

Zeke smiled at how hard Grandpa Buck laughed at his own joke, but became concerned when the laughing turned to coughing that went on for a while.

"You alright, old man?"

"I'm still breathing."

"You were coughing pretty good when I was back there. Maybe you need to get that checked out?"

"For what? I'm seventy-nine years old, son. When the good Lord thinks I'm ready to come home then I'll be ready to leave."

For all the death Zeke had seen, for all he'd created, he didn't want to think about it when it came to Grandpa Buck. Quickly changing subjects, he got to why he'd been thinking of him in the first place. About how he'd been told that he'd finished a job successfully, but felt that in the process he'd been demoted.

"I don't know how long I can take living in Missouri. I might reenlist, go where I can use all these years of training and make a difference."

"I can appreciate where you're coming from, but don't spend too many brain cells on it. Enlisted or not, you'll always be a soldier."

Zeke's father Daniel arrived at the house. The call ended after that. He pondered his grandfather's words, hoped they would soothe him and make him feel better. But the feeling of unease continued, even grew. Zeke felt an undercurrent swirling around his conversations with Van Dijk, and Bullet, too. Something was going on. Something wasn't right. He just couldn't put his finger on it.

25

The week had been crazy, beginning on Monday and Kennedy's conversation with Monica. She hadn't been looking forward to it. Was there any chance that her and Scott would be open to Kennedy working from a satellite office? Especially when less than two weeks ago she'd pledged her commitment to the company for the long haul, as part of the Chicago team? However she felt about it, it couldn't be helped. The horse was out of the stable. The train had left the depot. Her life was unfolding around the upcoming events. She'd have to set her cards out and deal with the consequences.

Not wanting to prolong the intrigue, as soon as she arrived at the office, she approached Monica.

"Hey, lady."

"KW! Good morning. Listen, I'm glad you're here. I want to talk to you about an event that's happening in two weeks that I'd like you to cover for the October issue. It's happening in one of our city's neighborhoods that rarely sees positive coverage. I think the photo layout from this can be incredible. Come on, I'll show you the event online."

Kennedy followed Monica to the office. Once both were inside, she closed the door. Monica immediately turned around, a question in her expression. Unless something confidential or controversial was being discussed, they never closed the door.

"Everything okay?" she asked.

"We need to talk." Monica sat behind her desk. Kennedy remained standing, in front of her. "Remember the stalking situation I mentioned awhile back?"

"Yes."

"The situation has escalated. It's reached a point where I no longer feel safe here, in the city. There's more to it that I want to share but I can't, not right at this moment. But it is critical enough that I am making plans to leave the city for a little while."

"How long is a little while?"

Kennedy shrugged. "A couple weeks, a month . . . I don't know."

Monica sat against the chair back, clearly unhappy. "How's that going to work, given your responsibilities here?"

"It will be challenging, but I love working here. I believe in this company and I feel horrible for having to come here with this, knowing how much building a team means to you and Scott. Maybe it will blow over quicker than I think and I can come back in a couple weeks. I just don't know, and I want to be honest about that."

"Did you have any idea that the situation might come to this? When you interviewed and I emphasized how important it was to have a commitment, somebody who was here for the long haul, who could oversee taking this company to the next level?"

"Perhaps I didn't want to see it," Kennedy admitted. She paced the room along the window, struck with how the world outside could be business as usual when one's own personal world was imploding. "I hoped that I could handle it myself, keep the situation contained. But it's bigger than what I can handle. I'm no longer confident that I can protect myself."

Monica got up and came around the desk. She pulled Kennedy into a hug. "I'm sorry," she said with a tone that showed she meant it. She stepped back. "I'm pissed off and don't know how we'll work this out if it's even possible. But nothing is worth risking your life and if you believe leaving town is what you have to do to save it, I can't be the one to hold you back, have something happen, and then have blood on my hands."

"Thank you, Monica. That means so much to me, it really does."

"When do you plan to leave?"

"This coming Saturday."

The story was set to break on Saturday, just as the Labor Day holiday weekend got underway. Papers would hit the stands at about the same time her flight left for Grand Cayman, just a little after six a.m.

"That means that for the next week I'm going to work my ass off and get as much of the October layout done as possible. I'll take a look at the event you mentioned, see if there are any shots I can do between now and then that will go with the story. I'll also outline the November issue. Hopefully I'll be back by then but just in case, I want to do as much as I can while I'm here."

With that hard conversation out of the way, Kennedy settled into work. As much as she didn't like staying late at work, she figured considering that she was leaving on Saturday it was the least she could do. On Wednesday, however, she left around eight to meet Gwen and Logan for drinks. When she entered the lounge where they were scheduled to meet, her eyes fell on them cuddled up in a corner booth. She stopped for a moment and observed their interaction. For a moment, she envied their normal life, having each other, having love. Once this drama was behind her, Kennedy figured it would be about time for her to think about more than work for a change, to figure out who she wanted to be for the rest of her life, and whether she wanted to be it alone. She shook off the melancholy and let her happiness at seeing them shine through.

"Hey you lovebirds. Get a room."

Hugs and greetings went around as Kennedy settled into the booth. They ordered drinks. Gwen eyed her keenly.

"First of all, Gwen, I owe you an apology."

"For what?"

"Well, maybe I don't owe it, but I want to give it to you anyway. You've been an amazing friend and were wise to be concerned about me. I know I brushed you off at some times, and got angry at others, but the truth of the matter is that I wasn't okay. I'm still going through it, and at some point, I plan to take your advice and see someone about all that has been going on."

"What has been going on?" Gwen asked. "I know it's more than what you've told me."

"You're right. It's a lot more than I've told either of you. And I'm still not at liberty to share everything but because the two of you have been there for me, I want to share what I can. Especially to you, Logan. You've been affected by what's happened and didn't know why.

"Gwen, remember the trip I took to the Bahamas?"

"With what all happened to you down there, how could I forget it?"

"I guess so, huh? While I was there taking pictures, I accidentally captured something, or more specifically someone, who's very high up in government, and wields a lot of power. I didn't even know what I'd taken until I had the pictures enhanced. And once I did, I understood that if they got out it could ruin the person's life. But they knew. I didn't see them, but they saw me take the pictures and they've been after me ever since, trying to get them back."

"Oh no, Kennedy." Gwen's eyes grew fearful. She reached for Kennedy's hand and unloaded a barrage of questions. "Is that who broke into your place? Is that why you moved? Are you safe?"

"No, Gwen, I'm not. Truthfully, I haven't been really safe for months. Logan knows about some of it because in helping me, he got caught up, too." Gwen looked at Logan, confused and annoyed. "No, don't be mad at him. I swore him to secrecy, figuring the less anyone knew the safer they'd be. When I was robbed in the Bahamas and all my electronics stolen, it was because they were looking for the pictures that at that time I didn't even know I'd taken. There's something else that I didn't know, and only found out recently."

She paused, ashamed to even mention the naked pics.

Logan leaned forward. "What, Ken?"

"While I was drugged, naked, and passed out, pictures were taken of me."

"Damn!" Logan spat.

Gwen's expression crumbled, "Oh. My. God. How'd you find out?"

"After turning down Anita's offer to sell the pictures to her."

"Who's Anita?" Logan asked.

Kennedy told him about the six-figure offer she'd gotten from someone she now believed worked for the man in the shots. "Not long after that the envelope was delivered. Somewhere around that time I also found out that someone had placed a GPS on my car."

"You can't be serious?" Logan said, now looking as concerned for Kennedy as Gwen did. "That's some mission impossible movie shit. Kennedy, you know me and law enforcement are none too friendly but you need to get somebody in on this, for real."

"Who's in this picture?" Gwen asked.

Kennedy took a deep breath. "Okay, guys. It's going to come out soon anyway and because of our association, I want you both to know. I mentioned him to you, Gwen, forever ago when this all just started. Anyway . . . I'll just tell you who it is.

But first you both have to promise, swear on your lives, that you won't say a word until the news breaks."

"Whoever this is can make breaking news?" Logan asked.

Gwen looked at her. "I remember." She turned to Logan. "He owns the news."

"Who is it? The president?" Logan asked, laughing.

Kennedy didn't crack a smile.

"It's not him," Gwen answered. "But someone just as powerful."

"The owner of TBC," Kennedy said.

"That racist network?" Logan asked.

Kennedy shrugged. "That's one way to describe it."

"What could he have possibly been doing to warrant all of this drama?"

"Probably stepping out on his wife," Logan said.

"Don't they all?" Gwen countered.

"Maybe," Kennedy said. "But in traditional circles, it's usually not with another man."

"Oh my gosh," Gwen breathed. "No wonder you're going crazy, Ken. Why didn't you tell me?"

"Because I didn't want anyone coming after you, like they came after me and Logan."

Gwen shot a look at Logan, who looked at Kennedy.

"You can tell her."

"Kennedy gave me a thumb drive to keep."

"You gave him the pictures?" Gwen asked Kennedy.

"I didn't know what was on it," she said. "Plus, you can't see anything with the naked eye, no pun intended."

Her comment lightened the mood a bit and the conversation shifted to other things. It was her last casual night before leaving. Between work and packing the last two days were a blur. But Saturday finally arrived. Kennedy was so ready to go, she hadn't even needed an alarm even though her flight left at six a.m. At just past four-thirty, she zipped and locked her luggage, took a last look around the room and tiptoed out the door.

She hated that it was still so dark outside. Rather than having to pull her luggage around the block to her car, she propped it by the gate and drove her car back there. After popping the trunk and tapping the hazard lights she left the car running and went to retrieve her luggage. She put the larger bag in, reached down for her carry-on and settled it beside the larger one. Just as she reached up to close the trunk she paused, sure she'd heard a noise. Before she could turn, one arm slammed her back against a hard body. At the same time a cloth was clamped over her mouth and nose. She clawed at the hand, raised her leg to kick him. And then her world went black.

26

Kennedy came to and found herself in total darkness. A panic attack threatened. She felt it from the tip of her toes to the top of her head. She'd never considered herself overly claustrophobic but now, bound and blindfolded in the backseat of what she quickly realized was her own car, she couldn't imagine that. Appropriate, since she was quite sure her destination was death. She'd been caught totally off guard by a kidnapper who wore some type of mask so she couldn't see his face. There were so many questions that would go unanswered with her death, including who kidnapped her, who was the man calling himself Jack Sutton that she'd met in the Bahamas, and would Dodie finish what they started? Would the American public ever know what a monster Van Dijk really was?

Her body rocked as the driver took a sharp turn. Where was she being taken? What statement would be made about her demise? What circumstances would be created to surround her death? She was a young Black woman living in America. She could be painted by the enemy with a very broad brush: prostitute, drug user, drug dealer, battered girlfriend, runaway. Any number of believable scenarios could be created. The possibilities were endless. She thought about her family, imagined two officers knocking on her mom's front door, Karolyn buckling after receiving the news, her brother's stoic presence at the funeral comforting their mom. Tears formed beneath the tape used to blindfold her. They ran down her face and into the leather. She forced herself to stop thinking that way. Her time would be better spent figuring out how to keep living. It wasn't over until it was over. She wasn't dead yet. Maybe if she engaged with her captor, made him see her as human, maybe she'd have a chance to see another sunrise.

"Who . . ." She paused, cleared the frogs out of her throat and began again. "Who are you?"

Silence.

"Why did you kidnap me? Where are you taking me?"

She heard the radio come on, stations being scanned. When the sound of heavy metal came through the speakers the driver turned up the volume. His meaning was clear. No talking.

The car shifted again and accelerated. Her body slammed against the back of the seat. She felt the car merge, heard speeding vehicles. They had entered the highway. Kennedy's heart thumped against her ribcage. Waves of panic washed over, causing beads of sweat to pop out on her forehead even as her teeth chattered with the chilly reality of what would be her final moments on earth. Tears rushed up from her soul, pushed against her eyelids and spilled over. Broken, resolved, she allowed them. Tears for a life not even half-lived. For her unfulfilled dreams. For her family and friends.

For yourself.

The thought slapped her senses like an open palm. It staunched the tears. Kennedy prided herself on being a modern woman, on being independent and forging a place for herself in the career of her choice. In middle school, she was sure that life would be lived on the stage. She'd idolized Alicia and Destiny's Child, imagined herself on *The Parkers*. Her talent didn't live up to the dream, so by high school the stage had been replaced by the race track. She attended meets and won medals but the day she saw a photographer and went over to ask if he'd taken a picture of her jumping the hurdles, her life changed. He showed the picture he'd taken, and many more, how he focused on different aspects of the subject, blurred backgrounds and varied exposures, she was hooked. She entered college determined to be an award-winning photographer working for a national magazine. Her life had been focused on education and career. She was on the precipice of realizing that dream. Until now it was all that mattered. But now, on what may be the last trip of her life, she realized there may have been something worthier, or at least equally worthy of her efforts—marriage, children, a legacy, something other than and greater than herself.

It wasn't until awakened by the slamming of a car door that Kennedy realized she'd fallen asleep. Despite her bound, vulnerable state, she kicked against the hand that reached for her and scooted as far into the car as she could away from him. The victory was short-lived. She was pulled out of the car and with no time to gain her balance or footing—as much that could be gained with bound ankles—she was half-carried, half-dragged into some type of shelter and down a hall, recognized because of how her body bumped against it. The hands squeezing her shoulder and arms released her suddenly, pushed her forward. She fell on a bed. No! Kennedy made a promise to herself right then. She would die before being assaulted and was so busy trying to roll to a sitting position and scoot to the headboard where she could brace herself and kick that it took a while before she realized there was no reason to fight. No hands grabbing at her, no pulling of clothes.

"Hello?"

She held her breath, the only sound in the room. Faint noises from another room told Kennedy she still wasn't alone. It pained her to not know who was in there or what he was doing. Minutes passed. She felt her life hang in the balance, wondered if her torturer enjoyed toying with her emotions, the power of setting the time she would die. Footsteps in the hallway suggested he'd made his decision. She struggled to sit up, but he placed a knee on her legs and held his torso against hers to hold her still. She felt the bonds being loosened on her wrists. The weight lifted, footsteps receded, the door closed, a car started. In that moment, Kennedy knew the only thing worse than being with her captor was being blindfolded, bound, and totally alone. Even though her captor had said not one word.

It took only seconds to shift her thoughts from dying to living. For reasons that did not matter, her captor had loosened the ropes. He'd removed her from Harriet, but the ancestor's spirit remained. Kennedy could get free! She stopped the frantic maneuvering against the ropes and after a couple calm breaths, she carefully twisted her wrists, this way and that, the ropes began to slide. For the first time since a wet cloth was placed over her nostrils, Kennedy felt hope come alive. A couple minutes more and her wrists were free. She shook them to get the blood flowing, rubbed them together so they could be used to remove the tape that had served as her blindfold. The tape was tougher, but she managed to push it up far enough to see her surroundings, then, while blinking to adjust to dim lighting, wrestled the rope from around her ankles, scrambled off the bed, and almost fell when she tried to run on legs that had been bound for a while. A few seconds to regroup and she ran for the door. Since the man hadn't killed her, he'd probably be back. She didn't plan to be there.

She raced to the door, grabbed the knob and prepared to yank it open. It didn't budge. She ran her fingers around and over the knob, looking for the way to get out. There was only a keyhole. She was locked inside. A jolt to her nerves, but Kennedy stayed focused. She crossed over to one of two windows in the front room and yanked the cloth shade. Bars. Her heart dropped. She quickly checked the other windows, already knowing what she'd find. Using one of the empty beer cans, she broke a pane of glass, hoping the bars were loose or maybe unlocked. Five windows, five sets of bars, and no such luck. The door to the home's only entrance was locked tight, the windows were barred shut.

Great. Now what?

It was becoming more difficult to stay calm. Kennedy took another turn around the small cottage, slower this time, looking for something, anything that could help her escape. The house was not only totally devoid of personal effects, it was almost empty. An old *Playboy* magazine and a newspaper sports' section were in the single nightstand drawer. The dresser drawers held nothing but dust which was also evident on the tabletops. A second bedroom was empty save a dartboard on the wall, a couple of chairs and some empty beer cans. The dirty bathroom's cabinet revealed little more than the rest of the room, an unopened toothbrush, mouthwash, and a used bar of soap. No shower rod. No tools. The kitchen was her last hope. Flinging open cabinet doors, her heart sank. There were canned goods, crackers, a jar of peanut butter, fast food condiments, a few paper plates. The drawers were no better. Aside from plastic utensils, fast food napkins and a rusty steak knife, they were empty. Clearly, whoever owned this place hadn't been here in a while. She looked around, fighting off thoughts that this mission might be impossible. She took a deep breath. That's when the situation went from bad to worse. That's when she noticed the distinct smell of gas. She raced to the stove where the smell was stronger, and a hissing noise releasing the gas. Turning the knobs was useless. Then came a glint off the steel. Kennedy looked up. There was a small skylight directly over the stove, maybe six square inches; hope, and on the heels of that sheer terror at the implication. Today was supposed to be hot, almost a hundred degrees. Could the sun get intense enough to cause an explosion? If this gas was confined and built up enough pressure, would it matter?

The ceiling looked to be about seven feet high. Kennedy raced for one of the chairs and placed it under the light. The cover was plastic, screwed in. She thought about the rusty knife in the drawer, but Kennedy didn't know if she had time to fuss with four screws. Instead, she took yet another turn around the house, throwing open a closet in the first bedroom she'd passed the last time. There were hangers, at least something, and then one thing more—the metal bar on which the hangers hung. It was set, unlatched, in plastic holders. She flung the clothes away, snatched up the bar and raced back to the kitchen. Adrenaline gave her the strength of ten men. She jabbed straight through the plastic and was rewarded with a hole that blessedly let in the sky. She didn't need much more motivation. She continued stabbing at the plastic, and once she accidentally hit the ceiling and pieces of drywall hit her face, she tried to punch through that as well. Her arms burned with the effort but there was no time for rest. She created enough of a hole around the skylight to pull it down, a space of about eight square inches. Jabbing the metal bar again, she hit a beam. Would wooden beams in the ceiling trap her inside as the metal bars had on the windows? Delirious with fear, Kennedy balanced the metal bar across two of the wooden beams, then used a third one to hoist herself up. With a portion of her weight now held by the back of the chair and one arm wrapped around the beam, she used her other arm to try and clear enough plaster, insulation and other stuff to make a hole big enough to crawl through. A set of clicking sounds stopped her movement. Whether real or imagined, the gas smell increased. Something told her she only had minutes to live. Scratched, bruised, bloodied, sore, exhausted—she called on strength from deep within her and lifted herself through the hole. There was a small attic, more of a crawl space really. But at the end of it . . . a window! Ignoring the pain of skin meeting rough wood, she shimmied over to the window and using the bar she held, broke out the glass. As she heard it break, another sound pierced the otherwise quiet morning. A car engine. *Shit!* Her kidnapper was back.

27

Plans changed. Not long after Zeke had crossed the Indiana state line, he'd gotten a call. It was Van Dijk.

"I need you to make a stop on your way to Springfield."

"That's no problem. Where?"

"Chicago."

It was the last city Zeke had expected to hear. "What's in Chicago, Mr. Van Dijk?"

"Not what. Who. The assignment you'd been working until a few days ago. You'll get to finish it after all. You're going to get a text from an international number, with an address for a place owned by . . . a friend. It's not far from the city, a place you can stop and rest a bit. But be sure not to leave any trash behind. We want to keep the place clean, understand?"

"Absolutely."

"Don't take too long. I'll expect to hear from you sometime tomorrow, from Springfield."

Zeke had shifted his thoughts as quickly as the gears in his Jeep, reprogramming the GPS and heading to Chicago. He didn't allow himself to wonder about the change or entertain questions unproductive to the job at hand. He'd followed the instructions as he would an order in combat. He'd arrived at the location, scoped the area, and in a stroke of luck had watched his target practically walk into his snare. That was the easy part. He found himself wrestling with what happened next, and didn't like the feeling at all.

Focus, Zeke. It's over. Forget and move on.

Over the years, Zeke had developed the ability to compartmentalize areas of his life, to stay focused on the orders he'd been given that were often ends justifying means. He didn't think about collateral damage as people. To imagine them with families, brothers and sisters, parents or even children, could lead to a crack in the armor around his heart. Before, it had always worked. It's what helped him get through four tours of duty and raw, heinous wars. It's what kept him sane through the knowledge of collateral damage created when drones hit the wrong targets, unsuspecting civilians, and bullets landed regardless of innocence or age. It's how he moved forward with assignments like this one, when he wasn't fully informed of the details, or other times when he hadn't totally agreed. He was able to carry out an assignment or hit, put the experience in a box, and forget it. Maybe it was the fact that he drove her vehicle, or had heard her voice, or felt her struggle, but for whatever reason, he remembered. Not the Wade that he'd ambushed, rendered unconscious with a drug-soaked cloth and taken to a designated location to meet an explosive end. The woman invading his conscious now was Kennedy, the sun goddess he'd seen in the Bahamas.

He should have paid more attention to that first tear, the moment she woke up and spoke and he felt an emotion. Feeling anything at all was a sign. But he'd ignored it, turned up the radio and zoned into hard rock. Once at the home she'd fought him, as if for her life. Bound and blinded, but still courageous. She did not want to die, and for an instant, a nanosecond really, he hadn't wanted to kill her. But he'd been given an order, and like a good soldier, he followed it.

Once inside the house he'd dumped her on the bed, witnessed the body language screaming that she thought he would sexually assault her. She had no need to worry. Dispose of an enemy? No problem. But he would never rape a woman. Instead he'd gone to the kitchen, and quickly, methodically, loosened a bolt on the gas line to create a leak that would take a couple hours to tip off the ignition, sort of like a detector, and explode. Then he returned to her and loosened the ropes on her wrists. Seeing what a hellion she'd been, he had no doubt she'd try to escape. But every window was barred and the doors were secure. There would be no exit for her until she woke up on the other side. He'd also loosened the ropes on her hands, knowing she'd struggle out of them. What she wouldn't know is that her actions would play right into his plans. Without those bonds, the scene would look like an unfortunate accident. He knew he could leave then, knew that two seconds after hearing the car take off, she'd be hell-bent to get free. It's exactly what he wanted, just as he'd planned. If firemen discovered bound remains in the ashes it would be investigated as a murder, not labeled an accident due to a faulty gas line, the way they would now. He figured there was enough time to wipe down the car, park it in a sketchy neighborhood, pick up his Jeep and continue on to Fort Leonard Wood. Ideally, he would have reported for duty by the time it happened. Though he was ninety-nine percent sure his execution was perfect, he never underestimated that one percent.

He'd walked back to the car and jumped in, fired it up, and hauled ass down the dirt road. He'd rolled down the window. That's when it happened. He'd caught a whiff of perfume that rent the tear into a hole. The fragrance unlocked the box where he'd put her and pulled out the memory of when he'd first seen her, when they'd first met. When she thought he was a nice guy and when for a minute he felt normal, like someone really out on a date. He'd been surprised by how much he'd enjoyed it;

how easy she was to talk to and how attractive he'd found her. He'd always leaned more toward the blonde-haired, blue-eyed babe. But there was something about how the sinking sun had hit her toasty complexion, turning it almost golden that moved him, something about how the light danced in her brown eyes. She'd been sarcastic, but playful, guarded but real. He didn't get real so much with his paid companions. The conversation had been enjoyable even though every word on his end was a lie. Something about Wade's easiness had calmed and relaxed him, even scared him a little. He knew that for her, the night would end badly. He shouldn't have cared about it, but he had, even attempting to prolong the friendly interlude when she was ready to call it a night.

"Are you sure I can't talk you into extending the evening? The company is amazing and it's a beautiful night."

"I agree on both counts but tomorrow will come early. I have a plane to catch."

"Where's home?"

"Chicago. What about you?"

"Virginia."

"Really? Where's the accent?"

"Back on my grandfather's farm, where it belongs."

"It's probably good you don't have one."

"Why?"

Kennedy shrugged. Stifled a yawn. "I think a southern accent is sexy and since I'm away from home and feeling relaxed, that could have gotten me into trouble."

She'd yawned again, proof that what he'd slipped in her coffee was working fast.

"Whew!" She began walking across the lobby, toward the elevators. "I'm more tired than I thought. Even decaf coffee usually gives me a bit of a bounce."

They reached the bank of elevators. He pushed the up button.

"Where are you going?" she asked.

"To my room." Zeke's smile was easy. "I'm staying here, too, remember?"

She'd offered her own sexy smile, then leaned against the elevator wall and closed her eyes. He'd asked for her room number, then pushed a button that was higher. Someone had waved from across the way for him to hold the elevator. Instead he'd jammed the close button, put his arm around Kennedy and once they reached her floor helped her to her room. Then he'd waved goodbye while discreetly placing a pin in the chamber so that it would not lock. Ten minutes later he'd entered the room to find Kennedy on the bed, fully clothed, and sound asleep. He disconnected emotionally, carrying out the orders that had been given. He didn't understand then, or now, the value of whatever pictures she'd taken. Nothing he'd seen pointed to a threat of any kind, unless it was to trees. Between the Bahamas and Chicago, every electronic device she had was confiscated, but the damning pictures of Van Dijk had yet to be found. She had to be eliminated for the secret to remain hidden. Even if someone else had the pictures, hearing of her "accident" would no doubt make them think twice.

The accident he'd set up to have happened to Wade was making him think . . . too much. He'd almost reached the main highway when he saw a sign showing the number of miles to the next three small towns. He took the exit for the second one and though it was barely after eight in the morning he soon found what he was looking for—a bar with a neon open sign, brightly lit. Meds would make him sleepy or too foggy for this stage of the game. But a shot or two with a cigarette would settle his mind down. Small towns were known for their tight-knit communities, able to see a stranger from a mile away. So he pulled on a red St. Louis Cardinals baseball cap and reached into a fanny pack for wire-rimmed reader glasses. He parked directly in front of the Grown Capone with a story ready to roll off his lips like gospel. He reached for the door and entered a dim room empty of patrons, with a pool table on his right side and three chairs facing the window on the left. A makeshift aisle ran between two sides of tables that led to a bar along the back side of the wall. The owner or whoever had been tasked with holding down a watering hole this time of morning was barely visible behind the counter, watching a fishing show on TV. Midway in the room was a jukebox, above it a large picture of Trout and a larger American flag. Zeke felt calmer already. This was going to be a piece of cake.

Pulling the bib of his cap a bit lower, Zeke slid on to a bar seat. Without looking away from the screen the bartender asked, "What can I get you?"

"Shot of Wild Turkey."

The bartender's eyes slid over briefly before returning to the screen. "Early morning or late night?"

"A bit of both."

The bartender picked up a glass, walked over to a row of bottles and picked up one in the middle.

"Make it a double," Zeke said.

The bartender set down the single shot glass and picked up a small tumbler. He poured a liberal amount of the amber colored liquor and slid the glass down the surprisingly smooth counter.

"Trying to forget something, buddy?" he asked, walking back to the chair.

Zeke didn't hear him. His attention and eyes were glued to the "Breaking News" banner crawling across the screen beneath pictures of Braum Van Dijk and the pharmaceutical heir Edward Becker juxtaposed over each other.

"Hey, can you turn that up?"

The bartender turned around. "You watch his network?"

Zeke offered a curt nod. "Damn right."

The bartender's broad smile revealed a checkerboard of tobacco-stained teeth. "Well, alright then."

He reached for the remote, turned up the volume and took a step back to see the screen.

. . . exploded today in the heart of Manhattan, after pictures of media mogul and owner of True Broadcasting Corporation, Braum Van Dijk and the newly married heir to Becker Pharmaceuticals, Edward Becker, were released by the news and entertainment magazine National Query. *These pictures are highly controversial and sexual in nature.*

The bartender looked over at Zeke. "What the hell?"

Zeke slammed down the double shot and had a feeling he'd need another.

Several photos accompany the National Query *article due out today, and state these highly questionable, deeply troubling shots were taken this past May as Becker honeymooned in the Bahamas on a private island owned by Van Dijk. According to the network's publicist, the images are photoshopped. She admits that Van Dijk was in the Bahamas at the same time as Becker, but stayed at a home owned by his wife on the main island. According to the article, Van Dijk gifted Becker and his wife a cabin on his private island and went there at the invitation and insistence of Charlotte Lee Winthrop, the new Mrs. Becker. She went on to state that Van Dijk had a horde of haters envious of his success and has callously tarnished the sacredness of a newly married couple's first days together to try and bring down the most powerful media mogul in the world. She says that both the Beckers and the Van Dijks are furious at the false allegations and are meeting with a team of attorneys to unearth the culprit behind this libelous act and prosecute them to the fullest extent of the law. The* National Query *stands behind the story and the pictures, which were captured by a professional photographer on assignment for the* Chicago Star. *The station is in possession of those pictures and will show a couple of them as much as we are able, but as I stated they are of a sensitive nature and even though we've blurred the most offensive parts of the pictures I do want to warn you that some viewers may still find them offensive. Viewer discretion is advised. That in just a moment but first . . .*

"What do they have pictures of, a foursome or something?" the bartender joked. Meanwhile Zeke had slid off the barstool to stand directly in front of the TV.

. . .photographer, who wishes to remain anonymous out of concern for their safety, says that the target being focused on for the shot was the island itself and only after having the photos magnified and enhanced was the realization made that there was a picture within the picture taken that if verified will turn out to be the money shot of the century, the most explosive media controversy since Patty Hearst joined the Symbionese Liberation Army. Again, we are advising viewer discretion. Here is the shot, purported to be in its natural state, meaning it was only enhanced so that the subject photographed from such a great distance could be clearly seen. The photographer has sworn in writing that otherwise the pictures are untouched, that there has been no photoshopping or other manipulation and that what she unknowingly shot is in fact what it appears to be here, some type of sexual tryst between these men. So far there has been no direct word from either Becker or Van Dijk . . .

One look at the blurred photograph and Zeke had seen and heard enough. He strode out of the bar, hopped into the car and turned back in the direction he'd just driven. With less than five minutes of breaking news, the questions regarding the Wade mission had multiplied. He wanted to call Van Dijk, have the story verified. Every TBC viewer was well aware of the nation's fake news. But until now Van Dijk's answers had never been satisfactory. Even worse, he couldn't ignore the fact that his superior may have straight out lied. He could have been sent out to eliminate a woman who was a threat to his boss's position of power more than the nation's security. If Van Dijk indeed had a dirty little secret that had been caught with the click of Wade's camera, then getting rid of her would have let it remain. Zeke knew that these were the pictures being guarded. What he didn't know was whether the photos were real or if they'd been doctored. And the only person who might have the answer was locked in a cottage with a fatal gas leak and was about to get blown up. He reached the highway, gripped the wheel, and pushed the pedal to the floor.

28

Kennedy held her breath, hoping her ears had deceived her. They hadn't. Although distant, the distinct sound of a car engine could be heard. She chipped away at the glass still clinging to the inner cross-like frame that held the four pieces of glass, now shattered. The wood was stronger than it appeared and the shards of glass prevented Kennedy from getting a good grip.

The engine sound grew louder.

Desperate, Kennedy turned her body around in the limited space and scooted her hips near the window. Then she laid down at an angle that allowed her to kick the pane with her sandaled foot. The wood cracked. A couple more kicks, and she was able to break away the narrow pieces. She looked out the window, which looked to be about ten feet above the ground below. She wasn't crazy about heights but didn't give the jump a second thought. She turned back around and edged out of the window feet first, gritting against the pain as the ragged wood fragments stuck through the thin cotton she wore and into her skin. There was nothing to brace her feet, so once her legs were through, she used the little strength in her arms that she had left to push her upper body through the small opening. Her thought was to hang from the opening and balance her fall. That didn't happen. Her fingers, weak and bleeding from her effort to break through the ceiling gave way. Kennedy free fell to the ground. The unforgiving soil knocked the wind right out of her. Kennedy groaned, rolled over and pulled in bits of grass and dirt with her deep gulps of air. She got to her knees and listened. Silence. What did that mean? Kennedy knew she didn't have time to find out. She stumbled to her feet and using the house to lean against began looking around to get her bearings, hoping to see a house, a barn, any sign of life where she could run to for help. Unfortunately, everywhere she looked, there was nothing but open space around her.

Her heartbeat was so loud she couldn't think. Instinctively, she crept toward the edge of the house away from the direction she thought she'd heard the car approaching. She passed the window to the back bedroom where she'd been taken, and the one on the front room's dining area side. At the corner of the house she stopped, took a breath and slowly, oh . . . so . . . slowly . . . peeked her head out the slightest bit, just enough to see beyond the front of the building. The coast appeared to be clear. She took one step forward. Then another.

The next footsteps she heard were not her own.

Kennedy froze, two steps away from the side of the house. She was afraid to turn around, fearing there was someone directly behind her. The thought propelled her forward. She stopped, listened. No further sound. Even on tiptoe, tall weeds blocked her view. There was no clear shot of the road. She had to take her chances and hope there was a house or something on the other side. She crept toward the road, hunched, listening. As soon as she reached the edge of the drive she'd be able to take a good look both ways, and see the car. She ran the few steps from the yard to the dirt road . . .

And saw a man jogging toward her.

No!

He broke out into a sprint. She could not get caught. Seeing the man she was sure was her kidnapper was like having a starter pistol go off at the beginning of the race for her life. Still wearing her sandals, she pulled on muscles she hadn't used in years and took off down the road.

"Help!" There wasn't another house or person in sight, but Kennedy yelled anyway and willed her legs to move faster. With the sandals on, that wasn't happening. But she didn't give up. Just ahead was a cornfield. She ran off the path and straight for the tall, leafy stalks. Three steps away from the first row of corn she stepped into a hole and fell.

Damn! You've got to be kidding! Is this a movie?

Kennedy crawled into the field, moving as far into the row as fast as she could. Her ankle was killing her, probably sprained, but focusing on that might cost her life. She reached shaky hands down to try and quickly remove the troublesome shoes. There was no time to undo the straps, so she pushed and stretched and forced the material over her ankle, removed the second one just as the man appeared in the row.

"Get the fuck away from me!"

She stood up, firing the sandals directly at the man's head. She hoped they'd connected, maybe taken out an eye, but she couldn't wait and find out. The dirt was chunky, her soles tender, but the adrenaline was running too high for her to feel the effect. She cut between stalks. He followed. It was as though she could feel his breath on her neck. In a last-ditch attempt to outmaneuver him, she broke out of the field and headed back toward the dirt road. Maybe the keys were still in the car. She could reach it and get away.

"Wade, stop!"

The sound of his voice made her abductor more real. Tears clouded her eyes. Her lungs burned and felt about to burst. Her legs were cramping, her ankle throbbing, and the bottom of her feet felt shredded and raw. She ran faster. But it wasn't enough. She felt rather than saw him. Her arms flew out as he tackled her and threw her to the ground.

"Let me go!"

She kicked, punched and tried to get loose.

"Wade, dammit, stop fighting!"

"No," she mumbled, trying to knee him in the groin. "You're trying to kill me."

"If that were the case, you'd be dead," he responded, his voice a deadly calm that stilled Kennedy's struggle. "Now I'm trying to save your life."

A giant explosion shook the earth beneath them. Kennedy sat up, dazed, as vibrant flames shot up in the air and clouds of black smoke seemed to cover the sun. She looked at the man who looked beyond her at the house she'd escaped from.

"How the hell did you get out of there?"

Kennedy slapped his rugged-looking face, paused, and slapped it again.

Knowing how loud noises could trigger flashbacks, so realizing he'd likely be close when the gas built up and exploded, Zeke had used techniques learned in therapy and prepared for the boom. He wasn't as prepared for Wade's vicious attack and grabbed her arm on impulse at a place he could snap it in two with one quick twist.

"Ow!"

Her scream snapped him out of combat mode. He rested his arms on his knees and caught his breath. Wade sat a few feet away breathing heavily, her eyes narrowed as she watched him intently while rubbing her arm. Her feet were bleeding. She seemed not to notice. As his eyes traveled upward, he noticed her dress was torn and dirty. Every piece of skin he could see was bruised, scratched or bleeding. He watched her change positions, saw her eyes shift from him to the road.

With the strength of an ox and the speed of a falcon, Zeke pounced on Kennedy, scooped her up and headed toward the car in a dead run. For once, his captive didn't fight him. She must have heard the sirens, too. They reached the car. He opened the passenger door and tossed her in.

With a finger in her face, almost touching foreheads, he said, "Run, and you'll regret it."

Zeke jumped into the driver's seat, gunned the engine, and after a quick look in his rearview mirror shot down the road. On the right side was a big black hole, where a house had stood moments before.

Zeke veered from one dirt road to another. When he felt a safe distance away, he engaged his GPS to lead back to the main highway. He felt Kennedy's eyes on him. A glance told him what he already suspected—they were full of questions. Did she recognize him, he wondered? Was she trying to reconcile a familiar face with brown instead of blue eyes and blonde hair once hidden beneath a brunette wig?

"Don't try anything crazy. This is not a part of the state where you want to end up lost."

Kennedy's chuckle held no humor. "Like you care about my welfare."

She shifted her legs and winced, lifted her feet from the floorboard. "I've got a first aid kit in my luggage. I need it."

Zeke shook his head. "Not yet. We need to put a lot of distance between this car and that blast."

She stared openly now. "Who are you?"

"Doesn't matter."

"Who hired you to kill me?"

"If I told you that, I'd have to go through with the order."

He glanced at her and smiled. She didn't smile back. She shifted as far away from him as she could, pressed against the door, and gave him a slow, perusing once-over. Zeke didn't notice. With the adrenaline rush slowing and reality setting in, he was thinking about what he'd just done and what acting on impulse may have cost him. He'd been given a direct order to eliminate Wade, to make her go away, to neutralize the problem. When the blurred picture came up on the bar's wide flat screen, it gripped his very core. When it came to the reason behind this assignment, he'd had several conversations with Van Dijk. He remembered snippets of one that in the present moment—barreling down the highway at a high rate of speed with the person he'd been ordered to kill beside him—was especially troubling.

Ah, hell, Foster . . . I was meeting with the son of one of those fathers. Now, the average person has no idea this family is a part of the order. In fact, they believe just the opposite, that they're part of the crowd bringing America down. He has successfully infiltrated Hollywood, politics, every bastion where secrets we need flow freely. To be seen with me would mean the end of that access, and usher in the end of the America that we now know.

He'd had meetings with influential men who didn't hold his conservative values many times. Their friendships had been left-wing fodder for years, dating back to before the election. It had never seemed to bother Van Dijk before. Why now?

Can you imagine what the liberal media would do if they had pictures of me chatting with someone seemingly opposed to our values? Say a faggot or atheist or one of those sympathetic Hollywood devils?

In the photo Zeke had seen before rushing out of the bar, Van Dijk and Becker hadn't been holding anything, except each other. They hadn't been wearing anything either.

They'd spin a web of lies the way they always do and the next thing you know there would be yet another probe with lawyers blowing smoke up our asses trying to find wrongdoing where there is none.

Even with certain aspects of the photos blurred out, words like probe and smoke up asses took on new meaning. Zeke had been there, had taken a boat tour after Wade caught her plane to go where she'd gone, to try and see what she saw, to have some idea of what she could have photographed that could topple America. He was no photographer and he sure as hell didn't know anything about programs like Photoshop, but still he wondered how someone could create a picture that looked so authentic. Wade had to know that if it were a lie, Van Dijk would sue the pants off her and her entire family.

Those liberal stations have hated me for years. They are jealous of the power our media yields, and how we've got the real American, the patriotic, God-fearing majority on our side. They want to turn our democracy into a socialistic, communist nation full of illegal immigrants taking the jobs, and people too lazy to work, living off the hard work of the tax-paying public and make that look normal. Now I know you don't want that to happen.

Zeke loved his country enough to die for it in a heartbeat. He admitted to not knowing a whole lot about communism and socialism except they were forms of government his party abhorred and because of that he did, too. He was all for keeping America for Americans and sending the people who didn't belong here back to their countries. Living in West Virginia, he'd known plenty of people on welfare. Some were lazy no-account bums to be sure. But most of them were upstanding, hard-working Christians who'd caught a bad break and landed down on their luck. Most were third and fourth generation Americans whose families had paid taxes for decades.

He should have put a call into Van Dijk. He should have left Wade in the house with the gas leak. He should be heading to Fort Leonard Wood right now, checking out guys for a security team. He hadn't done any of those things, and now he was in a world of turmoil bringing on the type of anxiety that squeezed his heart to the point it could bring on a heart attack. It was time to take a pill. He reached over for his fanny pack. The minute he did, he heard a click, and felt a whoosh of air. He grabbed Wade's arm as she prepared to tumble out of a car going ninety miles an hour.

29

It was the smile that did it. For Kennedy, that's when it all
came together. The fragmented images that popped up when
the man finally caught her. The moment when she finally had
the opportunity to give her captor a good look. It was him, except it wasn't. The hair was different. The eyes were brown,
not blue. But when he smiled, she caught that hint of a dimple
and the slightly crooked teeth that she once thought adorable.
That's when she knew who'd kidnapped her from the streets of
Chicago.

Jack Sutton.

From that moment until her hand reached for the door handle about two minutes later, there was only one thought on her
mind—escape. This was no longer a faceless kidnapper who'd
locked her in a death trap. This was now also the person who'd
befriended her in the Bahamas only to later drug and rob her,
take photos of her naked, and Kennedy would bet money, also
burglarized her and Logan's homes. He was the man she'd
seen in Peyton. In short, this was the motherfucker who for the
past few months had made her life a living hell. With that realization, there was only one option. Between staying in this car
and going to the second location, and risking her life by jump-

ing out of a moving vehicle, she chose the latter. Already bruised and almost broken, she'd take her chances with asphalt and speed. She opened the door, ready to drop and roll.

Only she didn't. Jack's hand was like a vise grip on her arm and more, the car veered left and right. She heard the sound of a long car horn and squeezed her eyes shut for the impending crash.

"Got dammit, Wade!"

She felt Jack pump the brakes and the car slowing as the car door swung jerkily in the wind. He pulled over to the side of the road where Kennedy noted more civilization. Road signs announced places to eat, sleep, and get gas just a mile away. It's all the motivation she needed. She swung a fist toward the side of Jack's head. He caught it, squeezed her wrists, and her world went black.

When Kennedy came to, her wrists had been tied behind her back and Jack was quickly binding her ankles with a belt he'd obviously pulled from her luggage. It was useless, but she couldn't help squirming and trying to pull her legs from his grasp.

He looked at her then with eyes that telegraphed more weariness than anger. "I don't want to kill you, Wade. But I will. If you want to live, here's what needs to happen. No more escape attempts. No more fighting. I'm driving you back to Chicago and between here and there will try and figure out how I'm going to . . ."

Kennedy watched his eyes dart around as his mouth continued to move with no sound, as though he were having a private conversation with himself. His gaze returned to her, intense and unblinking. Her blood ran cold.

"One more wrong move, and it will be your last one. So is this warning. Whether you live or die today is up to you."

Kennedy told herself she was done with the struggle. She wanted to live.

"Where's the first aid kit?"

"In the toiletry case, the flowered organizer at the bottom of the big luggage. It's white, plastic, with a red cross on top."

She heard him rattling around in her luggage. As he went through her things, her anger soared. Jack Sutton, the burglar and robber, rummaging through her personal belongings yet again. Much as he'd probably done in the Bahamas, and in Chicago. He'd warned that one more wrong move and he'd kill her. He might have to. Kennedy didn't know how far they were from Chicago, but she doubted possessing the kind of restraint that would stop her from trying to kill him first.

He returned to the passenger side of the car with the first aid kit and a bundle of clothes. She recognized one of her nighties, a pink, oversized t-shirt sporting a fat white cat wearing a glittery cap and glasses. Beneath it the caption: *I'm purr-fect.* She flinched as he reached for her.

"You need to put this on, cover your torn dress and all the scratches and bruises."

Blood rushed to her fingers as her wrists were freed. He stood blocking the door. There was no way to escape. Resigned, she snatched the tee from his hands and pulled it over her head.

As soon as it was settled around her, he shook the scarf he'd used and said, "hands behind your back."

It was one thing to be tied up but when your very own clothes were used to do so it took the audacity to a whole other level.

"Do we really have to do that? You've tied my ankles. I can't run anywhere."

"But you can try and punch me again. Hold them out front." Kennedy hesitated. Jack, just about out of patience, put a hand to her throat. "You're about to piss me off. Don't let that happen."

Kennedy was helpless to pry his fingers away from her throat and took a huge gulp of air when he released her. She held out her hands. He made an intricate loop secured with a Boy Scout style knot. She was bound, but her hands were in front of her and blood flowed to her fingers. It was way worse just a minute ago. Using another item of clothing, Jack reached for her foot.

"There's water in the back," Kennedy said. "A couple of bottles in the thermo pack."

He looked from her to the back seat, opened the back door and grabbed both bottles out of the pouch. He handed one to her, opened the other and poured a generous amount over her feet. She winced from the initial contact, but the water was soothing to her raw, split skin. He dabbed the area and then opened the small bottle of hydrogen peroxide from the kit and poured it over her feet as he'd done the water.

"Aw!"

"It'll sting but trust me, that's less painful than dabbing them. They'll feel better once they're wrapped up."

That said, he ripped apart one of her favorite dresses and formed two long pieces of fabric. He methodically and efficiently wrapped her feet and tied off the cloth. Kennedy wondered about the man who called himself Jack Sutton. Everything about him screamed military. That hadn't been evident in the Bahamas, but every action she'd seen since had been precise and calculated. Obviously, he had covert skills. And how had he been able to make her pass out with a press of his thumb to her wrist?

He returned to the car, paused for a moment before turning the key. He started to say something, stopped, then quickly started the engine, put the car in gear and eased on to the highway. Kennedy looked at the dash and noted the time. It was just after eight a.m. Was it really only three hours ago that she placed her luggage in the car, nervous but also excited about seeing Tamara for the first time in more than five years? It felt as though an entire lifetime had passed, all the moments since spent struggling to simply stay alive. For the first time since waking up bound and blindfolded in her own car's backseat, she thought about others. Tamara, Dodie, Gwen, her mom. They'd probably all placed repeated phone calls and were probably worried sick, especially her mom. Even without the whole story, she was still bewildered by all that had happened. Kennedy had promised she'd call before leaving the states which was scheduled to be less than ninety minutes from now.

"Where's my purse, my phone?" Kennedy asked.

"The trunk."

"I need my phone. There are people who were expecting to hear from me hours ago."

"They'll have to wait a couple hours longer, until you're back in Chicago."

Kennedy fell back against the seat and looked out the window. They passed a sign that let her know Chicago was sixty-two miles away. The life she knew was much further away from her. She wondered if she'd ever arrive back there again. Cars passed by. Anyone seeing them probably saw normal. A guy with a baseball cap behind the wheel. His friend/wife/girlfriend/captive on the passenger side. The pink tee covered her ripped dress and body bruises. Her hands told a different story. Scabs had begun to form on her palms where the shards of glass cut her. Scratches covered her outer hand and fingers. The manicure she'd gotten just yesterday was totally trashed. She still had a hard time believing that this was her life, the one that happened while she'd been busy making totally different plans.

Jack had slowed down and was driving the speed limit. Kennedy had always liked road trips. Were she not with her captor, she would have been able to appreciate the beautiful summer morning on this Labor Day weekend. At the moment, her gratitude was simply for being alive. She took a deep breath, tried to focus on that. Beside her it seemed that Jack had calmed down, too. The tension had dissipated. Somewhere between her feet being bandaged and these past few miles, the two must have reached an unspoken truce. The relative peace caused a shift in Kennedy's thinking. Until now all she'd thought about was getting away from Jack Sutton. She still couldn't wait to put a fair amount of distance between them. Until then though she needed something from him, answers to questions that only he could give.

"You're Jack Sutton."

He remained silent for so long Kennedy doubted he'd answer. Finally, he did. "That name works as good as any."

"But it's obviously not your real name."

He looked over with the lopsided smile that had won her over in the restaurant. That she was ever attracted to a man who could do all he'd done to her made her want to throw up.

"Obviously."

"Since you won't share something so basic as your name, you probably won't answer my other questions either. Like who hired you to kill me." He didn't answer. "If I had only one guess I'd go with the obvious, and say it was one of the people exposed, pun intended, in that picture today."

"Anybody can see that picture has been doctored."

Kennedy surprised herself by laughing, something that for the past few months had happened all too rarely.

"Have you seen the pictures? I can guarantee you Van Dijk has. That's probably who you work for and who ordered you to kill me. That they're real is why you were sent down to the Bahamas, why you drugged and assaulted me and stole all my stuff."

"I never touched you."

"No? I went out clothed and woke up naked. You had to have touched me, and had you been able to feel an ounce of the shame I did the next morning? You'd call it an assault, too."

"I'm sorry about that."

Kennedy's head whipped around. Amazing that he'd actually apologized and, even more crazy, she believed him. This situation just got weirder and weirder.

"Funny thing is, I didn't even know what I had. You can't see the men with the naked eye, even blown up on a computer screen. The average viewer's eyes are naturally drawn to the focal points of my design—the rainbow, the water, the gorgeous green foliage. Even when you followed me to Chicago and burglarized my place there, my friends and I chalked it up to bad luck. It wasn't until Logan was burglarized and his flash drive was taken that I became determined to find out what I was missing in those pictures. That's when I sent them to a friend because quite frankly, I was tired of looking at them, tired of them running and ruling my life. When I got back his enlarged pictures focusing on two guys having sex, I couldn't have been more shocked."

"I take it you're a fan of TBC?"

"I watch it from time to time."

"I didn't doctor those pictures, Jack. I'm not homophobic, either. Becker and Van Dijk can meet and fuck until the cows come home. But I believe America has the right to know."

Jack was quiet a moment. "So . . . you sold the pictures?"

It was Kennedy's turn to hesitate. "For my protection, copies of those pictures were sent to at least half a dozen people. The leak could have come from anywhere."

"I asked if you sold them."

"And I gave you an answer." Kennedy shrugged, and looked out the window. "It was as good an answer as any."

For the next thirty miles they were silent. Then Kennedy felt Jack glancing over at her, several times.

"How did you get out of the house?"

"Through the ceiling, and then through the window in the attic."

"I saw that window but didn't think . . ."

"I didn't either. I just reacted. Staring death in the face makes you very resourceful."

"I came back to get you."

"Tsk."

"My . . . the information I'd been given was that you had captured information that was a threat to our national security. As a military man, I've sworn to uphold and defend the Constitution, an oath that doesn't end now that I'm working a civilian post. Anyone threatening that democracy is treated like an enemy combatant, up to and including elimination.

"I left you to die, had created a timed gas explosion to make sure that happened."

The admission seemed to fill the car's interior. For a few seconds, Jack said nothing. Kennedy was unable to get her lips to move. She remained quiet as well.

"Down the road a ways from the house I stopped at a bar. The bartender was watching TV. Breaking news came on. It was the pictures you took. That's when I saw what I was helping to keep hidden and came back to get you out of the house."

"What if you hadn't made it, or I hadn't escaped?"

"Then you would have been collateral damage, a casualty of war."

Not much was said after that. Kennedy thought of everything and nothing at all. She was numb with shock, exhaustion and disbelief. Just outside of the city limits, Jack took an exit near a busy strip mall. He parked in an isolated area, then Kennedy watched Jack methodically and efficiently wipe down every area of the car's interior. He wiped the car handles. She heard him lift the trunk and close it. He wiped down the back seat. Then he returned to the front seat, started the car and drove off.

"Where are we going?"

"I'm going to park not far from your house, set up another explosive device."

He looked over to gauge her reaction. Even though she felt she could pee on herself, Kennedy kept her face a mask of stone.

"It will be on the door, set on a timer, controlled on my phone. Once I get out, you'll have to wait thirty minutes before you open anything—a window, door, trunk, anything. If you open it before the time is up, the car will blow up."

She didn't respond, but if thirty minutes was the price for her freedom, he could have that lead time. Kennedy intended to go after Jack, or whatever his name was, for what he did to her. But that wasn't the top priority on her list. For too many weeks the pictures she'd taken and at least one of the subjects in it had basically taken her life. It was time to get it back.

30

Kennedy waited thirty-five minutes after she'd watched him attach something to the driver's side door, adjust his ball cap and walk casually but quickly down a street leading into one of the busiest tourist areas in the city. He'd parked far enough away so that any potential bomb blast wouldn't kill too many people, but where within minutes he'd be absorbed into the crowd. She'd watched him until she couldn't see him anymore, remembered everything she could about him and filed it away with all the details she'd remembered on the drive back to Chicago. She waited, periodically checking the clock on the dash, trying to put herself back into her body after having an experience that only happened in movies. It wasn't easy. Her mind teetered on the brink of insanity, pushed by spending hours as the captive of her weeks-long hunter and the aftershock of knowing that earlier today she almost died. When she placed her hand on the door handle, a wave of panic overwhelmed her. She pushed through it, squeezed her eyes shut and opened the door. The only sound she heard was a crazy lady screaming. It took a few seconds to realize the noise was coming from her. Once she did, she chuckled. The chuckle became a laugh that grew into an all-out guffaw. She fell back into the car, laughing until it turned into a coughing fit, until tears filled her eyes. Then the pendulum swung to the other side of her emotions as she broke down and cried.

She didn't know how long she laid there, but Kennedy felt better when she sat up. She wiped her eyes, blew her nose and pushed the trunk button. Strange looks from the few who passed her reminded her of her dress rag-clad feet and her purrfect tee. She probably looked a hot mess and didn't give a damn. Have them get abducted, almost blown up, escape from a locked home and then get recaptured, and see how good they'd look. After retrieving her purse from the trunk, she hobbled on to the other side of the car and got in.

Being reconnected with her cellphone was an emotional experience. Tangible proof that she was no longer alone, she held it against her chest for a second before turning it on. Once it fired up indicators pinged like a song. It sounded as though the whole world had called her. She took a deep breath and instinctively placed the first call. There were others more important and whom she'd known longer but this first call had to be to someone she wasn't trying to protect. Less than an hour away from the trauma of her life, she didn't have the energy. The simple act almost brought on another crying spell. Once again, she was in the driver's seat of her life. It wasn't until she'd started the car, merged into traffic and driven away from the congested area that she finally engaged her Bluetooth.

Tamara answered, quietly frantic. "Kennedy! Oh my God. I've been calling you for hours."

Ironically, her friend's agitation calmed Kennedy's nerves. Good thing, because she could barely answer one question before Tamara fired off another one. "My phone was off."

"So you are in New York?"

"No, I'm still in Chicago."

"Why haven't you called Dodie?"

"I was . . . tied up." Again, maniacal laughter bubbled up from her stomach to her throat and pushed against her teeth. She swallowed it and began to understand what crazy felt like.

"She's been calling you, too. We've both been so worried. What is going on?"

Tamara finally took a breath, allowing the first moment of silence since her number was dialed.

"I'm alright now so please don't trip out when I tell you what happened. This morning, as I got in my car on the way to the airport, I was abducted."

"What?" Tamara's voice climbed at least two octaves to hit the note that word delivered.

Kennedy navigated the busy Saturday morning streets of Chicago with no destination, telling Tamara how her last few hours had been spent. When she reached a quiet, residential area with lots of street parking she pulled over and finished the tale.

"He put an explosive device on my car, walked down the block, and disappeared. I did what he told me, waited until the timer deactivated, then opened the door, got my phone, turned it on and called you."

Several seconds passed with no response. "Hello? Tamara?"

There was a slight sniffle on the other end. "Kennedy, I'm so sorry. You've been to hell and back this morning and here I was going off on you and putting you through it again."

"It's okay, Tamara. Were the tables turned I'd probably react the same way."

"Kennedy, how are you. Where are you?"

"Right now, I'm parked on a beautiful street with big houses, nice lawns and tall, old trees. It feels safe here."

"Kennedy, honey, you shouldn't be alone. You're obviously traumatized and probably still in shock. It sounds like you need medical attention. Obviously, you need to go to the police. But not by yourself. Is there someone you can call to come be with you while I arrange for you to get on the next flight here from Chicago? Don't worry about Dodie. I won't share what happened, but I'll let her know you're alright and that you'll call her soon. Okay?"

"Thanks, but she's my next call and yes, there's someone to help me."

"I can't believe the story you just told me."

"Yeah, well, it happened to me and I can't believe it, either."

"Thank God you're alive."

Kennedy nodded at the understatement. She was thankful for every breath she took and every second that moved her further away from Jack and what happened. She hadn't realized how much she loved life until it was almost taken away.

"Kennedy, I'm online now and there's a flight that leaves at one-thirty. Can you make it?"

Kennedy glanced in the rearview mirror. She couldn't get on anybody's flight looking the way she did. "No. I need to get cleaned up."

"Okay, look, don't worry about it. I'll handle rescheduling your flight."

"Thanks, Tamara."

"You'll be okay on that trip, right? You think you're able to fly?"

"Trust me, I'm ready. I can't get out of town fast enough."

"What's the earliest I should try and get you on a flight?"

Kennedy checked her watch. "Depending on which airport, Midway or O'Hare, I could try to make something between two and three."

"I'll keep you posted."

"I appreciate you."

She ended the call then phoned a very worried yet composed Dodie, the mark of a true New Yorker—unflappable. Just before tapping the phone icon to call Gwen she changed her mind and called a person she thought she'd never see again.

"Lydia, hi. It's . . . it's Kim."

"Kim?" There was a pause as Kennedy imagined her short-term roommate checking the time. "Shouldn't you be on a plane headed for your friend's house in Grand Cayman?"

"Yes, but something happened and I had to reschedule the flight for tonight. It's actually why I'm calling."

"If you want to come here until time for your flight, that's fine."

"Yes, I would like to come over, now if possible, but I'm hoping you'll be there."

"I will. I'm working the afternoon shift today and won't leave until around two-thirty."

"Okay. Thanks, Lydia. I'm on my way over."

"I'll put on a pot of tea."

Twenty minutes later, Kennedy turned on to the block where Lydia lived, the apartment that had been her temporary home. As she neared where her car had been parked that morning, a wave of fear washed over her. Kennedy slammed on the brakes in the middle of the street and was rewarded with the loud blare of a car she didn't even know was behind her. The horn startled her and dissipated the fear. She told herself that Jack Sutton was not there, over and again as she parked her car and walked the short distance to the apartment. She was uber-aware of every movement, every sound. When she reached Lydia's apartment and knocked on the door, she released a breath she didn't know she'd been holding.

There were shuffling noises. The door opened. Lydia's smile fled as she gasped. "Good God, Kim! What on earth happened to you!"

Lydia's maternal and nursing instincts took over. She pulled Kennedy inside and into a warm embrace as she closed the door and walked them into the living room.

"Never mind. You don't have to talk right now. Let me get you a cup a tea and then tend to those wounds."

It was the best cup of tea Kennedy ever tasted, laced, she

believed, with something stronger than your typical Earl Grey. The warmth from the mug soothed the scratches and deep cuts on her palms. She sat and sipped while Lydia went about her work, quietly, efficiently, pulling items from a large tool box that looked to have everything in it but an operating table. When she reached the most severe wounds she looked and told her, "This is going to hurt, but pain is a part of healing."

Lydia told Kennedy she needed to go to the hospital, that the bruises should be x-rayed and some of the gashes may require stitches. She also believed that once the shock wore off, Kennedy would be in a great deal of pain. Kennedy knew that a hospital visit would result in questions from people with whom she wasn't ready to share. It would probably also lead to authorities being called since she probably looked like she'd been in a serious fight, dragged down the street while tied to a car, or beaten with a tree branch, or all three. Kennedy wasn't ready for an interrogation and told Lydia she'd see a doctor once in Grand Cayman. Only after Lydia had attended to her face did Kennedy finally look in a mirror. What she saw was a woman who indeed looked to be a woman who'd run through the woods to escape an abuser, a variation of the story she told her angel nurse. But she saw someone else . . . a woman stronger than she could have ever imagined, and more blessed than she could have dreamed.

31

Tamara kept her word. Five hours after returning to Chicago, Kennedy once again headed to the airport. Taking no chances, this trip happened via taxi. Her car keys were with Lydia. Kennedy had removed all her personal items from Harriet. The car sat on the street where she'd parked it, waiting for Logan to pick it up with instructions that once she handled the title transfer online, he could do with her what he wanted. Her captor had spent time inside it. Kennedy never wanted to see that car again. She also texted Gwen and instead of Karolyn, her brother Karl. She wanted her best friend and family to know her trip was delayed but that she was alright. But an actual phone call would have meant going into all that had happened, or coming up with something close enough to the truth to suffice. She wasn't ready for that talk yet.

Her plane landed at Owen Roberts International Airport thirty minutes past midnight. Tamara was there to greet her, along with Dr. Roberta Jennings, a friend of a friend whom Tamara had talked into opening her private practice upon Kennedy's arrival so she could be examined right away. They hadn't seen each other in many years but Tamara was just the type of personality Kennedy needed in the moment—compassionate without being emotional, proactive, efficient and connected.

The doctor examined Kennedy's many scrapes, scratches and cuts, then took x-rays to make sure the deep bruising didn't indicate bones that were fractured or broken. All of what Lydia advised had been spot on, including that the pain would increase. Once the thorough examination was over, Dr. Jennings administered a shot for the pain, checked and redressed Lydia's bandages and stitched the deep gashes made during Kennedy's escape.

After finishing the last stitch on the deepest of Kennedy's gashes, she dressed the wound and smiled at her patient.

"Alright, young lady. I think we're all set. You obviously endured quite an ordeal, but the body is the most incredible instrument God ever created. With time the scars will heal and most of them will disappear completely. There will likely be scars from the deeper cuts that we've stitched up today, but also options to lessen their visibility."

"Plastic surgery?"

"That's one option. But there are others, including natural alternatives, oils and lotions that work well over time. We can wait and see what happens, how the body heals, and revisit the matter at a later date. How does that sound?"

Kennedy nodded, the long, eventful day combining with the pain medication to finally bring on the sleep that had lately been so elusive.

"Good. I'm sure you're exhausted so I'm going to give you an antibiotic ointment and write a prescription to help you through the next week or so. If you feel uncomfortable, have questions or need anything at all, please give me a call.

"Also," Dr. Jennings continued while writing on a pad. "I'm going to give you the name of someone who I believe can help with the scars from today that I cannot see. The mental and emotional scars on the inside." She finished writing, tore the sheets off the pad and held them out to Kennedy. "She is a good friend and an excellent therapist. Call her, even if you feel you're doing okay on your own. She can help you."

There was little conversation as Tamara drove Kennedy to her home, no talk of the island or tour of her lovely home once they arrived. Tamara settled Kennedy in the guest room, brought her a light snack, water, juice and a bottle of wine, gave her a heartfelt hug and wished her friend a good night.

Kennedy nibbled a couple crackers with a bit of soup, drank a glass of water, then crashed and slept soundly for the next twelve hours. She woke up in paradise, blinked her eyes and sat up in bed. The vision didn't go away. The "wall" of her guestroom was solid glass that offered a view of the most beautifully manicured lawn she'd ever seen and the turquoise blue sea beyond it. Throwing back the covers, she got out of bed and walked to the window. She kept staring, it felt like such a dream. This time yesterday she was in the clutches of a monster. She was in hell. A tear hovered on her eyelid as she took a breath of gratitude that she wasn't in hell anymore.

There was a tap on the door.

"Come in!"

Tamara stuck her head around the door before opening it fully. "Good morning, Sleeping Beauty."

"The sleep part is appropriate. Beauty is being kind."

"Oh, honey. Come here, give me a hug."

The two women embraced. "I'm so glad you're here," Tamara whispered. "So glad you're safe."

"Me, too."

"Are you hungry? Ryan's out playing golf, so we've got the house to ourselves. I can fix you whatever you want, we can do whatever you want, or nothing at all. I just want you to relax and feel at home. Okay?"

"Sure."

"Folks say I make a killer veggie egg white omelet. How does that sound?"

"You really don't have to go to all of that trouble. I don't have much of an appetite."

"Tell you what. Throw on a robe and I'll start with fresh-squeezed orange juice and throw a little something together. Maybe the smell of good food cooking will help it return."

Fifteen minutes later, Tamara and Kennedy sat at the breakfast nook, drinking tea and orange juice and nibbling on muffins. Tamara typed away on her laptop, giving Kennedy the opportunity to only talk if and when she wanted.

"My God, that asshole."

"What?"

"Oh, never mind. I shouldn't have said anything."

"I know you mean well but don't coddle me. I'm not made of glass. What is it?"

Tamara turned the computer screen around and unmuted the sound.

". . . categorically denying that anything untoward happened on my private island between me and a man on his honeymoon, for God's sake, whom I'd just gifted a cabin to share with his beautiful wife. Have you seen his wife, by the way? The beautiful Charlotte Becker, former Miss Globe, Ivy League graduate, Daughter of the Revolution? Not to mention my own wife, Elena. She's a beauty, too, even more now than when we married over twenty-five years ago. A quarter of a century. No affairs. No breakups. No sleeping around. So, don't believe it folks. Whoever this is, probably somebody from the opposition, taking these desperate actions to photoshop and manipulate a picture, a disgusting picture by the way, that is clearly fake. But you're smarter than they are. You won't buy this piece of garbage. As soon as we find out the lowlife who's behind this, we're going to trash them."

"Turn it off." Kennedy allowed her head to drop in her hands.

"I'm sorry for saying anything."

"No, I'm glad you did. I need to know what's being said. It's just that listening to his voice for more than a minute makes me want to throw up."

"A reaction I completely understand."

"Hmm." Kennedy broke her muffin into bite sized pieces and thoughtfully chewed.

"Hey, let's change the subject. Let's talk about how it feels for you to be a millionaire."

Kennedy gasped.

"She didn't give me specifics, just said that you did very, very well."

A slow smile spread over Kennedy's face. "I did alright."

"Woohoo!" Tamara held up her hands for Kennedy to slap. "Congratulations, woman. Who gives a damn what he says when you've not only exposed him, you just got paid!" She walked into the kitchen. "Let me add some champagne to that orange juice, girl. It's time to celebrate."

"Just a little for me," Kennedy said.

Tamara complied, letting two drops hit Kennedy's glassful of orange juice before offering a toast.

"To the woman who looks like she's been to war and lived to tell about it. You photographed a rainbow and found a pot of gold. Cheers!"

Kennedy sipped, thoughtfully, stopped and took another sip. "Say that again."

"What? Oh, about photographing a rainbow—"

"No, what you said before going to get the champagne."

"What, that you're a millionaire?"

"I think it's just now beginning to sink in. I'll finally have money that actually stays in my savings account?"

"Looks that way."

"Oh my gosh, Tamara. My life has really changed."

"Yes, it has."

"I'm a millionaire!"

"Yes."

"You know what. I think my appetite's coming back. Is that omelet offer still open?"

"Coming right up."

"Tamara, your home is beautiful. I didn't see any of this last night."

"You were a dead man walking when we got home, sister. Go out on the patio. We'll finish the meal out there."

Kennedy stepped outside. She closed her eyes and tilted her head as the warm breeze wafted over her. Thinking of what Tamara said made her soul smile. Kennedy couldn't have said it better herself. She'd beat back a witch, escaped his house, went over the rainbow and found her pot of gold.

32

It took a while, but after forty-eight hours of luxurious living in the jewel that was Grand Cayman island, Kennedy once again felt she lived in her skin. She was ready to face her family. She was ready to talk with Karolyn, share the truth, and answer the myriad questions her mom would likely have for her. There was so much to share. Any nervousness over finally coming clean with all that had happened, or guilt about leaving them out of the loop, was overshadowed by what else she had to tell them. That because of the experience, her mom's financial worries were over. Kennedy planned to be smart with her new-found wealth. She'd heard too many stories of lottery winners and other nouveau riche who won seven, eight, sometimes even nine figures, only to find themselves broke or bankrupt within five years. She'd speak with Ryan, Tamara's husband, and other professionals. She'd do her research. Then she'd assemble the proper financial and legal team to help manage her wealth. All that would come later. There were plenty of landmines in the road—the legal case on Jack Sutton, keeping her identity out of the press. Right now, all she wanted to do was tell her mom that basically . . . they were rich!

She'd spent much of the past two days in the expansive

guest suite. But with Ryan still in New York and Tamara out at a meeting, Kennedy went to the beautiful outdoor living space just off the great room so that she could take in the ocean view and enjoy its breeze while talking to her mom. She poured herself a tall glass of juice, flipped the switch that opened the floor-to-ceiling doors, and walked out on the veranda. For a moment she stood there, her face to the sun, listening to waves crash against the shore, feeling the wind on her face. She sat down and was just about to check her voicemail before calling Karolyn when the phone rang in her hand.

"Mom, hi! You're not going to believe this, but I was just getting ready to call you. I kid you not, I had the phone in my hand!"

"Better late than never I guess."

"I'm sorry, Mom," Kennedy said with a sigh, fully aware she deserved her mom's ire. "I know you've been worried and that I should have kept in better touch. But there was a very good reason why I didn't, why I couldn't, until now."

"Does it have anything to do with the men who showed up on my job with a warrant to search my house?"

"What?"

"You heard me. Two men looking like a slimmed down version of the Blues Brothers came to the hospital flashing badges and asking questions. Had everybody looking at me crazy, like I'd committed a crime. I'm sure by now I'm the talk of the town. It was embarrassing!"

Not even a day of relative peace and now this news. Kennedy picked up the juice and walked into the house. "What did they want? What did they ask you?"

"They told some kind of cockamamie story about me supposedly being in possession of classified information, or some crazy shit like that. I told them the only thing classified in my house were the ads from yesterday's paper. Then they showed me the search warrant and demanded that I either go with them and let them in the house or they would break in and search it without me. We were already short a nurse. Now my check will be short, too. And don't tell me to ask Karl about it. I called him thinking it might be connected to him running for city council. I never felt good about him getting involved in politics. That business is dirtier than throwing cans on a trash truck. Ray wouldn't even know how to piss off the feds. That leaves you and this strange behavior you've exhibited for over a month. So, I'm going to ask you again and this time, you'd better tell me. What is going on?"

"Mom, that's what I was calling to tell you. And even though I'm ninety-nine percent sure this call is being monitored, likely by the Blues Brothers who showed up on your door, I'm going to give you answers. I have nothing to hide. And after staring down the devil, dodging his pitchfork and escaping hell? I'm not afraid of Big Brother or any of his friends."

Kennedy spent the next hour telling Karolyn her story. She began at the beginning, with the Bahamas boat ride and meeting Jack Sutton, being drugged and robbed, first in the Bahamas and again when she returned home. She spoke of being spied on and followed and admitted the truth about her strange behavior at the Fourth of July parade, that it wasn't an old classmate she thought she'd seen, but Jack Sutton, her ongoing nightmare. Finally, she told of the abduction, surprising herself by leaving very little out. Her mom didn't ask many questions, but gasped, sputtered and delivered appropriately outraged, appalled, and shocked responses.

"I couldn't believe when I turned and saw him coming toward me. It felt like watching a horror movie, only I was in it. I pulled on all of that high school track training, Mom, and was ready to die to try and escape him. Then the house blew up."

"No, Kennedy! It actually blew up? You mean to tell me that if you hadn't escaped through the attic you would have been killed? Lord, no, I almost lost my baby. Don't tell me the rest, Ken. I can't take it. I swear my heart can't take anymore."

Kennedy heard Karolyn crying and second-guessed her decision to tell all. Any part of her two-month ordeal was a lot to digest. Getting it all in one hearty, fact-filled meal had probably given her mother heartburn of both the literal and figurative kind.

"The bottom line is that I got out, I got away from him and I'm safe now. But there is one last thing I feel I have to share with you, it's probably the most important detail of all, and the reason for everything that happened that I just shared with you. Did you see the news over the weekend, the picture of the owner of TBC Network?"

"Who didn't see that scandalous mess? It's all over the news, the internet the paper. People at work were shocked, thinking there's no way he could ever do something like that."

"What do you think?"

"I believe the pictures. With everything that man has done all these years, I wouldn't put anything past him."

"Mom, I can understand you sharing what I've told you with Ray, but please let me tell Karl when I'm ready, okay?"

"Okay."

"And what I'm about to say next, please keep this between the two of us for now."

"Okay."

"Do you promise?"

"Yes, Kennedy. What is it? I won't tell a soul."

"I'm the one who took those pictures of TBC's president and his boyfriend. That's why you got a visit from the Blues Brothers and why I've been running for my life."

33

After selecting three guys to join him in Springfield when the time came, Zeke rented a small home in the country near the Kyvas' land and tried to put what happened behind him. Easier said than done, when the media feeding frenzy continued, as did the war between the conservatives and the liberals, the alt-right and the far left, with no end in sight. Early in his military career, Zeke had tucked his opinions behind the oath, determined to suck it up and be a good soldier. But in the last couple weeks, for the first time in life, he'd straddled the political fence, a position brought on by seeing breaking news in a redneck bar that led to ignoring a direct command. Nagging questions had plagued his ride back to rescue Wade. Was his commander-in-chief fucking gay? Or was what they'd shown on television something that happened after too much vodka? Either way, did the depth of their "close" dealings spill over into business, trade and other areas as his detractors suggested? How did America's interest and the common good of her citizens factor into that? Had Van Dijk lied to him, knowing exactly what the photos showed but giving him the line about national security to stir up his patriotism? Finally, what would happen to Wade? He knew the type of people she was going up against. They were the same ones who'd ordered him to kill her, the same ones who'd then shipped him to Middle America to babysit billionaires. These men were ruthless, cutthroat. As calmly as they'd ordered a hit on Wade, they could be planning one for him.

That thought was enough to bring on an attack but there was also the difficult task of keeping his truthful opinions, real feelings, and love/hate relationship in check—loving the values that TBC stood for while hating its owner. Just thinking of that asshole made his blood boil to the point he could kill somebody. He didn't give a fuck that his opinion wasn't politically correct. Van Dijk was a faggot, a sissy, a got damn homosexual. There were troops he knew would serve him up a dose of friendly fire. Back home real men would string him up and show him exactly what they thought about guys like him, would serve him up the dose they administered to back door bandits.

It wasn't how he felt two weeks ago after leaving Wade in the car on a street in Chicago, hauling ass to his Jeep and getting out of town. That day he felt conflicted, as though he may have let down his boss. On that trip, he'd thought a lot about the military men in his family, wondered how they would have handled the assignment, what kind of journey they would have made if they were wearing his shoes. Would they understand, he wondered, or would they call him a traitor? For pissing on the vow he'd made to support and defend the United States constitution, and the men who upheld its laws? Or would they remember other lessons, like those the women in the family taught, especially his mother—that a real man would stand up for justice, even if he stood alone.

He'd felt justified leaving Kennedy alive that Saturday morning. But the longer he'd driven, his car radio tuned to AM radio and conservative pundits defending their man, he'd second-guessed his decision, more than once had almost turned the Jeep around to go kill that bitch. Then Bullet texted him out of the blue. It was the perfect opportunity to get answers, find out if this was why Bullet had responded so strangely the first time around.

WTF with Van Dijk? Bullet texted.

Is that what you saw? Zeke asked.

When?

The pics I sent you.

Hell, no!

Zeke didn't know whether to believe him. But whether he had seen them or not wasn't the most important thing to know.

Zeke texted quickly. **Do me a favor.**

Shoot.

Take another look. See if they're real.

Don't have 'em.

Will send again.

K.

Zeke had to return home to send them since the pictures were on his computer, not on his phone. He walked straight over to the laptop, fired it up, transferred the pictures to his phone and texted them to Bullet.

An hour later, Zeke received back an answer.

Those look real as fuck man, damn!

Are you sure it wasn't photoshopped?

If so, the best I've seen. I'm deleting this shit off my phone.

Zeke's jaw clinched. **Gotta go. But Mr. TBC? Playing in the backyard? Motherfucking faggot.**

Zeke checked his watch. He was scheduled to report to base at seven a.m. He needed to get himself together. Remembering what he wanted to forget had stressed him all the way out. He had to take something just to calm down, keep from giving in to instinct, and training. He'd been trained to kill, and he'd learned well. There were a few people he'd like to take down, namely Van Dijk, who'd deceived him at every turn with this assignment. He was sure assaulting one's boss would not be a good look. Zeke had given his years of service and sacrifice to this country, more than half of his life, and had the utmost respect and loyalty for the flag. Van Dijk was highly respected, almost a father figure, which made betrayal cut all the way to the bone.

Zeke walked into the kitchen, grabbed a beer and tried to calm down. He picked up his phone, scrolled to his father's number. Since on the assignment tracking Wade, he'd been distant. That wasn't unusual. His family was used to long spurts without hearing from him and vice versa. Right now, Zeke could use a talk with his dad. Or grandpa Buck. But he wasn't ready for words with them yet. Mainly because he was considering something for the first time since he was seventeen years old—getting out of the military and protecting others—of giving up the professional gun.

He knocked back the beer and headed to the Jeep. He switched from AM news to FM rock. Just as he pulled through the gates at the base, his phone rang.

"Foster."

"Good morning, Foster, it's Braum."

Zeke gripped the wheel. "Good morning, Mr. Van Dijk."

"I've been meaning to call you. It's been a hell of a circus over here, as you can imagine."

Zeke didn't have to imagine the circus. He'd been in the tent.

"Didn't feel a particular urgency, though. I read a newspaper article concerning an explosion that happened somewhere in Illinois. Gas leak, the paper said, blew the house to bits along with everything in it."

"That is correct, sir."

"Given your track record when it comes to carrying out assignments, I had faith that orders would be followed to the letter."

It felt as though a thousand thoughts flooded Zeke's mind all at once. Was this a test? Had they found Wade? He decided to take a page out of Van Dijk's book—not for national security, but his own.

"Absolutely, sir."

"We want you to know how much we appreciate you and your service to the country. I will pass on your achievement to the president and I wouldn't be surprised if he called to thank you personally. We'll get through this round of lies. Pictures sent anonymously," he spat out the word. "Of course they were. Because they were never taken. No one will ever come forward and say they were the person behind those disgusting, fake, manipulated shots."

Zeke hoped those words were true. If Wade had any sense at all she'd find a low, or even better, a no profile job and quietly fade to black.

"Don't get too comfortable in Springfield," Van Dijk was saying when Zeke began listening again. "You'll only be there for six months or so, just until you train the security team. After that I'll need you back here, in New York, the center of the world."

"Thank you, sir."

"Cassie is coordinating travel arrangements with the Kyvas. She'll let you know when they're set to travel. Should be in the next week or so."

"I appreciate it, sir."

The call ended. Zeke went to work and the world kept on spinning. As the days passed, an interesting thought took hold. Now that it seemed likely he'd move back to New York, he wasn't sure that's where he wanted to be.

34

Just two weeks after escaping death, Kennedy was on the road to truly reclaiming her life. The conversation with her mom was the clue that she hadn't done it yet. Yes, she'd released the photo. Yes, for the moment, she'd escaped Sutton's grasp. Yes, she had money and could pretty much do what she wanted. But the TBC Network seemed to be more popular than ever, a fact that bothered her to no end. So far, the enormous, relentless pro-Van Dijk propaganda machine had successfully refuted the picture's authenticity and drowned out the experts who said the picture was real. She'd moaned to Tamara and Dodie about it and received conflicting opinions.

"You did the right thing in exposing that asshole," Tamara told her that first week in Grand Cayman. "I'm glad the picture paid dividends but is that all you wanted?"

Dodie's advice was simpler, more direct. "Take the money and run, honey."

Along with the TBC president's seeming Teflon image, strange men still hounded the family. The two men who showed up at the mental hospital, most likely the Feds, had made her mom the center of small-town gossip. Karolyn did not like the spotlight. And for all her good fortune, Tamara was right.

Kennedy had still been living on the outskirts of her life. Not living, existing, when she viewed herself honestly, still bearing the residue of KW and Kim. The night after talking with Karolyn, and hours after meeting the therapist Dr. Jennings had recommended, Kennedy had sat in the middle of the gue-stroom's king-sized bed with a journal that the therapist Dr. Bobbi had given her, and following the therapist's instructions had made three lists regarding her life—what she was grateful for, what was working the way she wanted, and what she wanted to change. The third list was the longest by far and the one she'd begun tackling immediately.

In the past two weeks, she'd hired a "green team," an attor-ney, accountant, and financial planner to assist in managing her wealth. With their advice, she'd set up a trust so that trans-actions made through it would be done anonymously, in a way that it would be almost impossible to trace back to her. Through their consultation, Kennedy had discovered that Grand Cayman was one of the world's largest offshore banking centers. There were almost six hundred banks within the tiny island's twenty-two miles, including forty-three of the top fifty world banks. One of the first accounts made after the trust was established was one to transfer monies so her mom could buy a new home. Being able to do this added years to Kennedy's life. It had taken some persuading, but her mom had agreed to put their Peyton residence up for sale and for the first time in her life, consider living someplace other than where she'd grown up. Ray had family in Las Vegas and Karolyn liked slot machines. Plus, by moving there she wouldn't have to spend another win-ter "scraping ice off windows or shoveling snow." She'd agreed to make the payments on her brother's condo and bought him a shiny new truck, but because he was running for office and his finances would be scrutinized, he turned down her offer of more financial help.

"Let me take a rain check," he'd jokingly told her.

That she would share some of her windfall with her brother

was a given, but her first conversation after arriving in Grand Cayman had put the presumption into doubt. She'd decided to share with him what had happened to her, what had accidentally happened in the Bahamas, and why she was on the run. He'd listened, then put a knife in her chest with four curtly delivered words.

"I don't believe you."

He felt badly about her being robbed, but couldn't imagine that Van Dijk was behind it. "Being in another country made you a target," he'd reasoned. "Americans get robbed all the time."

He felt her being followed, hunted, spied on was a product of paranoia and an over-active imagination. Already shaking by this point with his summary dismissal, Kennedy left out the explosive ending to her two-month nightmare. An argument ensued, turned into a scream fest and ended with her abruptly ending the call. Their mother had intervened. Karl called back and apologized. He still doubted the picture's authenticity or his hero's involvement, but he congratulated his sister on "getting paid" for "whatever," and was sorry for the anguish it had obviously cost her. Half-heartedly, Kennedy realized, but the best her brainwashed brother could do.

Kennedy sold her condo and resigned from *Chicago Sightings*. Scott refused to speak with her. Monica was disappointed, but more understanding. Kennedy made a few phone calls and made the exit a little less painful by referring several lucrative advertising contracts their way—one a full-page ad that would run in their December issue. It was a close-up of the rainbow shot in the Bahamas, with the colors manipulated to bring out the reds and greens. She'd photoshopped out the island and replaced it with a blue-green ocean. Over the water was the simple caption: Photographer Kennedy Wade. Her website was listed at the bottom. One step closer to her life.

Both she and Karolyn became debt-free. At her financial planner's suggestion, a "fun money" account was established and a budget to handle major purchases and ongoing expenses. Eventually, she'd purchase a house. She had no idea where "home" would be, but just days ago she'd set up a temporary residence in a two-bed, two-bath condominium right on the beach. Just in time, since two weeks from now Gwen was coming to visit. Kennedy couldn't wait. Their friendship had suffered. She missed her friend. Part of rebuilding her life was restoring relationships. There was so much of what had happened that she hadn't shared with Gwen. That would change with her visit, and hopefully so would Gwen's cool demeanor. Once told of her life the past two months, Kennedy was sure Gwen would understand and forgive all. She'd bought a cute used Kia, a warm weather wardrobe, and top of the line electronic and photography equipment that she put to use on the beautiful island every single day. She'd returned to scouring websites for possible sales. Another step closer . . .

One of the best decisions she'd made in the past two weeks was making the appointment with Bobbi, the therapist Dr. Jennings had recommended. Her outer scars continued to heal, some had already faded. But there were emotional wounds still gaping, oozing anger, and stinging with pain.

Kennedy was on her way to see Bobbi now. It would be her second visit to the office. The first time, she'd been skeptical. Naturally pretty, with kind eyes and a ready smile, Kennedy had thought them around the same age. She'd imagined someone older, maternal, and didn't know how she felt telling her business to someone so young. When she found out Bobbi was closer to fifty than forty, she was shocked. Ten minutes into their first meeting, she was converted. Bobbi was an excellent listener. Her office was more that of a living room setting. That, combined with her relaxed, casual demeanor dispelled assumptions of getting counseling and made you feel like you were sharing confidential secrets with a good and trusted friend.

Bobbi's office was in fact in a condominium complex, where several other businesses were housed. She pulled into a parking space and took the stairs to the second floor, noting the beautiful surroundings and the clean, fresh air. *Is this my life?* Not long ago she'd asked that question and prayed the answer was a resounding no. Today it had a totally different meaning. She opened the door. A melodic series of sounding bells announced her presence. The condo opened into an outer office where last week a receptionist had handed her a series of forms to fill out before meeting Bobbi. She wasn't there now but Kennedy assumed someone had heard her enter and would be out soon. Meanwhile, she took in the tranquil blue walls, the beachy furniture surrounding the glass-top desk, and the big, leafy plants that brought the outdoors inside.

The inner door opened. "Hello, Ken."

"Hi, Bobbi."

"Sorry to keep you waiting. I was on the phone. Come right in."

Kennedy followed Bobbi inside to the main office where Bobbi counseled her clients. It was cozy yet inviting, its walls a warm yellow that contrasted with coral-colored floor tiles. Floral seating consisted of a couch on one side of the room and two matching chairs with a small table between them facing a view of the ocean on the other. Bobbi directed her to that area. The flow of water from an angel fountain on the patio provided a soothing, almost imperceptible energy. Himalayan salt lamps and the subtle smell of lavender completed an atmosphere that had obviously been designed to soothe the soul.

"Would you like something to drink?"

"No, thank you. I'm fine."

Kennedy noticed Bobbi's faint smile as she took the chair directly facing the ocean. Bobbi walked over to a table and retrieved a notebook before taking the other chair.

"Tell me how you're feeling other than fine."

"I guess that was a rote answer." She paused, rubbed her arms as a sudden chill hit her. "I think I stopped feeling because it was all too much. The abject fear followed by anger and sadness. The hurt, so much hurt. And guilt. What will this do to my family? Feeling sorry for myself for what it may have done to me."

Bobbi set down the pad. "Let's talk more about that."

"Before all of this happened the world made sense. I mean, it was crazy, but it was the type of crazy that happened to someone else. Going through what I did changed me. Not only does the world not make sense but now my life doesn't make sense. I don't make sense."

No longer able to sit as these feelings swirled around her, Kennedy stood and alternately paced and gazed out of the window.

"On one hand, I feel that releasing the pictures was the right thing to do. Then, the very next second I can't believe I ever made such a stupid decision. I almost died because of it. Then I get here and look online and there he is, the reason this all happened, looking smug and lying, expertly, with a straight face. He looks directly into the camera and says those pictures are fake."

"And that makes you feel . . ."

"Like I could explode with anger, just like the building from which I escaped. I'm livid at how he manipulates the American people and seems to get away with it time after time. He continues to be popular. He continues to win."

Dr. Bobbi didn't immediately respond. She picked up her pad, jotted down a few words. "How is that anger serving you, Kennedy? Wait, don't answer. Not yet."

She walked over to a cherry armoire and picked up a journal from a stack on the shelf. "I have an exercise I'd like you to try. It's another form of list building."

Kennedy returned to the seating area and took the journal. "Like I did before?"

"Yes, a way to organize the thoughts in our head, to put them in some type of form, some perspective. You write whatever question you want to explore at the top of the page. Then draw a line down the middle. On the left side you write what the benefits or positives are about the feeling, opinion, position, whatever. On the right side, you write the challenges to the aspect, the deficits, what it's costing you. There is no right or wrong. You shouldn't judge yourself or try and analyze the feelings. You simply want to write them down. Looking at them outside of your body can have a profoundly clarifying effect. Would you be willing to try it?"

"I guess."

"Good. Trying is all we can hope for. I have a few questions I'd like you to list build. The first I've asked already. How is your anger regarding Van Dijk serving you and your life? The second is, what are the ways this experience has changed you. And the third, how could what you've done potentially impact America. That obviously matters a lot to you. Explore what your actions could potentially mean to your fellow citizens."

"Wow. That's a lot."

"The enormity will lessen if you break it into tiny pieces, be patient with yourself and take your time. And remember, Kennedy, you're still here. With all the confusion and emotions and pain, through the healing, take a breath, and then another, and remember . . . you're still here."

35

"Gwen!"

Kennedy ignored the other traveler's curious stares as she enthusiastically waved at the best friend coming toward her.

"Ken!" Gwen's smile was wide, as she sashayed to meet Kennedy, wearing a bright red mini, high-wedged sandals and big, round black shades.

They came together with arms outstretched and enjoyed a rock-back-and-forth hug. Gwen stepped back. "You cut your hair!"

"I did."

"And ditched the blonde look. Thank goodness for that," she mumbled right after.

"I heard that."

"Good. Hopefully that'll help you not make that mistake again." She side-stepped Kennedy's playful punch. "I love you!"

"Yeah, whatever. I love you, too."

They reached the yellow Kia. Gwen squealed. "Is this you?"

"Yes. Cute, huh?"

"I never would have guessed this was your car but yes, here in the islands, it fits you somehow. And speaking of, what a beautiful place!"

Kennedy helped Gwen place her luggage in the backseat, then headed for the road to her home that bordered the ocean, underscoring the island's beauty and Gwen's remark.

"Living here must feel like a permanent vacation," Gwen said.

"It does, like living in paradise."

"Do you think you'll stay here?"

"I don't think so. I love it, and the island is really stunning, one of the most beautiful I've visited so far. But it doesn't quite feel like home."

"So, you'll return to Chicago?"

"I don't know what I'll do, still figuring life out. For now, I've rented a condo on the beach, not too far from my friend Tamara, who you'll meet later this week. She and her husband Ryan are taking us out to dinner. You'll love them. They're good people. She's helped me out a lot."

Gwen didn't respond. Kennedy immediately recognized her error. A woman she'd barely mentioned to Gwen knew more about her recent struggles than Gwen did.

Kennedy reached over and squeezed Gwen's hand. "I've missed you, girl. There's so much that I've wanted to share, so much to do on the island. Some of the guys are pretty sexy, too, but I guess you're not much into that."

"Slow down, now."

Kennedy glanced over. "You and Logan aren't together?"

"I guess you can say we're on a break. I went to the studio recently and felt he was being a little too friendly with one of the singers."

"Oh, no. He cheated?"

"He said he didn't, but you know that look a woman gives you when they've touched the dick you thought was yours?" Kennedy nodded. "She gave me that look."

"Ah, man, Gwen. I'm sorry."

"It happens."

"I haven't talked to Logan in a while. He's due a phone call, if for no other reason than to curse him out."

A convertible sports car passed by them. The tanned driver with wraparound shades smiled and waved. Gwen turned to watch him speed down the road. "Don't be too hard on a brother. Sometimes what looks like a bad situation can turn out to be a blessing in disguise."

"Do you think you could live here?" Kennedy asked.

Gwen looked at Kennedy, then beyond to the sea. "Absolutely, I could live here. In a heartbeat."

They reached Kennedy's condo. Gwen loved it immediately and told Kennedy she was crazy to even think about leaving this haven and returning to any city in the United States. After freshening up, Gwen was ready to sightsee. Kennedy gave her a quick tour, ending up on one of the main roads running through town at a place called Snorkel, the newest oceanfront restaurant creating a lot of buzz.

"Table or bar?" Kennedy asked, after Gwen finished gushing over the prime ocean view and the partially glass floor revealing the deep blue water beneath. It was early, around five-thirty, but the establishment seemed to be filling up fast.

"Let's do the bar," Gwen said. "I might meet a lonely stranger and prevent him from drowning in drink."

The bartender was friendly and a wealth of information on the extensive drink menu and the fresh, organic cuisine. While sipping bikini martinis they perused the menu, finally deciding on an appetizer of conch fritters and entrees prepared from the catch of the day. Gwen caught up Kennedy on all things Chicago. Kennedy finally told the whole story to Gwen.

"Ooh, girl, I'm glad you didn't share all that as it happened," Gwen admitted, once Kennedy was done. She placed a sympathetic hand on Kennedy's arm. "I couldn't have handled it."

"I can't believe I did."

"That sounds like the stuff you see in movies. Your life is a movie, girl. Or a book. That's what you should do while you're kicking it on the island."

"Write a book?"

"Why not? You're a writer."

"A copy writer, not a novelist."

"I don't know the difference. I just know that the stuff you told me sounds like something some people would read."

"It's hard enough just list building and trying to write a page a day in my journal."

"When did you start keeping a journal?"

"When I started going to therapy so I wouldn't lose my mind."

Gwen leaned back, a slow smile forming. "How much did you get for the picture?"

Kennedy gave her a look. "That's classified."

"For other people maybe, but not for me. This is Gwen, your best friend, remember?"

"I know and I love you," Kennedy said. "But part of the negotiations was that the amount couldn't be disclosed."

"Damn, the way you're dodging it had to be a lot. A million, maybe?"

"Something like that."

Gwen's mouth dropped. "Why are you holding back on the good news. This calls for celebration! Bartender! Bring us your best bottle of champagne!" A beat later, Gwen leaned over and whispered, "You've got that, right?"

Kennedy burst out laughing. "Yeah, I got it." *Best friends.*

Conversation flowed as smoothly as the libations, changing from one topic to another as the restaurant filled. As the women split a sticky, gooey, decadent dessert, the conversation drifted back to the picture.

"You know what's crazy," Gwen said, shamelessly licking toffee off her fingers. "You went through hell and made a bunch of money off of a picture that most of the country thinks is not even real."

Kennedy reached for her napkin and leaned back in the chair. "I try not to think about it."

"How can you not? Living in paradise is a just reward for your troubles but doesn't it bother you just a little bit that after everything you went through, Van Dijk is still rich and that Becker guy's brother is running for governor of his state. Hell, they're not making lemonade out of that lemon. They're making a lemon cake with lemon frosting served with lemon ice cream."

"Did you say Van Dijk?"

Kennedy leaned forward a bit to see the man sitting beside Gwen who she hadn't noticed until now. Gwen turned as well.

"I'm sorry for eavesdropping," the man said, his slightly glazed eyes and a rosy complexion suggesting that the tumbler he gestured toward them hadn't been his first drink. "But I couldn't help overhearing the name. It's like a stinger, you see. Every time I hear it a bit of a shock goes through me."

"We're in the minority," Gwen said, adjusting her seat to bring the stranger into the conversation. "It's like the picture that came out a few weeks ago didn't even happen."

"Are you surprised? That man has been burying secrets and scandals for years, since he was in his teens. He cut his teeth on bribery and theft. Blackmail and payoffs are how he climbed the corporate ladder. Then there's his father who's basically a white-collar gangster, holding on to political offices for decades, no matter what the cost or who it hurt. The guy learned from the best."

"Do you believe the picture is authentic?" Kennedy asked.

"Hell, yeah, I believe it. I know it's true." The man paused, looked around conspiratorially, and signaled the bartender to bring another round. "I know people," he continued, his voice low and secretive. "Van Dijk and his wife Elena live separate lives. Their marriage was a business arrangement, a power grab to expand the TBC empire. The rumor mill has her with a lover young enough to be her son. Van Dijk is bisexual. He's known the Becker family since he was a kid and slept with the father before dating the son."

"You've got to be kidding?" Gwen asked in a hushed voice.

"Did you see the picture?" the stranger asked.

The bartender delivered their drinks. The trio sipped in silence.

"I know whoever took that picture meant well," the stranger said, finally breaking the silence. "And I understand keeping their identity a secret. But in doing so, they've done Van Dijk a huge favor and helped him in ways they could never know."

"How do you mean?" Kennedy asked, not sure she wanted to hear the answer.

"Without the photographer, TBC's PR machine has no credible pushback. For every expert her handlers tout to the public, there are three that his camp can find to beat back what they said. He's raised questions, caused doubt. If the pictures are real, why hasn't the photographer come forward? Why are they hiding? I heard him bragging on television just last night. 'There is no photographer because there was never a picture.' He has successfully convinced his viewers and much of America that the picture paraded as authentic is fake. Even some who don't care for his network concede the point.

"He and his team will now take that momentum and shift it to all of the other allegations regarding the influence his network has in Washington and the part it plays in shaping politics in other countries." He began counting on his fingers. "The FBI's probe into Van Dijk's involvement in money laundering, appropriating weapons, and helping rogue factions topple elected governments. The questionable business dealings and conflicts of interest. The not-so-subtle moves to have a monopoly on the conservative narrative, both shaping and broadcasting the White House's political position. As horrific as those are there's even something more damning. His successful defense against one of the most scandalous, controversial, egregious pictures ever has given that narcissist super powers. Since that picture was published his base has increased, his popularity has soared, and his detractors are huddled in a corner licking their wounds."

The guy sat back, placed his drink on the bar. "The FCC has blocked his latest moves to merge with two other companies and create a juggernaut across most media platforms. But with this momentum, next time the sale just might go through. At that point, we might as well be like all those other countries who only get government sanctioned news."

"Do you actually believe that could happen?" Gwen asked.

"A man like Van Dijk lives for the type of power he enjoys, and will do whatever it takes to keep that type of control and media dominance in the Van Dijk family. If a man can convince an entire nation that what they're seeing with their own eyes is an illusion, then they'll drink any flavor of Kool-Aid he pours."

The stranger finished his drink and left. Not long afterwards, Gwen and Kennedy left, too. For the week her friend stayed there, Kennedy played the perfect hostess. Snorkeling and boat rides. Swimming with dolphins and shopping for diamonds. An upscale evening at the Ritz Carlton, enjoying fine dining with Tamara and Ryan. Everything great. They laughed, gossiped, flirted, and over-indulged. For Kennedy, everything that happened that week was under the blanket of that conversation with a stranger. A man at a bar who when she'd asked him his name had delivered the familiar line, that he'd have to kill her if he told her.

She tried to let it go, but his words about Van Dijk wouldn't leave her, especially when time spent online proved most of it true. The inner counter argument was that she'd just begun to get her life back. Thing was, taking that picture was a large part of that life. And very few knew about it.

36

Summer slid into fall and the inner turmoil continued. Still, Kennedy continued to restack the building blocks of her life. She sold a set of pictures showcasing Grand Cayman to a travel publication, and another of the smaller islands to *Mother Nature* magazine. As normalcy returned, and after Gwen's whirlwind visit, Kennedy's isolation was magnified. She began to feel lonely. Tamara, Ryan, and appointments with Bobbi made up her entire social circle. With that in mind, she'd sought out and joined a group called Sisters of Spirit, who practiced yoga and meditation, and gathered to listen to musicians playing down at the beach. Karolyn was a week from moving into her new home. Logan and Gwen were back together, and Karl had proposed to Kimora, the girlfriend she'd met the past Fourth. Life was good. Kennedy should have been happy. But she was troubled, a fact clearly evident when she and Bobbi began to chat.

"He was just some guy, some stranger," Kennedy said, after relaying what happened at the bar. It wasn't the first time she'd mentioned the incident to Bobbi. It was the third time, in as many weeks. "Who's to say that if I came forward anything would change?"

"No one can guess the future," Bobbi said quietly, writing notes in her ever-present pad.

"It's not only me," Kennedy continued. "I have to think about my family, my friends, and associates. The minute I put myself out there, then they're out there, too."

For the next forty minutes, Kennedy voiced the thoughts that kept her from sleeping. Half of the time she was ready to call a press conference, the other half she wanted to have the matter disappear. Without giving an opinion, Dr. Bobbi listened, encouraging Kennedy to continue talking through the mental chaos. She let Kennedy know that to do so was healthy, and that whatever answer was right for her mental, emotional, and spiritual well-being was the correct one.

As the session ended, Dr. Bobbi asked her, "Have you continued journaling, list building?"

"I've slacked up on the daily journal writing, but the list building has helped so yes, I've used it quite a bit."

"Consider using it for this dilemma that is causing such angst and unsettlement."

"The benefits to revealing my identify versus remaining silent."

"Do you think that would help you?" Bobbi asked softly.

"I don't know. Even if on paper it's better for me to go public, that may not be the best choice for me in real life."

"Remember, Kennedy. The right decision for you is the correct one."

That night Kennedy sat with her journal by the open patio door. She opened it to two blank pages. One page was titled "The Worst That Could Happen If I Reveal Identity." On the other page, she wrote "The Worst That Could Happen If I Remain Silent."

The next morning, she called Dodie.

After sharing the position her list building had produced, Dodie said one word. "Why?"

"Did you not hear what I just shared with you? Because I have a chance to make a difference. Because my work has been disregarded, even discarded. America, even the world, believes the truth is a lie. That's what this is about. Not about whether or not Van Dijk is gay. Not even about the length and depth of his and Becker's relationship. This is about telling the truth, the whole truth, my truth. The desire to do what's right is now bigger than my fears of what all could go wrong. Do you think you're the person to help me? Or would you prefer to recommend someone else?"

"I admire you," Dodie said. "I understand how you came to the decision you made. But I need you to understand something. As my client, it is my responsibility to make this very clear. Once you go public, we hold a press conference, your picture gets snapped, the Associated Press picks it up and it enters the world, your life will change in ways—good and bad—that you cannot imagine. Scrutiny will be intense. Your life, past and present, will become an open book. You will be ripped apart by the loyal viewers of TBC. Those connected to you will not be immune. There will be supporters but the pushback from his camp will be relentless and ruthless. What you're proposing to do is not for the faint of heart."

Kennedy was silent for a long moment, digesting what Dodie said. "I appreciate your honesty, Dodie. When it comes to Van Dijk and his minions, the threat is real. Were I acting from my head, we wouldn't even be having this conversation. I'm responding from my gut, trying to do the right thing. I love this country and am saddened by its decline. I'm nobody's soldier but this feels like a war. The picture is my only weapon. And the only way that the nation will believe it, is if they see who's pulling the trigger. I may regret some of the fallout from this decision. But I'll never regret the decision."

"Do me a favor?"

"What?"

"Consider getting protection, and I'm not talking about a gun. I'm talking about a guard. A person trained in protecting a life."

A face, clear and strong, came to Kennedy's mind. The thought was crazy enough to make her smile. Impossible. She'd made it her mission to be hard to find and had no idea how he could be located.

"I actually think that's a good idea, but don't know where to start."

"I can help you. So, you'll do it?"

"Sure. It will help my courage to have protection around."

"Alright, I'm all in. When do you want this to happen?"

"As soon as possible, Dodie. Before I lose my nerve."

Kennedy spent the next week in New York, prepping for battle. After meeting with several attorneys, she hired a legal team to help navigate the new minefield of being a public figure and to create the preventative language that would minimize the possibility for a legitimate lawsuit. They knew Van Dijk's camp would be recording and dissecting every word of the press release. The team was led by Dante Ross, a thirty-three-year-old wunderkind who had Johnny Cochran's confidence, Obama's education and intelligence, Kofie Siriboe's good looks and the Black Panther's swagger. He was also single, which was slightly problematic. Of course, she was attracted to him. In order to not be she'd have to be dead. But the task before them was enormous. A lot was at stake. "Catching feelings" during the process was simply not wise. These attorneys, led by Dante, along with Dodie, the speech writer and herself, spent the better part of three days on a five-minute release. A makeup artist, hair stylist, fashion stylist, and personal assistant rounded out the group who prepared Kennedy for her entrance.

The night before the scheduled press conference, Kennedy made three calls. Tamara told her that she'd be praying, that she loved her, and was so very proud. Ryan's message through Tamara was to "kick major ass" and that when she returned to Grand Cayman, he had good investment news to share. Gwen's response was more measured, clearly concerned for her friend.

"I probably would have sailed my rich behind happily in the sunset," she admitted. "But you know, I grew up on the South Side. If you need me for a beatdown, I've got your back."

The third call was to her mom. It didn't go quite as planned. When she told Karolyn she had news regarding Van Dijk and the picture, her mother had cut her off cold.

"Why do you insist on staying involved in that mess? Look, anything having to do with the TBC, the government, or anything that might send folk to my house, I don't want to know about it."

"But, Mom, wait. You need to—"

"I don't need to do anything but pay taxes and die. I mean it Kennedy Lynn. I don't want any part of you messing with that man. You know he's crazy, and it's rumored that his father had folk killed. God has blessed you, girl, given you the chance to have a good life, an amazing life. Mind your business. Live *your* life. And leave that man alone."

Her mom's words were sobering. They gave Kennedy pause. The next morning, she met Dodie at her stunning Manhattan office on the eighty-fifth floor of One World Trade Center. A sophisticated blend of stainless steel, leather, hardwood and glass, the rooms screamed success. Just entering the office increased Kennedy's confidence.

Dodie approached her with a steaming cup.

"Oh, no thank you," Kennedy said. "My stomach is roiling. I don't think I can get anything down."

"Even more reason for you to drink this." Dodie held out the porcelain cup. Kennedy took it. "It's a special blend I get from my OMD."

"That's a doctor?"

Dodie nodded. "Oriental medicine. It's got ginger and some types of roots. It's sweetened with a fruit that I can't pronounce. It soothes like a drug, but it's all natural."

"Thank you."

Kennedy took the cup and walked over to the windows that let in downtown Manhattan, New Jersey and the Atlantic Ocean.

"Here's the press release," Dodie said, walking over with a single sheet of paper.

Kennedy shook her head. "Is it the same one you sent over yesterday?"

"Yes."

"Then why do I need to read it again?"

"To let the reality of the moment wash over your soul. This release will be faxed to over one-hundred news outlets. Once I press send, there is no going back."

Kennedy took the picture. She sipped and scanned the words that were almost memorized, her mother's words running beneath them like the bass line to a song.

For immediate release.

Why do you insist on staying involved in this mess?

For months, there has been speculation as to the authenticity of a photograph. Understandably, a tsunami of speculation and accusations ensued. At the crux of the debate was the photographer's identity or the question of whether there had been a photographer at all. This because the photographer who released the pictures to the *National Query* chose to remain anonymous both for her privacy and for her safety.

You know he's crazy, and it's rumored that his father had folk killed.

Because of that decision, it is believed by a majority of the media and much of the nation that the photograph presented in the magazine was indeed fake, that the picture was created on the computer and there was no photographer. The photograph is real and untouched and the photographer has decided to come forth to defend the images shot some months ago.

Mind your business . . . leave that man alone.

Kennedy finished reading the release and handed it to Dodie. "You've done an excellent job on this, Dodie," she calmly said. "Press send."

37

For the press conference, Dodie had reserved a portion of an event space on the thirty-ninth floor of One World Trade. Attention had been given to every detail: the room's size, lighting, configuration. Furnishings were purposely minimal. The media would stand. A riser where Kennedy would read the meticulously-crafted statement had been erected at the front of the room. It was covered with a deep blue fabric and bare except for a podium fitted with a microphone. Behind the rafter was the room's only decoration—three photographs measuring six by four feet hanging from wires connected to the ceiling. The middle photograph was the one featured in the *Chicago Star*, a beautiful rainbow with an island below. On either side of that picture were ones of Van Dijk and Becker that changed Kennedy's life, each man clearly visible, clearly naked and clearly engaged in a sexual act.

The press conference was scheduled for nine in the morning. The team waited in Dodie's office. At 8:35, word was sent up that the room was completely packed. At 8:58, a focus group of twelve men and women went from Dodie's office to the rented space in another part of the building and more than forty floors down. Dodie, Kennedy, and a media consultant made up the female contingent. Dante and his team of attorneys, a press recorder and four men on security detail, rounded out the group. Anyone watching them cross the plaza could have mistaken Kennedy for a celebrity heading to a business meeting or high-level corporate executive surrounded by an entourage. She wore a tailored navy suit with a wine-colored shell and simple gold jewelry. Her makeup was natural, the short pixie cut, flawless. There was peace in her heart and strength in her stride. Until a figure walking in her direction caused her to falter. Even from a distance, his walk suggested authority and confidence and though partly covered by dark glasses, his was a face she recognized.

Kennedy didn't realize she'd stopped until Dodie addressed her.

"Kennedy, are you okay?"

A security guard moved next to her, while another blocked the path. "Do you know that man?"

"Yes."

"Friend or foe?" the head guy questioned.

Yes. Kennedy watched Zeke remove his shades and hold up his hands in a gesture of surrender. He spoke to the guard on the sidewalk, whose gestures suggested Zeke was getting nowhere fast.

"It's okay," Kennedy called out.

"Who is that?" Dodie demanded. "We can't do this now, Kennedy. We've got a whole room waiting."

"This will only take a second." Kennedy walked to where Zeke stood. The guard gave them a modicum of privacy by taking two steps back.

"What are you doing here?" Kennedy whispered.

"I heard about your press conference and thought I'd come and offer my services." He looked beyond her at the four men staring him down. "Looks as though you could use me."

"I think we've got that covered."

"Oh, yeah? Good thing I wasn't still on a mission. From the time you went to her office," he gestured toward Dodie, "until I met you here, there were half a dozen times you were exposed."

"What? How . . ."

"We'll talk about it later."

"Kennedy, we really need to go." Kennedy heard Dodie and knew she was right. She turned to rejoin her.

"Ken." Zeke reached for her arm and drew stern looks from her guards. He held out a business card. "I'm serious about looking for work."

She took the card, trying to read the message in his eyes.

"Okay. I'll call you."

"One more thing."

"Kennedy!"

She was drawn to the eyes and the smile of the guy she'd met on the island, the guy named Jack. "What?"

"I'm proud of you."

The security team surrounded her, blocked out Zeke, and led her through a side door. They entered the room from the back of the riser, mounted the three short steps and walked to the front. The buzz in the room quieted. Flashes went off from every angle in the room. Kennedy stood at the podium, her speech on a tablet. Dodie flanked her on the right side, Dante was to her left. Both Dodie and Dante had offered to introduce her, but she had declined it. This moment had been a long time coming. She'd introduce herself. With hands steadied on each side of the podium, she looked out at the crowd, took a deep breath and addressed the room.

"Good morning. My name is Kennedy Wade. I am a professional photographer with an undergraduate degree in photography and a minor in copy writing, and an MFA in Visual Arts from the University of Chicago. My areas of emphasis were photography and new media. I have worked as a photographer in a professional capacity since graduating eight years ago. In those eight years, I've had full-time employment and I've also worked as a freelance photographer, writing articles, and taking photographs for websites, newspapers and magazines. This year, during the third week of May, I was on assignment in the Bahamas for a major Illinois newspaper, the *Chicago Star*. For two days, I shot in and around the city of Nassau, and several other nearby islands. That Friday, on what was supposed to be my last day in the Bahamas, I wanted to be on the water, and hired a private tour boat for a casual sail. The captain, a native Bahamian, was very knowledgeable about his country and kept up a running dialogue as I snapped pictures for fun. Shortly before going out on the boat, there'd been a spring shower and as we rounded what the captain described as a private island, a beautiful rainbow appeared."

Kennedy motioned to the picture behind her. "It was stunning, even to the natural eye. I easily took thirty or forty shots of that scene alone—varying angles, focus, and using different lenses. I finished the boat ride, went back to my hotel and prepared to go home. Before doing so, I took the concierge's suggestion to eat at a restaurant not far away. While I was there, a stranger approached. He was alone, too, and introduced himself as Jack."

At that moment, something made her look up. There was Jack, real name Zeke, standing at the back of the room, offering a subtle nod of encouragement.

"We chatted, and it turned out that we were staying at the same hotel, or so he told me. After dinner, we returned there, and at his suggestion had an after-dinner drink. Mine was nonalcoholic, a decaf latte, one cup. I had an early flight the following morning so as soon as I was finished, I got up to retire for the night. He got up also and we both got on the elevator to go to our rooms. I began to feel funny, woozy. The next thing I knew, I was waking up, the sun was bright in the sky. I was completely naked, and all of my electronic equipment was gone.

"I filed a report with the hotel and the police. They checked their records. No one matched who this man said he was. I chalked it up to meeting a jerk who robbed unsuspecting travelers. And that would have been the end of it had I not been burglarized again, two weeks later, after the photos appeared in the *Chicago Star*. But I had still not connected the burglaries to the pictures I'd taken. It wasn't until I received a suspicious-sounding call from someone representing themselves as part of the Bahamas Tourism Department. This person was very interested in the pictures I'd taken during that visit, specifically those of the private island and the rainbow behind it. I was offered an unusually high amount of money to sell all the pictures that I'd taken, with the understanding that I would also sign a release giving this company exclusive rights to what had been shot. It was only then that I became truly curious as to why those photos were so important and began examining them closely to see if there was something in them that I had missed."

She paused, looked behind her, and said, "There was."

The room came alive with titters and murmurs. Flashes went off everywhere.

"It became my opinion that whoever had me drugged and burglarized not once but twice, and subsequently followed, harassed, threatened, and basically upended my life, knew these pictures existed." Kennedy pointed to the picture. "That appears to be, it is, allegedly, Braum Van Dijk. The other man appears to be, allegedly, Edward Becker, heir to the Becker pharmaceutical fortune and alleged member of the secret society, MAK. One can make their own decision about what is transpiring in the shot. I concluded that whatever it was, it seemed to be something the American public should know about.

"I consider myself an artist, one who doesn't get into the conservative/liberal fight. I rarely watch news, but will admit when I do, it's not TBC."

That admission drew laughs and comments. Their reaction helped to relax her.

"But the viewpoints promoted on Braum Van Dijk's network are not why I released the pictures and it is not why I stand before you today. I released the pictures because of the pain and suffering that was caused by my simply having them in my possession. I believed that releasing them was a safeguard to my very life. That with their release, all of the ways that my life was being invaded, and the lives of those around me, would stop. It hasn't. I am still being followed. My homes have been bugged with video and possibly audio equipment. Friends have had their homes burglarized. A GPS was put on my car. Most of this happened before I even knew what I had accidentally captured on camera. So, I had to ask myself a question. Who is behind all of this, and what are they working so hard to hide? Is it that this network owner with a large conservative, evangelical viewership was allegedly engaging in homosexual sex, and since he's married, adultery? Is it the fact that he was meeting a man married just hours before on the private island set for their honeymoon? Who has the power and the resources to do all that was done to me? A man as rich and powerful as Braum Van Dijk, with influential connections and a network encompassing government, law enforcement, and corporate America, has almost unlimited power. He has access to almost every industry in the world. I'm not saying Mr. Van Dijk was behind what I endured. I am saying that someone who seems to have a great stake in preventing these pictures from being released, is behind it.

"These pictures were not doctored. They were not photoshopped. They were enlarged and the blurriness was corrected. I took those pictures. They are not fake. I am not fake.

I am a photographer who captured a set of pictures that someone needs to explain."

Kennedy stepped back. The room erupted. Dante limited
the questions. Dodie wrapped up the interview. From the time
the press conference ended, Kennedy entered a whirlwind.
Requests for interviews came from news outlets and talk shows,
national and international, radio, podcasts, internet TV. News
magazines called with offers to pay for her story. For someone
who spent many hours alone taking pictures, the constant barrage of attention was almost too much. More than once, she
second-guessed her actions, whether she had done the right
thing. Then she'd see Van Dijk on television and know the answer.

38

Since seeing Kennedy and attending her press conference, Zeke hadn't been able to think about much else. Considering what happened twenty-four hours before that, he was still trying to figure out what possessed him to go in the first place.

The fireworks started with a phone call just as he'd pulled into a drive-thru to grab dinner. It was the network calling, but it wasn't Van Dijk. To Zeke's surprise, it was his long-time secretary, Cassie.

"I don't know what you did to piss him off," she said, her voice low and unfriendly. "But my boss wants you on the next thing smoking, and for me to have a car that will pick you up when you arrive at the airport and bring you straight to the office."

Orders like this could only mean one thing. Van Dijk had found out about Kennedy. Cassie told him she'd send a text with the information as soon as his flight was confirmed. He'd lost his appetite, but went ahead and ordered a burger and fries. The ground round was juicy and the fries were fresh. Might as well have been sandpaper. He didn't taste a thing. All he could take in was that he'd failed an assignment and was being called in for a job not done. For the first time in his life, he'd overridden command with conscience. It felt good as he'd rescued Kennedy from the abandoned house. Not so much right now.

He thought he'd at least have a night to sleep on what was probably a termination meeting. Instead, his text indicator sounded before the ice melted in his soda. The next thing smoking was leaving from Branson, Missouri, in less than two hours, a cargo plane owned by one of Van Dijk's rich friends. Zeke had hustled back to his house with just enough time to stuff clothes in a carry-on and catch the Uber Cassie had ordered. Later, he would barely recall the flight over and the ride from JFK to the TBC offices.

On the other hand, he couldn't forget what happened once he arrived at Van Dijk's office. People barely speaking, if at all. Cassie not meeting his eyes. Van Dijk, when Zeke was finally called into his office, looking out the window and beginning the conversation without turning around.

"Do you know why you're here?"

"I have an idea."

"You told me you killed her."

"Not exactly."

Van Dijk slowly turned around. "Are you calling me a liar? Because you're the only one in this room wearing that title!"

Zeke ground his teeth with the effort it took to remain quiet. This man thought his homo tryst was a threat to national security. The boss did not want to get him started.

"What happened?"

"I saw the news." With that simple statement of truth, something shifted. Zeke's direction became clear. He was not afraid. "I saw the pictures that had been leaked to the *National Query* and no longer wanted that woman's blood on my hands."

"Oh, it became your decision, did it?"

"I did what I could live with, Mr. Van Dijk. In the end, it's worked out okay. You've worked your magic and convinced the viewers that the pictures are fake, the story an attempt to assassinate your character. Wade's not dead, but she might as well be, since she won't face the public."

"The bitch has scheduled a got damn press conference!"

Zeke couldn't hide his surprise. "I can't imagine that being a good thing, sir. For her, I mean. There are a lot of people very upset about what was published in the Query. What she faces now might be worse than being in a gas explosion."

"You bet your ass it will, and you along with her. I don't like being crossed, Foster, and I can't stand traitors." Van Dijk picked up an envelope. "Come get your walking papers. Your last check will be deposited into your account."

There was plenty Zeke wanted to say, but none of it would change the outcome. Given it to do all over again, there was nothing he'd change, either. He walked over to take the envelope from Van Dijk's outstretched hand.

At this last second, it was pulled back. "You might want to pull out your military uniform, because this is your last security job if I have my way."

Right then was when Zeke decided to find out where Wade was having the press conference. He wanted to be there to hear firsthand what she had to say. He'd arrived early the next morning to the One World Trade Center, wanting to case the perimeter and find out where the conference would be held. It was luck that he'd seen Kennedy arrive at the adjacent offices. He followed her inside, watched the elevator she got on, then went to the directory and scanned the floors it had stopped on, and correctly guessed her destination was the fixer Dodie Ravinsky. He'd anticipated Wade would give a good speech. She was calm under pressure, a quick thinker, even in life-threatening situations. What he hadn't been prepared for was how he felt when he saw her, walking toward the building surrounded by security. Her shoulders were squared and her walk was steady. Facing a David versus Goliath scenario, she showed no fear. Whether in combat or in the streets, soldier or civilian, Zeke could appreciate that kind of moxie. Wade was totally badass.

He hadn't planned to approach her and hadn't seriously thought about working security as he gave her his card. But as the reality of his termination set in, Zeke hoped that Wade was hiring, and would give him a call.

39

Dodie was right. Kennedy's life changed in ways she could not have imagined. Perhaps in ways Dodie hadn't seen coming either. Both had been prepared for a reaction from the White House. Dodie warned her that Van Dijk's viewers would explode. Kennedy thought she was ready for the pushback, which was immediate. The day after their press conference at One World Trade, the White House press secretary held a press conference specifically to denounce most of what was said in Kennedy's statement. A standard rebuttal. What took it to another level was Van Dijk taking to the airwaves to say she was "lower than a cockroach" and a "lying bitch." Her statement and his comments blew up the airwaves. Sides were taken. Gauntlets were thrown. Kennedy immediately shut down all social media after receiving several death threats, being cursed out post by post and seeing hundreds of retributive comments against her that her team believed to be bots from who knew where. Becker's attorneys continued to state a case for felonious libel and called for her arrest. Beyond prepared statements, neither the heir nor his family had spoken out. Concerned for her safety and at the advice of the team, she retreated to her condo in Grand Cayman, and called Zeke.

He answered and she recognized his voice, but she kept it professional. "May I speak to Zeke Foster?"

"Speaking."

"Or should I ask for Jack Sutton?"

"He's here, too. Hello, Kennedy."

"I can't believe I actually called you."

"I can. Half of America is after your ass. You need all the protection you can get."

"You're right about that. Some of them want to hear everything I've got to say, and other others want to shut me up forever."

"How are you holding up?"

"I'm okay."

"Where are you?"

"Someplace safe."

"Good."

Kennedy paused, feeling all sorts of emotions and a little insane. She said as much to Zeke.

"You know this is crazy, right? Me calling the robber, abductor, and man sent to kill me to consider hiring him to now guard my life."

"It's a script that Hollywood couldn't have written."

"I shouldn't feel this comfortable talking to you. I'm kinda pissed that I'm not still angry, still not running straight to an attorney to have you put under a jail. That day when you left me in that wired car that could have blown up if the bomb malfunctioned—"

"There were no explosives."

"What?"

"That car wasn't wired. But I was fairly certain you'd believe it was, considering what we'd been through."

"Motherfucker."

"At your service, ma'am."

They laughed at that, but when Zeke spoke again, Kennedy heard a shift in his mood.

"I don't think there are adequate words to tell you how sorry I am for what I put you through. I've never allowed myself to consider another's emotions. One can't do that and be a good soldier. Emotions get in the way of doing a good job. They can also get you fired."

"So, you were working for Van Dijk."

"Yes, as his personal security and enforcer every now and then."

"Why'd he let you go?"

"Because I didn't kill you."

"Damn."

"You asked. As I said, even though this is a civilian job, I still think like a soldier. It's the first time I blatantly disobeyed a command."

"Well, in that case, thank you for your service. Especially that day. Are you seriously looking for a job in security? If so, I need a personal guard."

Kennedy flew Zeke down to Grand Cayman, and less than a week later he was attached like an appendage as she participated in more than sixty national and international radio and television shows. Interest in her and her story was wide and relentless. Released anonymously, the pictures of Van Dijk and Becker were easily dismissed. Now, their possible authenticity was back in play and everyone wanted to speak with the woman who admitted to having taken them. When Zeke felt Kennedy was being watched and followed, and it appeared that her Grand Cayman location had been compromised, they relocated to the exclusive Miami, Florida community of Fisher Island, where one of Ryan's stockbroker buddies owned a home. That's what they told Kennedy. When she arrived, she realized that was much too humble of a word to describe the gargantuan estate she found herself hiding in. Until arriving at the mansion, Tamara's home was by far the most opulent she'd ever resided in. The Fisher Island home felt more like a hotel. The team met her there and took advantage of the seventy-five hundred square feet of space, with its six bedrooms, seven baths, and uninterrupted ocean views from its almost three-thousand-foot terrace, and used it as the base of operation during the four weeks she spent there. Dante was a constant presence, interpreting law and helping her traverse the snarky waters entered when speaking of others, defining "one's opinion" and "allegations" and what exactly constituted "free speech." Before issuing the statement, Kennedy hadn't given much thought to the legality of words. But from the time they'd crafted the speech for the press conference, "alleged," "allegedly" and "I am of the opinion" took on new meanings. Kennedy stopped speaking publicly, with Dante issuing statements on her behalf.

"We stand behind what was said during Ms. Wade's press conference," he calmly stated over and again during the almost daily, sometimes hourly, requests for comments, rebuttals and reactions to whatever asinine statement either Van Dijk, the network publicist or his attorneys had said. "One can huff and puff, but our house will not be blown down. We have the law and the truth on our side."

"But isn't your client worried?" one reporter asked him. "These accusations—"

"Allegations."

"—have been made against some pretty powerful people."

"These allegations are what Ms. Wade recalls to the best of her knowledge, and there is proof to back up her claims. All the incidents that occurred were unfortunate and some were criminal in nature. But they happened, and Ms. Wade has a right to tell her story."

"Even if it means being sued or going to prison?"

"People are wrongfully sued every day in America. As for being incarcerated, those are empty threats made by those whose intention is to scare us. I don't frighten easily. Neither does Ms. Wade. We choose not to respond directly to anything being thrown at us from the other side. We're focused on fact, not fanaticism, and are saving our words for court."

Still, the public outcry and media barrage continued. Two of Dodie's partners joined in handling the massive amount of interview requests, along with full-time assistants, stylists, a makeup artist, and a full-time chef. Additional legal staff documented every threatening post made online. Private investigators and technology experts worked to reveal the IP addresses and identities behind death threats and heinously racist hate speech. It reached the point where Dante tapped his connections and resources, and quietly brought in law enforcement sympathetic to Kennedy's plight to help keep her safe.

In mid-November, the focus changed for the personnel gathered in Fisher Island. After a very public sparring between Dante Ross and members of her legal team with Van Dijk's army of attorneys and the Department of Homeland Security, Kennedy was subpoenaed to answer questions under oath regarding the photographs, her comments regarding the incidents that allegedly occurred as a result of said photographs, and the "felonious, damning and egregious" actions that Kennedy had alleged were at the hands of either the military mogul or the connections of the influential Becker clan.

It seemed, in those minutes after the subpoena was received, that Van Dijk ratcheted up the pressure, and subsequently her fear, and that even with her attorney's directions, she had completely stepped over a judicial line for which she could be fined, sued, imprisoned, or all of the above. Drama reached a new level when Van Dijk's close friend, President Dennis Trout, joined the fray. Often called the bully of cyberworld, he used a variety of platforms to send a flurry of messages.

The liberal media scum is at it again! Blaming Good Americans and our Allies for their misfortune. She will pay.

Seconds later, he underscored the consequence. *SHE. WILL. PAY!!!*

Over the next twenty-four hours, Van Dijk's online rant continued, courtesy of President Dennis Trout. The team was convinced that either he had someone else posting for him or the man got no sleep.

Kennedy Wade is a pitiful liar. Somebody ought to teach her a lesson.

I heard that Kennedy Wade is a gay lesbian. Maybe her lover is a flag-burning gang member.

Since Kennedy Wade has such disregard for America, maybe she should leave.

Our country is infested with roaches. Where is the bug spray?

Kennedy Wade will be prosecuted to the full extent of the law.

And then, seconds later—*To the FULL EXTENT OF THE LAW!!!*

If you are a God-fearing, flag-waving, proud American citizen, you should be appalled at this poor excuse of a woman's behavior.

She'll be found guilty. She'll go to jail. FOR LIFE!!!

Forty-eight hours into this new normal, Kennedy was on the verge of a breakdown. Medical experts who were compassionate and discreet ran a battery of tests and conducted evaluations. Dr. Bobbi was called for assistance, and phone counseling. Gwen took off work to bring the familiar into her circle. Kennedy had no appetite. Her weight plummeted. The high level of stress brought on insomnia and heart palpitations. Medication was prescribed.

During one outburst Kennedy neared the point of hysteria and threatened to fire everyone, especially Dodie and Dante.

"This wasn't supposed to happen!" she said to the high-powered attorney, after bursting into a meeting he was having with his partners, security, and Dodie. "You read the speech and gave me your word that I couldn't be sued. I asked you, over and over, if it was okay. I told you I didn't want to publicly speak about everything that happened. You're the one who convinced me to put it out there, saying that the more people knew the less likely I'd be further targeted. Ha! What a bunch of bullshit that was! I have a bullseye on my back as big as this fucking house!"

"Calm down, Kenne—"

Within seconds a stiff finger was in Dodie's face. "Don't you dare tell me to calm down. You with all of your high-profile connections and ins to everywhere. What's happening to me right now is your fault!"

She addressed the room. "It's all of your fault! If I hadn't listened to how knowledgeable you were and how I shouldn't worry because you were so professional and because you knew what you were doing. Really? Then why aren't you being posted about, huh? Why aren't you getting death threats? Since you've so got my back, will you take my bullet? I'm sick of looking at all of you. I mean it. Get the hell out!"

Dr. Bobbi flew in and stayed three days. Kennedy was asked if she wanted her family (or anyone else who could make her feel better) to join them on Fisher Island. It sounded like a good idea. Kennedy decided to call once her mom's shift was over. She went into a master suite the size of her Grand Cayman condo, closed the door and walked out to the private balcony that took in the calming sea.

"Hey, Mom."

"Hi."

The dry greeting had Kennedy second-guessing her decision to call. But it was late and Karolyn had just finished working. She tried not to take it personally.

"Where are you?" Karolyn asked.

"Florida."

Even though she'd called her mom on one of the temporary phones she'd shipped her, Kennedy still didn't feel comfortable saying more. She was dealing with a government who could tap conversations in caves, who could decode smoke signals and catch a pigeon midflight.

"You don't sound so good."

"I've felt better," Kennedy admitted. "I'm sure you've seen what's been said in the news."

"Who hasn't seen it? You're the talk of the town. Why'd you do it, Kennedy, put yourself out there like that?"

Kennedy felt her blood pressure rising. She consciously slowed down her breathing, as Dr. Bobbi had advised for moments like this.

"Lately, I've asked that question myself. But at the time the decision was made, I felt I had no choice. He was straight out lying about the pictures, Mom, and using them to further his sick, self-centered agenda. By staying quiet I was indirectly helping him. I couldn't do that. I felt it was my responsibility, my duty to speak out."

"Yes, but at what price?"

"You know what, Mom. I'd better go. I'm already stressed, and this phone call isn't helping."

"I'm just scared for you, baby. Those are some of the most powerful people in the country you're dealing with, even beyond this country, in the world. There are rumors swirling that Russia is after you, that Petrov dude. He's working with Trout to try and put you in jail. I don't want anything bad to happen to you, Kennedy. But I feel helpless to stop it."

"I can understand your feelings, Mom. I'm worried and scared, too. But I've looked death in the face before and figured out a way to cheat it. If I spent every waking moment worrying about dying, there'd be no time left to live. Besides, if something went down now the whole world would think that van Dijk was behind it."

"There's worse things than dying."

The comment gave her pause, as Trout's threats rushed to mind. She'd chosen not to tell her family about the subpoena, or about the numerous threats she'd received. But her mom seemed to have that mother's wit, already imagining Kennedy being imprisoned, or tortured, or ruined financially. Any number of bad things could happen.

"I'd rather not think about them," she finally said.

"You should think about them, Kennedy. You should have thought about it before going public. And not just about you. You should have thought about how your actions would affect the rest of us. I can't go anywhere without being stared at as though I've done something wrong."

"I'm sorry, Mom."

"Are you, Kennedy? Are you sorry for all this trouble you've caused?"

"Karolyn . . ."

Kennedy heard the deep sound of her stepfather's voice before the voices were muffled by a hand being placed over the phone's microphone.

"Mom, what is it? What's going on?"

Another few seconds went by. When she could hear clearly again it was Ray, not Karolyn, on the phone.

"Ken, it's Ray. Don't let your mama get to you. She's worried and has been under a lot of stress. The media has been camped out on the block so long they should pay taxes. Neighbors are mad, sick of the streets being clogged up and their privacy being violated." He stopped, sighed. "Then there's the job."

"I thought she'd put in her notice?"

"She did, but you know they're always shorthanded. She'd agreed to continue working until the closing finalized, which should be in a week or two."

"Does she work with a bunch of TBC supporters?"

"It's more than a few. Unfortunately, one of them is her supervisor."

"Put her on," Kennedy demanded. "I'll cover you guy's expenses until you get moved and she finds a job in Vegas. She doesn't have to put up with any of their crap."

"She's in the bathroom, but I'll tell her what you said. Don't worry about us, though. You've got enough on your plate."

It was decided that in Kennedy's best interest, Karolyn would not come to Fisher Island.

Two days before Thanksgiving, Kennedy, along with Zeke, Dante and two other attorneys, and one man from the press conference security detail, entered a nondescript building not far from the U. S. District Court in New York City. They were there for the deposition, for Kennedy to repeat under oath what she'd claimed during her press conference speech. She was calmer than two weeks ago when she'd had the conversation, and when she'd blown up at her team, learned Karolyn's troubling news and spiraled to the point of almost being out of control. Dr. Bobbi had returned to Grand Cayman, but continued her counseling by phone. What had really helped were her suggestions just before leaving. For the past ten days, Kennedy spent at least forty-five minutes with a personal trainer and another two hours working with holistic practitioners involved in yoga, meditation, energy healing, and a weird looking practice called tapping or EFT. Zeke often joined her for the workouts. His presence made a difference, too. Together, it seemed to work. Just before entering the office where her testimony would be given Dante had placed his hands on her shoulders, looked her squarely in the eyes and said, "Be fearless. You've got this. Just tell the truth."

The cross-examination was brutal, but Kennedy got through it, even though the prosecution felt assured of a win. Their cockiness shattered her confidence. Dante assured her they were bluffing, that it was one thing to say what they'd be able to do and another to actually do it. He reminded her of the proof they had to back up her claims. The police reports taken in the Bahamas and Chicago. The naked photos sent to Lydia's condo that Kennedy had saved. The pictures of Kennedy's injuries that Lydia had wisely taken before beginning to treat them. The testimonies of friends and family on the Kennedy they'd known before her trip to the Bahamas and the very different one that returned. Yes, they had all of this, but was it enough? On its face, none of this could be tied to Braum Van Dijk. Would the word alleged really hold up against strongly delivered claims of libel, trespassing, and a few other charges? Could "in my opinion" keep her out of federal prison?

Kennedy was quiet as they walked out of the building, so deep in thought she forgot that Zeke was beside her.

"This doesn't have to be as hard as you're making it," he said.

"What do you mean?"

"You've got firepower in your arsenal that you're not using." She continued her blank stare. "Me, Kennedy. The only other person besides you who was there from the beginning. I know Van Dijk is lying and that what you've been saying is true. I know it. You know it. The world needs to know it. This is a way I can make up for all the pain I caused. I mean it, Kennedy. If you need me, I'll testify."

Against everyone's orders, Kennedy went home for Thanksgiving. A visit home to see her family was long overdue. She'd been given a reason to be grateful, to feel cautiously optimistic, and hoped sharing good news with family would make them feel better, too.

40

After Zeke volunteered to be a witness, life took a turn. The timing was perfect, as the week Kennedy had spent at home with her family had helped her regain her equilibrium and gave her a different perspective of her life's forest that couldn't be gained when surrounded by its trees.

The visit had been good for other reasons. Her mother was hurt and angry at what she felt was being ignored as Kennedy went through the scandal. She didn't agree with Karolyn, but she did understand. In ways, she'd been right. Her mom had suffered, along with the neighbors and the town. There was a saying that money didn't buy happiness. That was true, but it definitely allowed one to rent a bit of it. Money also gave one choices, the ability to change things, even to make some problems go away. After a long discussion with Karolyn, she learned it wasn't just waiting until the house sold prolonging the relocation to Vegas, but her mom's growing reluctance to leave the town where she'd lived her entire life. That Saturday Kennedy talked her and Ray into dropping whatever plans they had for the day and fly to Vegas. On the way to the airport she'd located a realtor online and scheduled an appointment by text. The next day the realtor offered to pick them up. They learned a lot about Las Vegas, the city beyond downtown and the strip that most people never saw. They visited the suburbs of Henderson and Summerlin. They were shown half a dozen houses, one with a yard and a pool that her mom loved. They returned to Peyton. Karolyn gave her two-week's notice. The day before Kennedy was scheduled to fly to New York, her mom requested that she put in an offer. Movers were hired. They'd be arriving next week. Ray and Karolyn were leaving Peyton. Kennedy knew it was time to make a move too, and not just about her location.

"I'll give this one more month," she announced when she arrived at Dodie's office in New York.

"Give what one month?"

Kennedy spread her arms to encompass the room and as she spoke, continued to the windows and included the world beyond them.

"All of this, every way my life has been since revealing my identity. Every way I've had to live because of those pictures. I rented a place in Harlem," she continued.

"Did you speak with security?"

"Yes."

"What did they say?"

"They'll be close by. There will never be a perfect time to take back my life and start living like a human being instead of a fugitive, albeit one with means. Dante knows about it. He lives there, and to make you feel even better, Zeke will move in with me."

"I still don't get that."

"Except for Zeke and I, nobody will."

"So are the two of you—"

"No, we're not."

Dodie raised a brow. "You may have answered that a bit too quickly."

"Only because I want to remain on topic. Zeke is an experienced security expert and easy on the eyes, but the only relationship I'm focused on right now is the one with myself."

"I get that," Dodie responded, all sarcasm gone. "I couldn't have withstood what you've been through."

Kennedy smiled as their camaraderie returned. "I think you could. It wasn't only your expertise as a publicist or your extensive connections. It was your strength that I recognized the most, that helped bolster me up during challenging times. You always came through with a word or a look. I didn't always agree with you, but I always respected you and felt you truly had my back."

"Thank you for saying that, Ken. This has been ugly, but worth it."

"As for your partners, they've been great and for a while they were needed, but I'd like to go back to working solely with you, effective immediately. I'll retain the attorneys but only one bodyguard. I'll speak with the other assistants, the stylists, the makeup artist and inform them that their services are no longer needed. I'm sure there are aspects of this whole operation that I've left out, which is why I rented the place for a month. But I'm not staying a day past that."

"Wow." Dodie walked over to a seating area and sat. "You've obviously thought this out."

"When visiting small towns, there's a lot of time to think."

They laughed.

"So, after Harlem, and once your focus isn't on 'all of this' as you say, what then?"

"Coming up with an answer for that wasn't as easy as the previous steps mentioned. I know I'll return to Chicago, at least for the time being. It's where I've lived my entire adult life. A city I know and love."

"And continue freelance photography?"

"I don't know," Kennedy said, and then chuckled. "My friend Gwen says I ought to be a novelist."

Dodie thought for a moment. "You have a very smart friend."

"I think she was kidding."

"Really? I'm not. Think of all the wild and crazy things that have happened to you, because of something you did by accident? Your life is the poster child for the truth being stranger than fiction. You do have a degree in writing."

"Yes, but not creative writing, not writing a book."

"You could do it, Kennedy. And you should give the possibility serious thought. You received a sizeable chunk for that picture, but it wouldn't hurt to add the cushion of a *New York Times* bestseller."

"You really think that many people would be interested?"

Dodie rolled her eyes in exasperation. "In the woman who literally exposed a media and political conspiracy? Um, yeah, I think one or two people would want to read that book. It has everything," she continued, becoming more excited. "It has action, drama, politics, scandal. It crosses state lines and continents. There is intrigue and betrayal, and the conversation that has been raised as to what counts as patriotism and who should get to define it. And you've got a decorated war hero switching sides for his country! I think, no, I know, if written correctly, a book like that could go all the way to the top. It could be number one."

"I don't know, Dodie."

"Think about it, will you?"

"Okay."

"And when answering, consider giving me a slow yes instead of a fast no."

Once Kennedy met with the team and put the ball in motion to dismantle it, things moved quickly. Dante and his team met the federal prosecutors and pushed back hard against their innuendos and veiled threats. They revealed a new development, a witness who admitted to having participated in many of the events that Kennedy had described in her deposition. In an offensive move, they shared a statement Zeke had written with the prosecution, a letter expressing pride in having served his country, and how in coming forward he felt he was serving it still. They assured the prosecution that their witness was prepared to go to prison for the American public to be protected and for truth to prevail.

"No bother threatening him with a jail sentence, boys," Dante had drawled after dropping his trump. "This man has seen horrors of war beyond what we can imagine. Prison would be a walk in the park."

Relaying this information to Van Dijk's team changed the network's tone regarding Kennedy and the pictures she'd taken. Van Dijk retreated like a tornado all out of wind. The posts stopped. The pundits shut up. With no director leading the choir, the TBC viewers backed off. In the middle of all of this, President Trout suddenly announced a potential trade deal with North Korea. Capitol Hill went crazy. The media went wild. What Dodie suggested when the media frenzy began, finally happened. A news story broke that shifted the attention away from her.

Interest surrounding the pictures didn't end. But the American public's attention span was short. They quickly moved to the next headline. Media requests slowed, and even though Kennedy no longer gave interviews, they didn't stop completely. Those opposed to the hold Van Dijk had on the media went out on a majority of airwaves, keeping the story alive, aided by news channels with twenty-four hours to fill. Still, Kennedy felt she'd been released from prison, was able to walk around rather freely, and could get back to some semblance of a normal life.

By the end of the third week of Kennedy's four-week stay in New York, the legal battles had calmed to a simmer and her team had been redefined. Publicly, Van Dijk and his buddy President Trout continued to blow smoke about bringing traitors to justice. But he no longer posted about the pictures and he no longer mentioned her name. Still, the attorneys told her that the case was far from being settled, that legal matters like this could drag on for years. At this point, time was on her side. And so was a man named Zeke Foster. When it was time for her court close-up, she'd be ready, and Zeke would be there. In the meantime, another project had captured her interest. Dodie, and her endless list of influential contacts, had connected Kennedy with a high-powered literary agent to shop her book idea. By the time Kennedy left New York, several publishers were interested, and three weeks after returning to Chicago and signing the lease on a six-month rental, Kennedy decided on the publisher that was right for her and signed a lucrative contract. An opportunity that came about because of her true love and passion—finding beautiful objects and having others see them through her lens. It was often said that a picture was worth a thousand words. Kennedy was going to write more than that about the snapshot she'd taken that changed her life, and put them in a book.

Don't Miss

Stiletto Justice

Available wherever books are sold
*Camryn King's sizzling debut novel delivers an intriguing tale
of three resourceful women with a ruthless senator in their
sights—and even more explosive ways to take him down . . .*

A successful businesswoman who used to play by the rules. A
cautious single mother who never took chances. A gorgeous
rebel out of money and almost out of time. Each loves a man
unjustly sentenced to long prison terms by former prosecutor
Hammond Grey. They've tried every legal remedy to get justice—only to see Hammond climb ever higher up the political
ladder and secure himself behind power and privilege. So
when Kim, Jayda, and Harley meet in a support group,
they've got no options left. It's time for them to launch Plan
B. And they won't stop at infiltrating Hammond's elite world
and uncovering mass corruption. Exploiting his deepest
weakness is the ultimate delicious payback—and the kind of
justice they'll gamble everything to get . . .

Enjoy the following excerpt from *Stiletto Justice* . . .

PROLOGUE

"Is he dead?"

"I don't know, but seeing that lying trap of a mouth shut is a nice change of pace."

Kim Logan, Harley Buchanan, and Jayda Sanchez peered down at the lifeless body of the United States senator from Kansas, Hammond Grey.

"I agree he looks better silent," Kim mused, while mentally willing his chest to move. "But I don't think prison garb will improve my appearance."

"Move, guys." Jayda, who'd hung in the background, pushed Harley aside to get closer. She stuck a finger under his nose. "He's alive, but I don't know how long he'll be unconscious. Whatever we're going to do needs to happen fast."

"Fine with me." Harley stripped off her jacket and unzipped her jeans. "The sooner we get this done, the sooner we can get the hell out of here."

"I'm with you," Kim replied. Her hands shook as she unsnapped the black leather jacket borrowed from her husband and removed her phone from its inside pocket. "Jayda, start taking his clothes off."

"Why me?" Jayda whispered. "I don't want to touch him."

"That's why you're wearing gloves," Harley hissed back. "Look, if I can bare my ass for the world to see, the least you can do is pull his pants down. Where's that wig?"

Kim showed more sympathy as she pointed toward the bag holding a brunette-colored hair transformer. "Jayda, I understand completely. I don't even want to look at his penis, let alone capture it on video."

Harley had stripped down to her undies. She stood impatiently, hand on hip. "I tell you what I'm not going to do. I'm not going to get buck-ass naked for you two to punk out. It's why we all took a shot of Jack!"

"I'm too nervous to feel it," Jayda said as she wrung her hands. "I probably should have added Jim and Bud."

"Hold this." Kim handed Jayda the phone and walked over to the bed. After the slightest of pauses, she reached for the belt and undid it. Next, she unbuttoned and unzipped the dress slacks. "Jayda, raise him up a little so I can pull these down."

Harley walked over to where Kim stood next to the bed. "Don't take them all the way off. He looks like the type who'd screw without bothering to get totally undressed."

Kim pulled the pants down to Hammond's knees. The room went silent. The women stared. Kim looked at Harley. Harley looked at Jayda. The three looked at each other.

"Am I seeing what I think I'm seeing?" Jayda asked.

Harley rubbed the chill from her arms. "We're all seeing it."

"*Star Wars*? Really, Hammond?" Kim quickly snapped a couple pics, then gently lowered the colorful boxers and murmured, "Looks like his political viewpoint isn't the only thing conservative."

She snapped a few more. Harley donned the wig, looked in the mirror, and snickered. "Guys, how do I look?"

"Don't," Kim began, covering her mouth. "Don't start to laugh . . ." The low rumble of muted guffaws replaced speech.

The liquor finally kicked in.

"Come on, guys!" Jayda harshly whispered, though her eyes gleamed. "We've got to hurry."

"You look fine, Harley. As gorgeous a brunette as you are a blonde."

Harley removed her thong and climbed on the bed. "Remember . . ."

"I won't get your face, Harley. What the wig doesn't cover, I'll clip out or blur. You won't be recognizable in any way."

"And you're sure this super glue will work, and hide my fingerprints?"

Jayda nodded. "That's what it said on the internet."

"I'm nervous." Harley straddled the unconscious body and placed fisted hands on each side.

"Wait!" Kim stilled Harley with a hand to the shoulder. "Don't let your mouth actually touch his. We don't want to leave a speck of DNA. I'll angle the shot so that it looks like you're kissing."

"What about . . . that." Jayda pointed toward the flaccid member.

"Oh, yeah. I forgot. Look inside that bag." Harley tilted her head in that direction. "With the condom on, it looks like the real thing."

Jayda retrieved a condom-clad cucumber and marched back to the bed as though it were a baton. "He won't like that we've filmed him, but he'll hopefully appreciate that we replaced his Vienna sausage with a jumbo hot link."

The women got down to business—Jayda directing, Harley performing, Kim videotaping. Each job was executed quickly, efficiently, just as they'd planned.

Finally, after double-checking to make sure her work had been captured, Kim shut off the camera. "Okay, guys, I think we've got enough."

Harley moved toward the edge of the bed. "Pictures and video?"

"Yep. Want to see it?"

"No," she replied, scrambling into her jeans. "I want to get the hell out of here."

"That makes two of us," Jayda said, walking toward the coat she'd tossed on a chair.

"Three of us." Kim took another look at the footage. "Wait, guys. I have an idea. Jayda, quick, come here."

"What?"

"No time to explain. Trust me on this . . . please?"

Five minutes later they were ready to go. "What should we do about him?" Jayda asked, waving a hand at his state of undress.

"Nothing," Kim replied. She returned the phone to its hiding place in her pocket. "Let him figure out what may or may not have happened."

They'd been careful, but taking no chances, they wiped down every available surface with cleaning wipes, which they then placed back in the bag that once again held the condom-clad cucumber. Harley almost had a heart attack when she glimpsed the wineglass that if forgotten and left behind would have been a forensic team's dream. After rinsing away prime evidence, she pressed Grey's fingers around the bowl, refilled it with a splash of wine, and placed it back on the nightstand. After a last look around to make sure that nothing was left that could be traced back to them, the women crept out of the bedroom and down the stairs. Harley turned off the outside light and unbolted the side door.

Kim turned to her. "You sure you don't want to come with us?"

Harley shook her head. "I have to leave the way I came. Don't worry. The car service is on the way. See you at the hotel."

After peeking out to make sure the coast was clear, Jayda

and Kim tiptoed out the back door as quietly and inconspicuously as they'd arrived. A short time later Harley left, too.

Once down the block, around the corner, and into the rental car, Jayda and Kim finally exhaled. The next day, as the women left the nation's capital, hope began to bloom like cherry blossoms in spring. Until now their calls for help and cries for justice had been drowned out or ignored. Maybe the package specially delivered to his office next week would finally get the senator's attention, and get him to do the right thing.

Connect with U s

Visit us online at
KensingtonBooks.com
to read more from your favorite authors, see books
by series, view reading group guides, and more.

for sneak peeks, chances to win books and prize packs,
and to share your thoughts with other readers.

f 🐦

facebook.com/kensingtonpublishing
twitter.com/kensingtonbooks

Tell us what you think!

To share your thoughts, submit a review,
or sign up for our eNewsletters, please visit:
KensingtonBooks.com/TellUs.